Miranda's mouth went dry when she saw Allessandro standing in the shadows.

He was wearing nothing but a pair of well-worn camouflage pants and a white undershirt that emphasized the darkness of his tan, the strength of his chest. In his hand he held his semiautomatic, as if it were as an impenetrable shield between him and the world. In his eyes glittered a harshness she didn't understand, a look that was equal parts pain and pleasure.

Dangerous, she thought. Not just because he held a gun in one hand and her life in the other, but because his brutal exterior couldn't hide the glimmer of compassion deep inside him.

He didn't move, didn't speak. He just watched her, the light from across the street slashing in, momentarily rescuing him from the shadows, then returning him to darkness.

Something deep inside her started to tremble. *Dangerous...*

Dear Reader,

"In like a lion, out like a lamb." That's what they say about March, right? Well, there are no meek and mild lambs among this month's Intimate Moments heroines, that's for sure! In *Saving Dr. Ryan*, Karen Templeton begins a new miniseries, THE MEN OF MAYES COUNTY, while telling the story of a roadside delivery—yes, the baby kind—that leads to an improbable romance. Maddie Kincaid starts out looking like the one who needs saving, but it's really Dr. Ryan Logan who's in need of rescue.

We continue our trio of FAMILY SECRETS prequels with *The Phoenix Encounter* by Linda Castillo. Follow the secret-agent hero deep under cover—and watch as he rediscovers a love he'd thought was dead. But where do they go from there? Nina Bruhns tells a story of repentance, forgiveness and passion in *Sins of the Father*, while Eileen Wilks offers up tangled family ties and a seemingly insoluble dilemma in *Midnight Choices*. For Wendy Rosnau's heroine, there's only *One Way Out* as she chooses between being her lover's mistress—or his wife. Finally, Jenna Mills' heroine becomes *The Perfect Target*. She meets the seemingly perfect man, then has to decide whether he represents safety—or danger.

The excitement never flags—and there will be more next month, too. So don't miss a single Silhouette Intimate Moments title, because this is the line where you'll find the best and most exciting romance reading around.

Enjoy!

Leslie J. Wainger
Executive Senior Editor

Please address questions and book requests to:
Silhouette Reader Service
U.S.: 3010 Walden Ave., P.O. Box 1325, Buffalo, NY 14269
Canadian: P.O. Box 609, Fort Erie, Ont. L2A 5X3

The
Perfect
Target

JENNA
MILLS

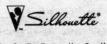

INTIMATE MOMENTS™

Published by Silhouette Books

America's Publisher of Contemporary Romance

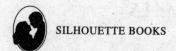 **SILHOUETTE BOOKS**

ISBN 0-373-27282-0

THE PERFECT TARGET

Copyright © 2003 by Jennifer Miller

This edition published by arrangement with Harlequin Books S.A.

Visit Silhouette at www.eHarlequin.com

Printed in U.S.A.

Books by Jenna Mills

JENNA MILLS

grew up in south Louisiana, amid romantic plantation ruins, haunting swamps and timeless legends. It's not surprising, then, that she wrote her first romance at the ripe old age of six! Three years later, this librarian's daughter turned to romantic suspense with *Jacquie and the Swamp,* a harrowing tale of a young woman on the run in the swamp and the dashing hero who helps her find her way home. Since then her stories have grown in complexity, but her affinity for adventurous women and dangerous men has remained constant. She loves writing about strong characters torn between duty and desire, conscious choice and destiny.

When not writing award-winning stories brimming with deep emotion, steamy passion and page-turning suspense, Jenna spends her time with her husband, two cats, two dogs and a menagerie of plants in their Dallas, Texas, home. Jenna loves to hear from her readers. She can be reached via e-mail at writejennamills@aol.com, or via snail mail at P.O. Box 768, Coppell, Texas 75019.

For my terrific editor, Stephanie Maurer…
this one is all yours!
Thanks for the inspiration and collaboration.
I'll always remember our thunderstorm in New Orleans.

Thanks also to Patrick and the rest of the SPSS gang,
for helping make this book possible.

And always, my husband, Chuck.
You are my light. I love you
more than words can express.

Prologue

Two roads diverged in a wood
And I took the one less traveled by
And that has made all the difference.
— *Robert Frost*

"Turn on your TV."

Alessandro Vellenti squinted through the darkness of his Lisbon hotel room. He'd seen closets bigger, closets dedicated solely to shoes and handbags. But the small room had a shower, and that's all he'd really wanted.

Well, maybe not *all* he wanted, but all he could have.

Night had fallen while he'd stood under the spray of a lukewarm shower, trying to ignore the metallic smell of the water. Now, flashing lights from the discotheque across the street cut through the threadbare curtains like something straight out of a macabre horror flick.

"My TV?" He positioned the mobile phone against his

shoulder and fumbled for the bedside lamp. Anticipation increased his heart rate. Javier was hardly a television kind of guy. Sandro doubted his partner wanted him to see the newest reality show to disgrace the airwaves. "What's going on?"

"Something big. What took you so long to answer the phone? I'm not *finally* interrupting something, am I?"

Sandro ignored the jab and wrapped a threadbare towel around his hips. Rivulets of water clung to his chest and slid down his legs, but he didn't finish drying. There was no need. The room reeked of stale cigarettes and harsh antiseptic, but the temperature was only slightly cool. Sandro had certainly endured colder. And hotter.

He preferred the hot. "I'm not a kiss-and-tell kind of guy," he muttered, looking for the remote. "What's going on?"

"Jorak Zhukov was arrested crossing into the United States from Canada. The ambassador to Ravakia is giving an interview right now."

Finally, the urgency in Javier's voice made sense. Implications and questions immediately surfaced, raised more questions. "Was he by himself?"

"Apparently."

Sandro went down on one knee, locating the remote under the narrow bed, adjacent to a skimpy black bra and slinky white scarf. He didn't even want to *think* about how the erotic garments had found their way under the bed. Doing so would be too depressing. Instead, he aimed the ancient control at the pathetic excuse for a television across the room.

Nothing happened. "Has he been charged with anything?"

"Just traveling on a falsified visa. So far. But I can't imagine the United States letting him slip through their fingers, not after what happened to those agents."

Sandro hit the power button again, still with no luck. Banging the useless instrument against the nightstand, he recalled the countless reports he'd reviewed about Jorak Zhukov and his father Viktor, the overthrown leader of the Eastern European country Ravakia. The two were wanted in connection with the deaths of eight undercover operatives. Word on the street had it something even bigger was going down.

It was Sandro and Javier's mission to find out what.

"What of Viktor?" Anticipation whirred deep inside Sandro. Nailing the notorious father-son duo would save countless lives. "Any indication they were traveling together?"

"The State Department doesn't think so."

Sandro gave up on the remote, took the room in three long strides, and jabbed the on button. A bright light yawned across the screen, but no picture and only the sound of static.

"They think Viktor's holed up somewhere in Europe," Javier added.

Maybe. Probably. When the U.S. got determined about finding something, safe hiding places became scarce. "Do they know where?"

"If they do, they're not saying."

A distorted picture finally formed. Sandro flipped through channels on the old black-and-white until he found the familiar CNN logo. The picture remained fuzzy, however, the sound garbled.

"The State Department's heightened the travel warning for American citizens and interests," Javi added. "With Jorak in custody, Viktor will be desperate. They fear retaliation."

Sandro slammed his palm against the side of the television, still no sound. Against a backdrop of a proud American flag, Ambassador Peter Carrington grew more animated by the second. Defiance glowed in his eyes, hardened the lines of his patrician face. His hands moved as he talked, slicing through the air like a chop to the neck of an invisible opponent.

"What's he saying? I can't get any volume."

"The usual. The United States is not in the business of negotiating with criminals on the FBI's Ten Most Wanted list."

Sandro stepped back from the television, suddenly cold. "Zhukov will take that as a direct challenge."

A hard noise broke from Javi's throat. "I don't understand people like Carrington, so snug in his ivory tower that he doesn't realize he's not insulated from the real world."

"He was born with a silver spoon in his mouth," Sandro pointed out. The highly revered, much loved Carrington family skirted as close to royalty as America got. "He's never had his world blow up around him."

"That's about to change," Javi warned as the interview ended. A shadowy image of General Viktor Zhukov replaced that of the newly appointed ambassador to Ravakia. "Viktor's already on the move, knows he needs leverage."

Leverage. The word snaked through Sandro like rancid meat. "You mean a hostage."

"Viktor made contact about thirty minutes ago," Javi said, his voice practically drowned out by a siren somewhere in the city. "He's already got a plan. And a target."

The news didn't surprise Sandro. "Who?"

"Miranda Carrington."

The name did. An image immediately formed, of leagues of chestnut hair and exotic green eyes. "The ambassador's daughter?"

"A child for a child," Javi muttered cryptically. "Word on the street is she's in Europe indulging some gypsy fantasy. She was last seen in Seville."

Only a few hours' drive from Lisbon.

"Cristo." Sandro knew little of the ambassador's youngest child, other than that in her late twenties, she seemed the exact opposite of her perfect, politically correct older sister and brother, Elizabeth and Ethan, dubbed the E-twins

by the press. Not that Miranda wasn't perfect in her own right...

She sure as hell could kiss, he thought, then wished he hadn't. Vividly, he recalled a tabloid photo of a bikini-clad Miranda wrapped around some Ivy League frat boy, mouths locked in a pose more suited to the cover of an X-rated video.

Sandro sucked in a sharp breath and shoved wet hair back from his face. His body groaned in frustration.

Don't go there, he warned himself. Don't even think about there. Especially not with a woman targeted to become a pawn in a high-stakes international game. Especially not while he stood wet and naked in a hotel room that reeked of sex by the hour. He couldn't afford to be distracted any more than he could afford the nasty kink in months of grueling undercover work. His mission was clear: gain the general's trust, learn his secrets, then bring him down.

"It gets worse," his partner added, seemingly reading his mind, as always. "That's why I'm calling."

Sandro braced himself. "Lay it on me."

"The general wants you to get her for him, *amigo*. Said if you can deliver the girl, he'll know where your loyalties lie."

Sandro went very still. A test. The irony of it burned clear down to his bones. If he failed the test, he failed his country.

But if he succeeded...

Reeling, Sandro dragged the phone back to the narrow cot and slipped his hand under the pillow, where his 9mm awaited, silencer intact. "Tell him I'm onboard."

He'd always excelled at tests, wouldn't fail now. Training and loyalty left him no choice. He had to find her. Find the ambassador's daughter. Find her fast, find her first.

Before the long-awaited chance to cozy up to the general went up in flames.

Chapter 1

No one recognized her.

Miranda Carrington lowered her tortoiseshell sunglasses and glanced around the open-air market, savoring the sense of liberation. No one watched her every step. No one shoved a camera in her face. There was no one grabbing a mobile phone to excitedly report her outfit, her language, the drink in her hand. No one waiting for her to commit a faux pas worthy of splashing all over the covers of every grocery-store tabloid.

Exhilaration tumbled through her hard and fast. Miranda wanted to twirl around the crowded cobblestone sidewalk, to laugh. Instead, she smiled. Last night a storm had raged, but the morning held nothing but clear blue skies and cool Atlantic breezes.

And freedom.

Here, in the small Portuguese village of Cascais, no one gave a flip about her or her prestigious family. No one noticed the two glasses of port she'd nursed the night before. No one paid attention to her slightly off-kilter sense of fashion. No one watched. No one cared.

Here, she was just another woman, on just another day. She could dance in the street without speculation that she was practicing witchcraft. She could laugh out loud.

Smiling, Miranda reached for the camera draped over her shoulder, lifted it to her face, and snapped several shots of the vendors working the market.

"*Bom dia,*" she greeted the older gentleman who'd moved from South Africa to Portugal, where he now made his living carving wooden toys for children by night and selling his crafts by day. He offered her a big smile, which she captured on film.

"Astrida! Astrida!"

Down the cobblestone walkway, an older woman grinned despite her missing front teeth.

"Rosita," Miranda greeted, then snapped a shot of the woman standing proudly in front of her stall, with a fine array of brightly colored scarves blowing in the April breeze. Miranda had purchased one just yesterday, and now used the slinky turquoise fabric to hold blond hair back from her face.

"*Obrigada,*" she said in thanks, then continued on her way. A few feet away, she took a shot of a young woman showing off handmade seashell wind chimes to a group of older tourists.

Years of sweltering under the public eye kept Miranda walking at a brisk pace. She didn't want to draw attention to herself. She wanted to savor anonymity as long as she could.

The thrill never went away. Sometimes, she still couldn't believe she'd finally convinced her father to let her live her own life. Eleven years before tragedy had forever changed their family, and in its wake, he'd tightened the net around his family to near unbearable restrictions. But Miranda hadn't seen Hawk Monroe or any of his men in weeks. And she'd certainly looked. She knew the tricks, knew the small tests to figure out if someone was shadowing her or merely living their own lives.

More than anything, Miranda wanted to live her own life.

At the end of the street stood a trendy boutique, boasting the seaside village's finest collection of European perfumes. Miranda was tempted to dash inside but didn't want to waste the hazy morning light. She'd seen a fleet of old, rainbow-colored fishing boats bobbing in the harbor from her hotel window, and—

The all too familiar feeling of dread slammed in from nowhere. She stopped abruptly and sucked in a sharp breath, but the icy fingers at the back of her neck didn't go away. Slipping her sunglasses back on, she turned slowly, carefully scanning the crowd milling about the bazaar.

Nothing. Nothing out of place, anyway. No one hurriedly ducked into a shop. No one covertly turned away. No one quickly raised a newspaper to cover their face. She was only imagining things, so used to living in a fishbowl that even here, in this small seaside village, she felt the eyes of the world watching.

Posh, she scolded herself. *Get a grip.* She flat-out wasn't that important, even if her family was.

Her heart, however, refused to slow. The uncooperative organ kept pounding, spewing adrenaline with every hurried beat. Dismayed, Miranda forced herself to round the corner and head for the ocean. No way would she let paranoia spoil the perfect, storm-washed morning.

Beyond the battered seawall, the glistening blue of the Atlantic stole her breath. The day before, she'd stood in just this spot, staring over the water and imagining what it must have been like for those long-ago Portuguese sailors, who left their familiar worlds behind, in search of something new.

Freedom.

Odd, she thought. Her own quest for freedom had carried her across the very same ocean, but in the opposite direction.

Silently, she thanked God for airplanes.

Through the camera's lens, she scanned the swelling waves and bobbing fishing boats, over to the palm-lined promenade along the shore, where pigeons flocked and a young couple kissed with what could only be described as desperation. They were wrapped around each other so tightly, not even the breeze could squeeze between them. The man had one hand buried in the woman's dark brown hair, the other hand securely around her waist. Their mouths moved like a ballet, not overtly sexual, but erotically intimate, as though they were making love right there—

Miranda caught herself. She of all people knew better than to aim a camera at intimate moments. Returning her attention to the harbor, she tried to focus on the weathered fishing boats practically begging to be photographed, and not the unwanted longing yawning through her.

"No, no, no. That's not right at all."

The rough-hewn voice rumbled through Miranda, causing her pulse to surge like one of the waves against the seawall. She abandoned the perfect close-up on a battered blue boat and turned. Felt her body tense.

A tall, dark-haired man stood less than a foot away, closer than American manners dictated, invading her personal space in a style common to European men. She'd grown accustomed to the practice, but this man's nearness kicked her nerves into high gear. Dark sunglasses concealed his eyes, the frames and lenses the color of the whiskers shadowing his jaw. They were the kind worn by rock stars to create that edgy, mysterious persona that drove women wild. In hiding his eyes, he concealed his intent and sent a current streaking through Miranda, as indefinable as it was unsettling.

"I beg your pardon?" she said with a refinement that would have done her perfect older sister proud.

He nodded toward the camera in her hands. "The picture you were about to take. It's all wrong."

"Wrong?" She felt her spine stiffen. She may have been a novice when it came to political intrigue, but she knew photography inside out. "How so?"

He slid the sunglasses from his face, revealing eyes as dark and impenetrable as the lenses that had shielded them. A slow smile touched lips too full for a face of sharp angles and hard planes. "Because you're not in it."

The breath stalled in her throat. Her heart thudded against her ribs. Not just because of the unexpectedly provocative words, but because of the way he looked at her, like she was the coveted trophy at the end of a long, hard fought battle. She'd never seen a gaze so full of secrets and promises, never seen eyes that dark, like the color of midnight.

Walk away, countless hours of security training commanded. This man wasn't what he seemed. He watched her way too expectantly; his stance held the same deceptive casualness as the bodyguards who'd followed her around at Wellesley. But instead of finding his nearness threatening, Miranda found herself curious. No one knew her here, she reminded herself. No one lurked in the shadows, ready to hurt her or shame her family.

"I'm not in it?" she repeated with a smile of her own. He was tall, she noted, well over her brother's six feet. And his hair matched the color of his eyes. "I see myself in the mirror every morning. I hardly need a picture of myself."

His voice dropped an octave. "Then give it to me."

This time she did step back. "Now why would I do that?"

His eyes met hers. "So I can remember the way you look standing here, with the sun in your hair and the smile on your face."

Something inside Miranda turned hot and liquid. Fascination whispered louder. The man's dark hair and unshaven face lent him an aura of danger, but he spoke like a poet. He was dressed like a tourist, but held a professional-looking briefcase. His swarthy skin hinted at Mediterranean ancestry, but he wore his loose-fitting black shirt and olive slacks like only an American could. He spoke accented English, but used perfect grammar.

"I should be going," she said, pulling away before she stepped in too deep.

He reached toward her. "Let me take your picture first."

Miranda went very still. She looked down at her arm, where his warm fingers curled around her wrist. The sight jarred her, of a blatantly masculine hand on her body. For the past few years, if a stranger so much as brushed against her in a crowd, agents or bodyguards emerged from the shadows, alert and ready.

And Miranda had hated it. She'd hated being watched, monitored, hated being denied a normal life because of her family's notoriety. She hadn't asked to be born a Carrington. She didn't care about politics. She had no interest in carrying on the family legacy.

She'd just wanted to live her life, to laugh and dance and even fall down sometimes, without the whole world watching.

Butterfly, her maternal grandfather had called her. The only butterfly in a family of eagles.

Instinct had her covertly scanning the surrounding area, half expecting to see Hawk Monroe running toward her. But just like before, she found only a dazzling fountain spraying toward the pale blue sky, pigeons, street merchants and tourists.

Slowly, the stranger released her. "*Bella?* Did I say something wrong?"

Bella. There it was. The first clue to the puzzle. Italian. "No," she said. "You didn't say anything wrong."

"Then why do you look so...nervous?"

That got her. She didn't want to be nervous. She didn't want to react with paranoia to the very situations she'd come to Europe to experience. "What makes you think I'm nervous?"

"The way you're standing, like you're about to take off running. The fact you've yet to let me see your eyes."

She lifted her chin, smiled. Very slowly, very deliberately, she slid the Euro-chic tortoiseshell sunglasses from her face.

"Should I be nervous?" she challenged.

"That depends upon what makes you nervous," he answered in that faint but drugging accent. He glanced toward the showy fountain, then around the open-air market, as though looking for something. Then he stepped closer. "If you're worried that I'm a serial killer, I assure you I am not. This is Portugal, not America. That kind of thing is rare here."

Laughter broke from her throat. "I don't think you're a serial killer."

He didn't grin or smile as she expected. Instead, his gaze turned serious. "Don't let down your guard quite so easily," he muttered darkly. "Just let me take your picture. That's all I ask. Here," he said, reaching for her camera. "What harm can there be? Just one shot."

The man could no doubt talk her cousin's four-year-old into surrendering her favorite teddy bear, Miranda thought absently. Intrigued, she decided to play along.

"Just one," she agreed, uncurling her fingers from the sleek 35mm she'd purchased before leaving the States.

"Back up a little," he instructed. The camera hid his eyes, but she knew they would be focused and intense.

Odd, Miranda thought, stepping against the seawall. He held her camera in his left hand, but he'd yet to put down his briefcase.

"Perfect," he murmured. "Now untie the scarf."

She blinked. "The scarf?"

"Hair like yours is too pretty to confine. Let the wind play with it."

Heat streaked through her, completely unrelated to the burgeoning warmth of the day. Something about the word *play,* she knew. And that raspy voice. "I prefer it off my face."

"Just for the picture," he coaxed. "Just for me."

Caution warned her to call the whole thing off, but her newfound sense of freedom refused to be denied. Having a man flirt with her, with no ulterior motive, felt too good. Charmed, she reached for the turquoise scarf she'd purchased from Rosita and pulled the fabric free. The breeze blowing off the ocean instantly sent long strands of blond hair fluttering around her face and tangling over her shoulders.

"Perfect," the stranger said. "Perfect."

Miranda fought an odd jolt of self-consciousness, as though she stood before the man completely naked, rather than in an off-the-shoulder crimson shirt and a long, gypsylike skirt she'd purchased from one of the locals. Every nerve ending felt charged and exposed. Her heart strummed low and expectant. The stranger had her posing for him, and she didn't even know his name.

For the moment, she didn't care.

Identity had nothing to do with what was scrawled on your birth certificate, but rather, the ideals you carried deep inside. If she asked the stranger his name, he'd ask hers.

She wasn't ready to taint the moment with either the truth, or a lie.

"What are you waiting for?" He almost seemed to be stalling.

"The sun," he answered without hesitation. "You're not a woman for shadows."

His voice was hoarse, like a man who lived on cigarettes and whisky. No one had ever talked to her like that. No words had ever drifted through her like a feathery caress. She studied him closer, that full mouth and those dark whiskers sprinkled across a strong jaw, the thick neck leading to the kind of chest women dreamed about—

Miranda jerked her gaze back to his neck, where a nasty scar slashed across his throat, a faded testimony to a brutal attack. This man's raspy voice did not stem from pleasure or vice, but from pain and violence.

"Hurry up," she said. Well-honed instincts kicked harder. He may not have asked her name, but he'd skillfully pinned her between his big body and the ocean behind her.

"Don't be so impatient, *bella.* Some things aren't meant to be rushed. There can be tremendous reward in lingering."

The words were soft, but they robbed her of breath like a punch to the gut. Miranda hungered for freedom and adventure, but she also knew when she'd stepped in over her head. She could fend off attackers and wield a knife like a pro, but when it came to playing cat and mouse with outrageously good-looking, mysterious men, her defenses jammed like traffic in gridlock.

Fortunately, her legs didn't. Pushing away from the seawall, she strode toward him, hand outstretched. "Give me my camera back."

"But I haven't—"

"The camera," she said, firmer than before.

He refused to hand over her prized possession. "Have lunch with me. Maybe the clouds will clear by the time we're done."

"No." Fascination crumbled into determination. This man was not what he seemed, and she knew better than to teeter on a rocky outcropping with the tide rushing in around her.

"Look, I really need to get going, so just give me my camera," she said, extending her hand, "and—"

He took her wrist and started to tug. "Relax, *bella.* I know just the place—"

"Miranda!"

The urgent voice came from behind her and had her spinning toward the shopping district. A large Viking of a man broke from the crowd of older tourists and sprinted toward her. "Miranda!"

Hawk.

Her heart started to race, adrenaline spewing like a geyser out of control. They'd found her.

She didn't know whether to laugh or cry. The second a man touched her, one of her father's men always, always came running.

"Miranda!" Hawk shouted, gaining ground.

The stranger's grip on her arm tightened. "Do you know him?" he asked with an urgency that hadn't been there before. But before she could answer, the sound of gunfire ripped through the late morning and sent the crowd scattering like leaves in the wind. Pigeons took flight. Hawk went down.

Miranda screamed, lunging toward her fallen bodyguard. But the stranger wouldn't let her go.

"Get down," he commanded, shoving her toward the nearest merchant's stall. He crouched beside her, sandwiching her between a display of rooster tablecloths and his big body. "Stay low."

A large man dressed in army fatigues bolted around the corner, with what looked to be a semiautomatic in his hand. "Hold your fire!" he was shouting. "We've got you surrounded!"

"Too bloody late," the stranger muttered.

The man in fatigues kept running. He was beside the fountain when another volley of gunfire ripped through the chaos. His arms flew out as though he'd slammed into an invisible wall, and he crumpled to the ground.

"Cristo." The stranger glanced around sharply. "Where the hell are the shooters?" He held his briefcase in front of him, scanning the crowd. "I've got to get you out of here."

"But Hawk—"

"—is probably dead."

Horror convulsed through her. *Hawk.* She'd spent the past year evading the unyielding man at every turn, but she didn't want him dead. Until now, everything had always seemed more like a game than life or death.

"Look!" she cried, "he's getting up."

"Fool," the stranger hissed, just as the first police officer arrived, running from the perfume boutique to dive behind a nearby stall. Sirens screamed nearby.

"Stay down," the stranger shouted. "Be ready to run when I tell you." Then he took aim on the police officer's hiding place and sprayed the area with bullets.

From his briefcase.

More screams. And Hawk went back down.

The sirens wailed louder.

But there was no movement from behind the stall.

The stranger didn't stop firing. He pointed his briefcase toward a tree, unleashed another volley and brought a slender man with a ponytail crashing into the fountain.

Miranda cringed as the water turned red.

Her heart was beating so crazily she could barely breathe. And when the stranger faced her, she felt her eyes go wide with shock. He hardly resembled the man who'd brought her senses humming to life barely minutes before. Seduction no longer glimmered in his gaze. Those black pools were hard and dark and empty. The planes of his face were severe. Even the whiskers covering his jaw looked forbidding now. Dangerous. "Run!"

She did. Miranda shot to her feet and turned from the violent man who'd just mowed down her bodyguard, ran as fast as she could. The playful skirt tangled around her legs like vines, forcing her to grab a handful of fabric and yank it above her knees. She ran past a local vendor and down an alley, around the side of the building. She ran through muddy puddles and around trash bins. She ran until her sides hurt and her lungs protested.

Then she ran some more.

He was behind her, she knew. Running. And his legs were longer, stronger. She could hear him gaining on her, the pounding of heavy footsteps, the harsh edge to his breathing. She tried not to think about what would happen if he caught her, all the things he could do, but years of security lectures echoed insidiously through her mind. Small dark rooms. No windows, no light. Cold. Darkness. Blindfolds. No contact with the outside world. Favors for food. Bloodlust.

Comparatively, Hawk's fate was a gift.

The truth spurred her on, the knowledge of what a critical mistake she'd made. She knew better than to trust strangers. She knew better than to let a stranger's smile, no matter how seductive, lure her into lowering her guard.

But, God help her, here so far away from American soil and the media who hounded her family, she'd thought she could live a little without inviting disaster.

Wrong. Wrong, wrong, wrong.

The man with the enigmatic eyes and seductive words had only been playing her, melting her guard by claiming he wanted a picture of her, then trying to lure her away. That's when the shots had started. When he'd put a hand on her body, Hawk had broken from hiding and tried to fulfill his duties.

And now he was probably dead. Because of her.

The thought, the reality, chilled as badly as the knowledge the stranger was gaining on her.

"You can stop now, *bella.*"

The raspy voice tore through her as though he'd used his lethal briefcase and not his vocal chords. "Stay away from me!" she gasped, racing around a corner and into a narrow street. A car horn blared and brakes squealed, but she didn't slow, not even when the driver shouted at her.

"*Bella!* It's okay now."

God, no. A cramp cut deep into her side, but she refused to let the pain deter her.

"Please," he roared. Closer. Harder. "It's not safe to be on the streets."

Determination pushed her forward, when fatigue had her stumbling. She didn't know where she was now, just knew she had to make it back to the embassy. The ruthless stranger had already killed.

She doubted he would hesitate to do so again.

"Help!" she shouted as she ran down a narrow alley. Laundry flapped in the breeze from second-story windows and dogs barked rambunctiously, but no one came to investigate the commotion.

Because they didn't understand English.

Before, she'd liked knowing little of the Portuguese language, had reveled in the sense of anonymity. Now, her inability to communicate sent her heart hammering furiously against her ribs.

"Someone help me!"

"No, *bella,* no!" the stranger shouted, just as his hand clamped around her arm. She struggled against his grip, but he was too strong, and she couldn't move.

"There's a safe house not far from here," he was saying, but she barely heard. Training kicked in, and in one fluid move she reached down to the strap around her ankle and came back up with her last line of defense. She'd never thought to need the hunting knife which once belonged to her maternal grandfather as anything more than a token to prove to her father she could take care of herself, but now...

She jutted the weapon toward the stranger. "Let go," she said through clenched teeth.

Surprise registered in his dark eyes. *"Bella—"*

"You're making a terrible mistake," she warned, trying to twist her wrist free of his hand. Shallow breaths tore in and out of her. "Trust me when I say I'm not someone you want to mess with."

"I know you're scared," he coaxed in a surprisingly gentle voice, "but you don't need to be afraid of me. I'm not going to let anyone hurt you."

She swallowed hard, fighting the lure of his words. Deception came in all shapes and sizes, she knew. Seduction made a perfect disguise. She looked at him standing there, the heat radiating from his body fighting with the chill in her blood. His black shirt was damp now, clinging to a powerful chest. In his hand, he still held his briefcase.

That was really a gun.

Cold fingers of certainty clawed at her. No matter how badly she wanted to believe him, the fear pounding through her refused to go away. He'd approached her with a hidden agenda. He'd been trying to coax her away with him, out of the public eye. He'd wanted her alone…like he had her now.

And somewhere by the ocean, Hawk lay bleeding, maybe dead.

The truth reverberated through the narrow alley as explosively as the gunfire in the marketplace. She'd always known life turned in a heartbeat, but nothing had prepared her for the abrupt transformation from seductive Casanova to machine-gun-toting commando. Nothing about him even looked the same here in this shadowy place. Everything was harder now. Darker.

"Lower your weapon," the stranger warned. His gaze flicked to her fingers curled bloodlessly around the hilt of the knife. "Don't make me force you."

Because he would.

She didn't stop to think any further. Knife in hand, she lunged.

The stranger swore hotly, dropping the briefcase and grabbing the blade before impact. Just as quickly he tossed the family heirloom to the ground and retrieved his briefcase.

Never once did his left hand leave her body.

"Are you out of your mind?" he growled incredulously.

She looked at the fingers closed around her wrist and realized she'd gravely underestimated him.

"What do you want with me?" she asked, not sure she really wanted to know, but determined to meet her fate with at least some modicum of dignity.

"I want to get you to safety."

"You killed Hawk," she accused in horror.

"I saved your life," he corrected. "I almost took a bullet for you, damn it."

There were worse things, Miranda knew, than death. "You shot at the police."

His jaw tightened. "I shot at a known criminal, who just happened to be wearing a police uniform. *He* killed the man you call Hawk. If I wanted you dead, *bella,* you wouldn't be standing here right now."

There was a cool logic to the claim, but Miranda warned herself not to fall for his verbal skills once again. Her thoughts tumbled back to the scene by the ocean, the way Hawk had fallen that first time, then staggered to his knees. Shots had erupted only moments later. Which way had he fallen? she tried to remember. Toward the man in the police uniform, meaning the stranger had shot him? Or toward her, meaning—

"No," she muttered. "No."

For the first time since the shooting, the stranger's face softened. His eyes didn't look quite so ominous, and that mouth which had been a grim line returned to the almost sensuous fullness of before. Around her wrist, his fingers loosened.

"Look, *bella,*" he reasoned. "There's nothing I can say that you'll believe right now, but think about this. Someone who wanted to hurt you wouldn't waste time coaxing. If that's what I wanted, I'd have you over my shoulder and out of sight before you even realized I'd moved."

Miranda cringed at the realization of how easy it would be for him to do just that. She could fight him—she *would* fight him—but kicking and thrashing would not overpower a man of hard muscle and brutal determination, a man who enjoyed a six-inch, hundred-pound advantage. A man who could shoot with a briefcase.

Toward her, she remembered abruptly. Hawk had fallen toward her. The shots that felled him had come from the opposite direction, not the tall man who looked at her through eyes burning like chips of black ice.

If I wanted you dead, you wouldn't be standing here.

Her thoughts returned to those frenzied moments, but this time, she saw his actions through a different lens. When shots had sprayed the plaza, he'd shielded her with his body. When he'd told her to run, he'd covered her back. Even now, when she'd pulled a knife, he'd simply disarmed her, not using her weapon to teach her a lesson, as her father had warned an attacker would do.

Hawk had always chided her not to expect a kidnapper to politely ask permission. They would act first, consider damage later. Men who lived on the fringes of civility didn't show restraint. This man did.

His actions almost seemed...protective.

"Look, I appreciate what you did back there," she said, "but I've really got to go." The rational side of her brain realized he was right; if he'd wanted to hurt her, he would have by now. But he held a briefcase that turned into a semiautomatic. That made him dangerous, her uneasy. "I need to contact the embassy in Lisbon."

He frowned, but before he could speak, a nearby door flung open and a middle-aged woman with a baby on her hip stepped into the shadowy alley.

"Paulo?" she called, then continued speaking in Portuguese.

Miranda took advantage of the momentary distraction to break away and bolt down the alley. "I need your phone—"

She only made it two steps. *"Bella, bella, bella,"* the stranger murmured, taking her arm and drawing her against the hard planes of his body. His voice was drugging, his eyes liquid. *"Mi dispiace,"* he muttered, pressing the hand with the briefcase against her lower back.

"Stop it," Miranda said, struggling against him. She had no idea what he said, but the Portuguese woman's sappy smile seemed to approve.

"Anima mia," he continued, leaning closer.

Anima mia she recognized. My love. She tried to push

him away, but he simply released her wrist and slipped his hand up through her hair. He held her tightly now, securely against his hard body.

"Tu hai le labbra le piu morbide del mondo," he whispered, gazing into her eyes. *"Baciami."*

Her heart changed rhythms, from a frantic pounding to a frantic thrumming. Her limbs seemed to thicken. The world around her dimmed, blurred. She didn't understand the words he spoke, but his glazed gaze gave away his intent. Miranda opened her mouth to protest, to somehow convince the smiling Portuguese woman that the man was playing her for a fool, but the words never had a chance to form.

The moment her lips parted, the stranger lowered his head and settled his mouth against hers.

Chapter 2

"Stop it," Miranda struggled to say, but realized her mistake too late. In trying to speak, she moved her mouth against his, a sensuous rhythm that felt more like invitation than protest. Her body reacted instinctively, betraying her clear down to the tips of her toes. Her blood heated. Her bones went liquid. She tried to yank away, but her hand settled against his shoulder instead.

Shock, she told herself. That was all. Nothing more.

But then his hold on her shifted, tightened. She struggled against the arms that held her like steel bands, but instead of releasing her, he groaned, a sound that rasped from deep in his throat, one that sounded more of pain than pleasure.

"*Dio,*" he muttered against her parted lips. He tasted of desperation and brute strength, iron will and...coffee. His hands moved possessively against her back as he changed the angle of his kiss, all the while his mouth moving with relentless slowness, coaxing and promising, persuading.

Dizzy, off-balance, reeling, Miranda held herself completely still against the onslaught, resisting the temptation to play his dangerous game. She knew she should pull away. She *told* herself to pull away. Wipe the taste of him from her mouth. This man was a stranger. And he had a gun. But she was desperately afraid that if she moved, she'd be grabbing the damp cotton of his shirt and pulling him closer. Maybe it was leftover adrenaline or the stark realization that she could have been killed, but there was something blatantly masculine about the way he kissed her, and it sent her defenses into complete meltdown.

Swaying, she lifted a hand to steady herself, but found her fingertips skimming the stubble along his jaw instead.

And this time, the ragged cry came from her throat, not his.

He ripped his mouth from hers, staggered back almost violently.

Miranda groped for a nearby trash can and braced her hand against the cool metal lid. She struggled to breathe, to *think,* but could do little more than stare at the man who'd just kissed her with a gentle urgency that muddled her senses. His eyes were dark, but somehow managed to glitter. He stood alert, ready, as though face-to-face with one of Portugal's famous apparitions. If she hadn't known better, she would have sworn he didn't know who she was or where she'd come from.

At the moment, she wasn't sure she did, either.

''Dio,'' he whispered again, shoving dark hair from his face.

The thrill streaking through her made absolutely no sense. She sucked in a jerky breath, tried to calm the surge of craziness, but her lungs had other ideas. Her pulse tripped along at an alarming rate. She felt like she'd just run a dead sprint, rather than shared a kiss with a stranger.

Who held a gun on her.

That thought jarred her out of the sensual haze and forced her to swing toward the woman with the baby. But she no longer stood in the alley, and her door was firmly closed.

Panic crawled up Miranda's throat. The trembling started then, first deep inside, quickly racing to her extremities. She pivoted toward the stranger, only to find he'd recovered from their encounter. He looked taller than before, broader. She couldn't see the alley beyond him, only the width of his shoulders and the solid wall of his chest. He watched her carefully, the mouth that had kissed her so gently now a hard line.

Unable to look away, not trusting her voice, she lifted an appallingly shaky hand to her mouth, only to find her lips moist and swollen.

"I know, *bella,* it surprised the hell out of me, too."

For one of the few times in her life, words failed her. So did movement. Coherent thought. She should do something, she thought wildly. Tell him to go to hell. Slap him. Run from the man whose briefcase turned into a gun. She could, she knew. He'd finally released her. But her legs wouldn't work. Nothing, it seemed, not Emily Post nor boarding school nor Secret Service training had adequately prepared her for the shock of this man's mouth moving against hers, the reality of his body pressed to hers. The unmistakable evidence that he reacted to her as strongly as she reacted to him. The regret and desire warring brutally in his midnight gaze.

The completely misplaced blade of fascination.

"Who are you?" she whispered.

"I'm someone who's trying to help you," he answered vaguely, impatiently, and she realized she believed him. Then he reached for her. "Come on. We need to get out of here before anyone else sees us."

She pulled back from his touch, but couldn't stop staring at his hand. He held it outstretched, square palm up and callused fingers extended, exposing dried trickles of blood from where he'd grabbed the hunting knife instead of twisting her wrist. He hadn't winced, hadn't cursed, hadn't given any outward sign of a pain she knew he had to have felt.

And he hadn't made her suffer in return.

Confused, she looked up. She'd been seeking his eyes, but never made it past his jaw. His lips were slightly dry, a hint of her coral lipstick smeared against the olive skin at the corner of his mouth.

"If I didn't know better, *bella,* I'd think you've never been kissed before."

Squaring her shoulders, she met his eyes, those enigmatic pools of midnight, determined not to let this man who wouldn't even disclose his identity see the absurd curiosity that had her wanting to push up and brush her mouth against his once again.

Nonchalance, she reminded herself. That was the Carrington way. Cool, calm, collected. Unaffected and untouchable. Meet adversity with a smile, and no one ever had to know you bled.

"I haven't," she said with a saccharine smile. "At least, not by somebody holding a briefcase that's really an Uzi."

God help her, he laughed. It was a deep sound, rich and amused. "It's an MP5K submachine gun," he said, stroking the weapon in question like a man would caress a beautiful woman. "Uzis are Israeli. This baby is German."

A shiver ran through her, but she hid the reaction with a perfectly executed shrug. "Yes, well. Thank you for clarifying."

"And you hardly left me a choice. I couldn't let you tell that woman I'm some kind of monster."

"If the shoe fits…"

A sound of pure male frustration broke from his throat. His English may have been accented, but American slang was no stranger to him. "Relax, *bella.* You can add kissing to my list of formidable crimes, if you like, but rest assured, there will be no repeat performances. I'm not here to get you naked."

No emotion underscored his words, or his expression. Not threat or regret, not ferocity or hostility. He sounded matter-of-fact. Almost…indifferent.

And in that moment, Miranda realized a fundamental truth. She'd stopped being afraid. Somewhere along the line she'd forgotten about the fear that had chased her down the streets and alleys, forgotten the cold certainty that this man wanted to hurt her. Or worse.

She'd forgotten to think at all.

But she was thinking now, more clearly by the second.

Vividly, she recalled the scene along the promenade, Hawk breaking toward her, the way he'd gone down, the stranger reacting without hesitation, the man in fatigues racing from around the corner, then falling only feet from her. Everything had unfurled almost methodically, carefully orchestrated step by carefully orchestrated step.

Horrified at her own gullibility, she swallowed hard.

"Think about it," the man who'd just *happened* to be in the right place, at the right time, was saying. "How many kidnappers stand around and beg their prey to leave with them?"

The last of the fog cleared, leaving the truth shivering in the glare of the sun. The family net had closed around her once again. No wonder there'd been no warnings.

They'd have ruined her father's pop quiz.

"Is that what you're doing?" Incredulity drilled through her. Disappointment whispered along behind. "Begging?"

His gaze turned smoky. "Do I need to?"

Down the alley a door opened and closed, destroying the heated moment. Suddenly he was all warrior again, looking around, ready and alert. His eyes were dark, his mouth hard. Even his grip on the briefcase tightened.

And in that moment, she made her decision. "Give me back my knife."

"What?"

"You want me to believe you're on my side. Fine. Show me I can trust you. Show me I have no reason to be afraid." *Prove to me you're who I think you are.* "If I really have nothing to fear from you, you'll give me back my knife."

The man looked as though she'd just asked him to roll

naked over hot coals. "So you can try to skewer me again?"

"I won't try anything, so long as you don't."

He narrowed his eyes. "You're testing me."

"I'm asking you to trust me, no more, no less than you asked of me." She stuck out her hand. "Actions speak louder than words, after all. So do we have a deal, or are you going to make me scream?"

That light glinted in his eyes again. He held her gaze as a slow smile curved his lips and bared startlingly white teeth.

"Trust me, *bella,*" he said, squatting to retrieve the knife, then placing the ivory hilt in her hand. Never once did he take his eyes off hers. "When I make a woman scream, it doesn't have a damn thing to do with a knife."

Miranda curled her fingers around the cherished gift from her grandfather, trying to focus on something, anything, other than the stranger's smoky words and clever mouth, those big battered hands...

She had absolutely no business thinking about just how he might carry out his promise.

"Now come on," he growled. "I doubt our shooter was traveling alone. I've got to get you off the streets before the bullets start flying again."

He was good, she'd hand him that. The take-no-prisoners words destroyed any lingering doubt about his identity. And his employ. She'd heard those words, that tone, before. Many times. They were the hallmark of security personnel.

The words of a bodyguard.

"So what's it going to be?" her father's man asked. "Are you going to take your chances with me or wait for those thugs back there to find you? I doubt they'll be as patient as I am."

For now, she realized, she had few alternatives. This man meant business. She could go along with her father's latest orders willingly, or she could resist and leave the stranger no choice but to exert force. And while the latter carried a rebellious little thrill, Miranda thought it wiser to lull him into the same sense of complacency her father had used with her.

She put her hand in his. "If we're going to trust each other, the least you can do is tell me your name."

"I thought the knife was all you wanted."

Now that she knew what she was dealing with, she lifted a single eyebrow, determined not to give him the upper hand her father's men always wanted.

"Since when has a knife been all a woman wants?" she challenged. Her mother constantly warned her about rattling cages, but she'd never been one to back down.

His smile was quick, blinding, devastating. "A man can dream, can't he?"

"Is that really what you dream about? That a woman wants nothing from you but a blade?"

His gaze dipped from her face to where her blouse had fallen over her shoulder, down lower to her brightly colored skirt, all the way down to her leather sandals. Then he reversed his perusal, just as slowly, just as thoroughly.

"You really want to know what I dream about, *bella?*"

Heat washed through her, as though he'd touched her with those big capable hands and not just a look. The image formed before she could stop it, of what a man like him would dream about. She could see him too well, his big nude body thrashing about among tangled sheets—

"I'll settle for a name," she said.

"Smart lady." He glanced toward the end of the alley, where two children ran after a scrawny black dog. Only when they turned the corner did he return his attention to her. "My friends call me Sandro."

"And your enemies?" she couldn't help asking.

He didn't hesitate. "They'd like to call me dead."

The brutally frank words made her wince. She couldn't imagine this vital, capable man dead. Didn't want to.

"Sandro what?" she asked instead.

"Just Sandro."

Miranda didn't know whether to laugh or slug him. "Watched a few spy movies growing up, did we?"

But his smile was gone now, replaced by that same grim expression she was already growing to despise. "Just Sandro, okay? It's safer for us all."

Safer from what, she wanted to ask, but knew she'd only be wasting her breath. Her father's men never shot straight. They were always engaged in their little intrigues. If this man's orders were to conceal his last name, not even cruel and unusual torture would pry the information free.

For now, it was better to indulge him.

Later, she would outsmart him.

Sandro picked up the pace, practically dragging her around a corner and down an even narrower alley.

"What did you say when that woman came out?" she asked. *Before he put his mouth to hers and knocked the foundation from beneath her feet.*

He kept walking, his long legs gobbling up the cracked cobblestone. "It doesn't matter."

She refused to break into a run to keep up with him. "It does to me."

"Sweet nothings don't translate well."

"Sweet nothings?" She didn't understand the little jolt of disappointment. "Sure sounded like something to me."

He stopped abruptly, landing her in a lingering puddle from the storm the night before. Muddy water splashed up over her sandals and against her calves.

"If you must know," he said, lifting a hand to her face and easing back the tangled blond hair, "I told her we'd had a lovers' quarrel and I was trying to earn your forgiveness."

The words, his touch, seared through her, the image they created as dangerous as the lingering feel of his mouth on hers. A quarrel. Lovers. A man and a woman, intimately involved. Big battered hands skimming along smooth—

Surprise flashed through her. Not only was this man a stranger, but he was one of her father's chosen few. Men like him thrived in a world of intrigue and betrayal, a world where nothing was as it seemed and the truth often hid secrets more dangerous than lies.

A world she wanted desperately to leave behind.

"Does that usually work?" she wanted to know.

He quirked a dark brow. "What? Kissing a woman senseless?"

The smile broke before she could stop it. "No, lying through your teeth."

He streaked a finger down the side of her face. "If I'm lucky."

"And if you're not?"

He took her hand and started down the street, his strides long and purposeful, determined. "There's always Plan B."

Plan B lay in ruins, much like the abandoned villa hiding behind an overgrown wall of olive trees and cork oaks, oleander and hibiscus.

Sandro bit back a virulent stream of frustration. He was a careful man. He did his job efficiently, and he did it well. He left no room for error.

But this time, with the stakes so dangerously high, error had found him anyway.

Plan B featured Miranda Carrington safe and sound with a bodyguard, not dragged through the dirty alleys of Cascais. He'd arranged the scenario carefully. He'd approached Miranda just as the general had ordered, making it appear he was luring her away. But he'd also arranged for his kidnapping attempt to be thwarted. He'd even planned to go down in the process.

But the agents he'd had breakfast with only an hour before had not arrived.

Straddling a thin dark line was a hell of a way to live. He'd been forced to stall, to keep Miranda in the open, in front of witnesses who would see the ambassador's daughter forcibly wrested from him. Whether with Hawk Monroe or Plan A's fatigue-clad security agent Pedro Vasquez, she should have been nearing Lisbon by now, hustled onto a plane out of the country. But an unknown assailant had mowed down both plans and both men, leaving Sandro with an angry woman and one hell of a problem.

Possession of Miranda Carrington didn't figure into any of his plans, not C, not D, not even Z. Possession of Miranda Carrington went against every strategy, every rule, in the International Security Alliance operations manual. And unless Sandro played his cards right, the ominously silent ambassador's daughter could not only ruin years worth of work, but get them both killed in the process. Again.

This time for good.

Staying alive demanded he find a way to unload his unwanted charge before anyone realized he had her. Her disappearance would be viewed as kidnapping, and the fallout would create an international fiasco. The United States government couldn't sanction his actions, nor could the ISA claim him, not when doing so would forfeit years of undercover operations.

The low burn in his shoulder intensified, forcing Sandro to bite back a muttered curse. He had to maneuver out of this jam all by himself, just like he'd fallen into it. He'd long since learned the risk of putting his life into the hands of others. No way would he jeopardize the fate of an innocent woman.

The term collateral damage turned his stomach.

Frowning, he glanced at the woman walking beside him. He held her hand securely in his, but instinct warned touching Miranda Carrington required more than flesh to flesh contact. She held her chin high, shoulders back, those fascinating gypsy eyes focused on some point in the distance, as though being shot at and pursued through back alleys was an everyday occurrence.

"Almost there," he said, unnerved by her silence. She hadn't uttered a word in over thirty minutes, but he could tell she was thinking as rapidly as they were walking. He could only imagine the questions racing through her, the uncertainty.

He would get her inside, get her safe, then tell her what he could.

Which wasn't much.

"Almost where?" she asked, but didn't look at him.

He, on the other hand, couldn't stop watching her, all that thick blond hair cascading around her face and over a shoulder bared by her loose-fitting crimson blouse, that lush mouth set in a mutinous line and those defiantly high cheekbones. He knew where he wanted to take her, all right.

He knew where he wanted *her* to take *him*.

He also knew he was flat out of his mind.

Javier was right. Sandro had been living in the shadows far too long.

But he felt the light now, the heat, and that was the problem. All because of one stupid kiss. A reckless, desperate measure to keep her from rousing suspicion in the local woman. An insane curiosity to see if her mouth would feel as welcoming as the long-ago tabloid picture had promised.

A smart man would erase the encounter from his memory. A smart man would forget the feel of her lips, the soft little sigh that had escaped. He'd expected her to slam her fists against his chest and shove him away, to stomp down on his feet, to *fight*. But she'd barely resisted. It was as though he'd laid siege to her with a stun gun rather than his mouth. She hadn't been angry as he'd expected, as he *deserved,* but…frozen.

The realization should have brought him great relief.

It didn't.

Stopping adjacent to a crumbling stone wall, he pointed toward an overgrown oleander, dotted by a showy display of bright pink flowers. "Just through here."

She leaned closer. "Through where?"

He pulled a tangled clump of honeysuckle aside, reveal-

ing a broken-out section of the wall. The sun beat mercilessly against his back, but in the forgotten world beyond
the opening, shadows beckoned. He itched to step through
to the other side, to the familiar, secretive world in which
he thrived.

"Through there," he said.

Miranda pivoted toward him. In the space of a heartbeat
the unflappable facade faded, replaced by a vulnerability he
hadn't sensed before. Hadn't expected. Wariness glinted in
the near-translucent green of her eyes, as though he'd asked
her to go skinny-dipping in the frigid waters of the Atlantic,
rather than crawl through a hole to safety.

"Where are you taking me?" she asked.

There was a threadiness to her voice now, one that unnerved him more than her earlier silence. Whereas she'd
been all fire and defiance when she thought herself threatened, when he offered security, she pulled back.

"Somewhere safe," he told her.

"This isn't the way to the U.S. embassy."

"No, it's not."

"Then I'll ask you again. Where are you taking me?"

"Relax," he said, glancing up and down the narrow
street to ensure no one watched their movements. "I'm not
going to let anything happen to you."

Her gaze remained wary, her stance alert, prompting
Sandro to give her hand a gentle squeeze. Her flesh was
clammy now, making her hand feel smaller. More fragile.

The temptation to pull her into his arms made absolutely
no sense, so he discarded the misplaced notion and urged
her toward the opening. "Hurry up. We need to get off the
streets before anyone sees us. You can bet the shooter
didn't come alone."

The reminder of the danger did the trick. She turned from
him and climbed through the jagged opening in the stone
wall. He followed, letting the thick vines swing into place
behind him.

Only then did he breathe easier.

"My God," she whispered. "It's like stepping back in time."

An old wall separated the overgrown grounds of the abandoned villa from the rest of the world. Exiled aristocrats had constructed the Moorish-influenced home in the waning years of the nineteenth century, the pastel-washed, stuccoed limestone walls providing shelter and security to generations of a family on the decline. Not even two world wars had penetrated the safe haven.

Only death had possessed that right.

When the great-grandson of the original owner passed away some ten years before, none of his seven children expressed interest in taking over the villa. They'd scattered to Italy and France, a daughter in Scotland, two sons in America, and the prospect of returning to the less modern culture of old-world Portugal had held little appeal.

"This place looks deserted," Miranda said.

He tossed her a wicked little wink. "That's the point."

The villa stood abandoned now, a shadow of its former glory. Red clay roof tiles were cracked and faded; vines had long since taken over pale yellow walls that retained only a hint of their former color. Even the blue and yellow clay tiles framing the broken-out windows were chipped. *Azulejos* they were called, imitating familiar patterns of Moorish rugs.

Miranda walked toward a crumbling statue of the Virgin Mary, who rose from a tangle of thigh-high sage and stood with her arms outstretched toward the old house. "She looks…sad."

Sandro joined her. "She'll keep us safe," he said, reclaiming Miranda's hand and leading her toward the entryway.

Like so many other houses of central Portugal, the neglected villa boasted a wide front porch, framed by a series of three archways. The second story featured two smaller verandas, with the third story reserved for windows, dark now, almost gaping, like an old woman smiling through missing teeth.

The scent of rosemary grew stronger with every step, escorting them through an overgrown herb garden sprawling over the steps and engulfing the porch. Miranda broke off a stem as they passed.

"Through here," Sandro said, leading her inside.

"It's dark."

"You'll adjust." He kept her hand in his and headed along the familiar path to the back of the house, carefully checking for signs of unwanted visitors. Only a few hours had passed since his last inspection, but a man could never be too careful.

Beneath the stairs at the back of the house, he opened a small closet and pulled Miranda into the darkness.

"Just stay close," he instructed, whispering even though he didn't need to.

She stopped abruptly and tried to pull her hand free. "Where are we?"

Her voice was sharp, frightened. And in the ensuing silence, he could hear the frenetic rhythm of her breathing. The pounding of her heart. "Just a little further."

"But—"

"Shh," he soothed. "Trust me."

She didn't bother pointing out that she had no choice. He hadn't given her one.

Against the back wall, Sandro reached up and knocked twice against a hollow portion. A panel slid open, granting them access to a narrow stairway. He retrieved a flashlight from the ledge where he'd left it that morning and turned it on, drenching the narrow corridor in light.

"Straight up there," he said.

Disbelief flooded her expression. "A secret passageway?"

He shrugged. "Sometimes paranoia is its own reward."

At the top of the stairs he opened another panel, this one leading to the small room where he'd slept the night before and on several other occasions when he'd needed to melt into the shadows for a few days.

Miranda stared at the threadbare sleeping bag crammed against the far wall.

"There's no electricity," he told her, "but thanks to a well outside, we're okay for water."

She followed his gesture toward the small chamber off the side of the room, where a primitive toilet and shower stood in equal abandon.

"We're staying here?" she asked, hugging her arms around her waist.

Compassion tugged at him. Compared to the ritzy resort she'd been staying at back in town, this small dank room rated somewhere between slum and prison. "You'll be safe here, Miranda. I promise. That's what counts."

She stiffened for a moment, then spun toward him, eyes flashing with a fire he hadn't seen since before he'd put his mouth to hers in the alley. "What did you say?"

"This is a safe house," he explained, trying to restore the calm. "No one will find us here."

She shook her head almost violently, sending tangled blond hair over her shoulders. "No. What did you call me?"

"Miranda."

"Miranda?" She stepped back from him, her stance alert. "You think my name is Miranda?"

"I know it is."

Her gaze sharpened, her expression pensive. "Well, that explains that," she muttered. "I don't know how to tell you this, but there's been a mistake. You've got the wrong woman."

Now it was his turn to stare. He studied her standing there, all that blond hair spilling over her shoulders, those unusual eyes imploring. Could he have—

No. He hadn't made a mistake. No way.

Mistakes got men like him killed.

"You're the right woman," he insisted, battling an admiration he didn't want to feel. "I'm a very thorough man. You're Miranda Carrington, youngest daughter of Peter Carrington, the U.S. ambassador to Ravakia and youngest granddaughter of the late Albert Carrington, former U.S. senator and one-time presidential hopeful."

She shook her head. "Didn't you see that man and woman kissing by the boardwalk?"

"Yes." But only for a moment. The second he'd locked onto Miranda, the rest of the busy promenade had dissolved.

"I overheard them talking. *She's* Miranda." Sincerity and conviction laced the claim. "She has dark brown hair, not blond."

Sandro crossed his arms over his chest, wincing when the motion pulled against his shoulder. He knew she had a penchant for giving her bodyguards hell, had played enough games to recognize a pro when he saw one. She clearly thought she could play him.

He just didn't understand why she wanted to.

"Let me see your passport."

"By all means." She dipped a hand into the satchel slung over her shoulder and pulled out a well-worn blue passport bearing the emblem of the United States. Flipping it open, he studied the picture of a gorgeous blonde, the accompanying name and address.

As far as forgeries went, the ambassador's daughter had a beaut in her possession.

"Astrid, huh?" Somehow, he kept the laughter from his voice.

She nodded. "That's right."

"Astrid Van Dyke of Stockholm," he mused, "who just happens to have Carrington eyes. And," he drawled, executing a lightning-quick move to bare the shoulder still covered by the crimson blouse, "her tattoo."

She froze, like an exquisite dragonfly captured in amber, wings forever in flight. Just like the one imprinted on her upper arm. Her face drained of all color, all expression.

And then she started to shake.

Regret hit hard and fast, but he shoved the useless emotion aside before it muddied the waters any further.

"Don't look so confused, *bella,*" he told her, his voice deliberately husky. He kept his hand on her arm, his fingers tracing the tattoo. "A woman like you doesn't go unnoticed. A woman like you doesn't just fade into the shadows or melt into crowds. A woman like you cannot hide, not even from yourself."

She backed away. "What do you mean, 'a woman like me'?"

The way she spat the words, Sandro would have thought he'd accused her of something hideous. He looked at her standing there, green gypsy eyes too big and dark against her pale face, that lush mouth he wanted to taste again still swollen from his earlier mistake.

"Beautiful," he said. "Intelligent. Full of life. Living, breathing sunshine."

She lifted a hand to her mouth, but said nothing.

"Why the games?" he asked, steering the conversation to safe ground. The questions rattling through him didn't bear answering. "Did you really think I'd just let you waltz out of here?"

She shoved the hair from her face, managing to look alarmingly provocative as she did so. "Maybe I'm just playing the same kind of game you are. The same kind of game *he* is."

Game? "What are you talking about? Who is *he?*"

Resentment flashed in her gaze, bringing color back to her cheeks. "Look, I know who you are, okay? I know what this is all about."

"Of course you know who I am. I told you."

"Not your name—names don't matter. I know what's going on here, why you were on the promenade, why we're here now. I know who you work for and what you want, and I can tell you right now it's not going to work."

Sandro went very still, all but his heart. It slammed

against his ribs. She spoke with fire and conviction, making his blood run cold. She couldn't know. She couldn't. Only a handful of people did.

And only that handful knew he was still alive.

Chapter 3

For the first time since they'd met alongside the ocean, Mr. Confident didn't look quite so sure of himself. He stood unmoving, his midnight eyes wild, his mouth a hard line. Even the shadow against his jaw seemed darker. He stood with his feet shoulder-width apart, arms at his side, hands curled into semifists.

He looked like a man ready to pounce.

The breath stalled in Miranda's throat. She'd only been playing him, testing him, gauging his competence. She hadn't expected him to react so strongly. She hadn't expected the air in the small dank room to thicken, her heart to start hammering.

"Who am I?" he asked in a chillingly soft voice. "Who do I work for? What do I want?"

Her mouth went dry. Suddenly, she wasn't quite so sure herself. "You tell me."

"I already have. I'm the man who's not going to let anyone hurt you."

The take-no-prisoners words curled though her like an

ominous mist rolling in from the ocean. She held his inscrutable gaze a moment, then glanced at the nasty scar slashed across his throat, then over to the briefcase he'd finally set down.

"You're the backup," she said.

"Backup?" He spoke slowly. Quietly. "Backup for what?"

"Not what, but who. My father. He's a very careful man. He knew I'd try to give Hawk the slip the second I saw him, so he sent a backup." The mere thought caused her chest to tighten. Betrayal slashed brutally. She'd believed her father this time. She'd believed that for the first time in eleven years, he was willing to let her live her own life.

Now she knew everything had been staged, just like so many times before. Hawk was probably throwing back a cold one somewhere, congratulating himself on a job well done, indifferent to the trauma he'd caused.

Just like he'd done with Elizabeth.

"You casually come on to me, then I see Hawk, run, shots are fired, and voila, there you are, ready for me to run gratefully into your arms."

Like a perfect little puppet.

Over the years, she'd become adept at sniffing out her father's security drills, but she hadn't seen this one coming. She'd been too intrigued by the man with the penetrating eyes and flattering words.

Humiliation left a bitter taste in her mouth.

But Sandro didn't seem to notice. He wasn't frowning anymore, wasn't glowering, didn't look like a warrior primed for battle. A purely male smile curved the mouth Miranda found entirely too erotic for a face of such hard lines and sharp planes.

"You were already in my arms," he reminded.

Miranda narrowed her eyes, wondering where the commando had gone and half wishing he would return. At least she knew how to defend herself against him.

"Your hands, not your arms," she corrected tartly. "There's a difference."

"Not always," he said, "but we'll save that nuance for another time. Right now I'm more interested in knowing why your father would expect you to run from someone assigned to protect you."

Miranda stiffened. With skillful precision Sandro was steering the conversation down a path she had no desire to travel.

"It's not like that," she defended, but knew he wouldn't understand.

"Then tell me how it is."

An emotion she didn't understand tangled through her. She couldn't summon one single memory of any of her father's men asking her opinion on anything. Ever.

"I'm just…tired," she admitted, and with the words, the fight drained out of her. Weariness took over, a bone-deep fatigue sharpened by the chase through back alleys and the unexpected kiss, the battle of wills, the long walk to the abandoned villa. She slid down against the wall and sat on the pathetic excuse for a sleeping bag, pulling her knees to her chest as she did so.

The family net had closed around her once again.

"I thought for once I was…free," she said, surprised by her candor. She and Hawk had rarely spoken, certainly not about anything personal. Of course, she'd never had any desire to confide in the smooth-talking yes-man who'd almost shattered her sister's life, and he'd never regarded her as more than an escape from the mess his heartlessness had created.

He was ridiculously lucky her father had no idea what had really gone down between his perfect daughter and the hardened bodyguard he'd assigned to protect her.

Intimacy always carried a price.

But Sandro seemed different from the clowns her father usually sent to shadow Miranda's every step. He seemed… more human. He seemed more real. And the way he looked at her, that dark gaze concentrated fully on her, loosened the tight flag of indifference she normally kept furled close.

"As Astrid, I could go places," she told him with a smile her grandfather had called impish. The one her father called willful. For two months she'd been traveling the European countryside with her camera as her companion, capturing slices of a life she'd never known existed. "I could do and see things without worrying about attracting unwanted attention."

Her smile faded, along with the sense of freedom she'd embraced only a few hours before.

"Now I realize these past weeks were just an illusion. I never left the Carrington fishbowl after all." The sting of disappointment burned her throat. "He's been watching me every step, hasn't he? All his talk of trust and freedom was nothing but lies."

Sandro frowned. "You don't know that."

But she did. Sandro with the machine-gun briefcase was living, breathing proof of that.

She looked at him standing in the hazy light creeping through the dirty window, but for a moment didn't see the man who'd chased her through alleys or followed her father's orders. She saw only the man who'd approached her alongside the ocean.

The picture you're about to take. It's all wrong.

Wrong? How so?

Because you're not in it.

Her heart staggered. Moisture stung the backs of her eyes.

I see myself in the mirror every morning. I don't need pictures of myself.

Then give it to me.

Now why would I do that?

So I can remember the way you look standing here, with the sun in your hair and the smile on your face.

Emotion swelled through her. She'd wanted him to be real, damn it. She'd wanted the moment to be real.

But like everything else in the Carrington world, the encounter had only been a carefully orchestrated means to an end. Just like her first drink. Her first kiss. Except those hadn't been arranged by her father but, rather, pathetic scum who wanted to use the Carrington name as a meal ticket.

"Miranda?" Sandro asked, going down on one knee.

The gesture struck her as foolishly gallant. "I'm sorry he dragged you into this," she said, forcing a smile and pushing to her feet.

"I'm tired and I'm hungry," she added. "So why don't you take me back to my hotel, so I can call my father and tell him I'm not interested in playing any more of his games." If he insisted on having someone shadow her, she didn't want the man to be Sandro. She couldn't look at him without remembering the ray of anticipation she'd felt by the ocean. She couldn't stay with him in a small room like this without remembering the way he'd made her feel for those first few minutes, that seductive sense of intrigue, the intoxicating glow of discovery.

If her father had to keep tabs on her, she'd rather Hawk or Aaron or any other of his yes-men, not this tall man with the midnight eyes and rough voice, who reminded her how foolish she'd been to hope, for even a few minutes, that she could have a life beyond the Carrington mystique.

Slowly, Sandro rose to his full height. "You think this is a game?"

"Not a game. A drill. A lesson. A powerplay." Eleven years before, a tragic accident had forever changed the Carrington family. After burying his oldest daughter Kristina, her father had never left anything to chance, ever again.

Equal parts grief-stricken and naive, a seventeen-year-old Miranda had been unprepared for the measures Peter Carrington had implemented to protect his remaining children. Only months later, during her freshman year at

Wellesley, she'd been horrified when the caring, considerate girl with whom she'd shared secrets, clothes and a dorm room turned out to be a female bodyguard, hired to keep an eye on her. Watch her. Report back to her father. Since then Miranda had become skilled at spotting his setups. It burned her that she hadn't seen this one coming.

But then, never before had her father sent someone who looked like temptation and spoke like a poet.

"You're not the first, you know," she said, deliberately dismissing him. "Dad excels in orchestrating little security exercises to prove I need to be more careful."

"Security exercises?"

"You know. Because of Kris. Friends that turn out to be federal agents, bouncers that turn out to be bodyguards. Once he arranged for a raid at a college bar, just to prove that if he could find me drinking, so could the media or a kook."

Sandro swore under his breath. "You think the scene by the ocean was staged for your benefit?"

She lifted her chin. "Wasn't it?"

"Bella," he said in that hoarse voice of his, that seeped through her defenses like a smoky mist no matter how hard she worked to reinforce them, "I hate to shatter your illusions, but this isn't a drill or a lesson. This is as real as it gets." His gaze on hers, he lifted his hands to his chest, his fingers practically brutalizing the buttons of his black shirt.

Her heart started to hammer again, this time in a halting, irregular rhythm. "What are you doing?"

"Those shots back there were the real thing," he said, his voice softer than before. Almost strained. Reaching the waistband of his pants, he shrugged out of the cotton shirt.

Miranda braced herself for the sight of darkly tanned flesh and hard muscle, but instead found herself staring at a thick gray vest.

A vest she instantly recognized.

"The man trying to hurt you was real," Sandro continued, working the buckles and snaps of the familiar body armor. Impatience snapped through his voice. "And come morning," he growled, dropping the heavy vest to the floor and turning his back to her, "this will be a real damn bruise."

Shock cut through Miranda. She stared at the nasty green and purple already discoloring the center of a back otherwise magnificently perfect. His shoulders were broad, bronze, thickly muscled. They tapered to the center of his back, which in turn tapered perfectly to the waistband of his pants.

Perfect, that was, save for the nasty streaks of dark red.

Abruptly, she followed the trail of dried blood back to his shoulder, where a crust tried vainly to conceal blood still oozing from a nasty wound. *"You're bleeding."*

Sandro twisted around to look at his upper back. "Am I?" he asked, then grimaced. "Son of a bitch. No wonder my shoulder feels like it's on fire."

Deep inside, Miranda started to shake. The chill came next, starting in her heart and seeping through her blood. This man had risked his life for her. He'd been not only shot at, but shot.

Because of her.

"Here, let me," she said, stepping closer. She lifted her hands to his back, not really knowing what she planned to do, but knowing she had to touch him. Help him. Very gently, she touched her fingertips to the heat of his flesh—

"Cristo!" he shouted, then continued in a language she didn't understand.

She jerked back. "I'm sorry. I—"

"Your hands are like ice!"

And his skin was like fire. She stared at him, but the room started to revolve. The walls pushed closer. The air grew too thick to breathe. Thoughts and possibilities crashed around inside her like bullets in a mausoleum. Horror stabbed deep.

It was real. Everything that had gone down in the

crowded marketplace had been authentic, not staged. The shots and the shouting. Hawk going down, then pulling himself back up, only to be mowed down again.

Dear God, Elizabeth. Her sister said she didn't love Hawk, had never loved him, but Miranda had always believed—

"Miranda?"

She blinked rapidly, working desperately to bring Sandro's face into focus. He was moving closer, his big body blocking out the meager light seeping through the window, until her world consisted only of him.

"If there was a th-threat, he should have told m-me," she whispered in a voice she barely recognized as her own. "He should have warned m-me. T-told me about you."

"Miranda—"

"I wouldn't have been on the street like that," she insisted, gazing up at him. She widened her eyes, imploring him to believe her. She'd seen how her sister's death had shattered her family, would never do anything willingly to put them through that again. She wasn't foolish. She didn't have a death wish. She'd taken countless self-defense classes. Had a few tricks up her sleeve. "I would have been more careful."

"Miranda." Sandro took her shoulders in his hands and gave her a gentle squeeze. "Your father loves you," he said softly but firmly. "He wants to keep you safe. Where's the crime in that? If I hadn't been there, don't you realize where you would be right now? What could be happening to you?"

She did realize, that was the problem. If he hadn't been there, she could be with the horrible man who'd killed Hawk—or dead. But in not warning her about the threat or telling her about Sandro, her father had left her equally vulnerable.

"What if you'd been shot somewhere besides your chest or back? What if I'd stabbed you? Then what would have happened? Both my bodyguards would have been down, and because my father chose an underhanded method of protecting me, I wouldn't have had a clue what was really going on.''

Sandro lifted a hand to her face, his fingers skimming her cheekbone. ''None of that happened. I have you now, and everything's going to be okay.''

There was an unmistakable gentleness to his touch, a persuasiveness that sent an unwanted rush through her. ''Why didn't he warn me? Why didn't he tell me about you?''

''Everything happened too fast. There wasn't time for warnings.''

''He should have found a way!''

''Bella, bella, bella,'' he said, his voice like velvet. ''Are you always so tough? Do you always malign those trying to help you? Protect you?''

The softly spoken questions hit with unerring accuracy. ''You don't know what you're talking about,'' she said, ripping away from his touch. She needed to think, but couldn't gather her thoughts when he stood so close she felt his every breath, his every heartbeat.

''Don't you have something more important to do than psychoanalyze me?'' she asked with a sharpness he didn't deserve. ''Like report back to my father?''

His expression darkened. ''Actually,'' he said, glancing at the nasty wound on his shoulder, ''I do.''

Regret hit hard and fast. This man had been shot because of her, was bleeding. This man had put his body between her and a bullet. And here she stood, berating him because he willingly followed the orders she'd grown to despise.

''I'm sorry,'' she said, appalled at her thoughtlessness. But when she started toward him, he lifted a hand to stop her.

''Don't, *bella*. I can take care of this myself.''

''But I can help you.''

''That's not necessary.''

She didn't know what she heard in his voice, bitterness

or resolve, maybe regret, but she recognized the look in his eyes, that hard, cold look of a man who didn't allow others to interfere with his code of conduct.

"You've been shot," she said.

"It's only a flesh wound." He turned from her then, reached for the body armor. "Bullet barely grazed me."

"What are you doing?"

He fastened the vest around his upper body and retrieved his black shirt, wincing as he slid the wrinkled cotton over his injured shoulder. "This is wrong, *bella*. This isn't how things were supposed to go down."

"What are you talking about?"

"You're not supposed to be with me," he growled, and almost sounded pained. "There are things you don't understand. Things I need to find out. What went down back there was a mistake. You're right. I was the backup. I wasn't supposed to end up with you. Hawk was. Now I've got to figure out what went wrong and what happens next."

She watched him fight with little black buttons far too small for his fingers. "Why can't we just go to the embassy?"

"Too risky," he answered without hesitation. "Too public."

"What if someone sees us?" she asked, glancing toward the window. Not much light made it through the grime and the overgrown foliage surrounding the villa, but beyond this secluded world, the sun shone brightly.

"No one will see us," he said.

"How can you be so sure?"

"Because *we* won't be anywhere. You'll be here, and I'll be doing what I do best."

Miranda just stared at him. "You're leaving me?"

He strode toward the small window and peered outside. "You'll be safer here than out there with me."

She hugged her arms around her middle, not wanting to be left alone, but unaccustomed to asking one of her father's men for anything. "What if you don't come back?"

"That's not going to happen."

But what if it does? she wanted to ask, but the words jammed in her throat. He was hiding something, she realized with cold certainty. Holding something back. It was there in his eyes, an edgy, unsettled look, like he wasn't quite sure what he'd find when he turned the corner.

"What aren't you telling me?"

He picked up his briefcase. "Nothing you need to worry about."

"Nothing I need to worry about?" She crossed to him and took hold of his forearm. "A man shoots at me and my bodyguard goes down, then I'm dragged through alleys to some abandoned old house and led through a secret passageway to a room that looks more like a jail cell and you tell me not to worry about it?"

His lips twitched. "You do have a way with words, *bella.*" He glanced at the black-banded watch around his wrist. "Give me an hour, two tops. When I get back, I'll tell you everything you want to know. Until then, I need you to try and relax."

"Sandro—"

He took her hand and led her to the door. "Here," he said, pressing a metal object into her hand. "This lock works both ways. When you hear me turn it from the other side, I want you to do the same."

She looked at the small silver key in her palm. He was trusting her, she realized. He was giving her a small measure of freedom, of respect, just like when he'd given her back her grandfather's knife.

Beware of strangers bearing gifts, she'd always heard.

"How do you know I'll let you back in when you return?" she asked softly.

"I don't."

Surprised, she looked up, just in time to be blinded by his smile.

"I'll have food, clean blankets, and flashlights," he said matter-of-factly. "If you'd prefer to spend the night hungry, cold and in the dark, that's your decision." He slipped his hand into his pocket and pulled out a small black device, which he pressed into her palm, as well. "If anything happens, if you hear anything, if you get frightened for any reason, push this button, and I'll be back before you can catch your breath."

Her throat tightened. God help her, she wanted to believe him. "When I'm scared, I breathe pretty fast," she said with a small smile.

His expression gentled. "There's no need to be scared." Reaching down to the bottom of his pant leg, he came back up with a sleek black semiautomatic. "Do you know how to shoot a gun?"

He had no way of knowing how many memories a simple question could unearth, memories that tumbled hard and fast, of long afternoons spent at the shooting range, determined to prove to her father that she could take care of herself.

He'd been furious when a tabloid photographer had found her instead, splashing her photo over the cover, along with a headline that insinuated she didn't trust the government to protect its own. "Yes."

Sandro put the butt of the gun into her hand. "If anyone comes through that door besides me, shoot."

She swallowed hard. "You're trusting me not to shoot you?" she tried to joke, but his expression remained grim.

"You're a smart woman," he said, lifting a hand to her face. An odd light glimmered in his midnight eyes. "I think you realize someone out there wants to hurt you. I also think you realize that as much as you don't want to be with me, you want to be with him even less."

And then he was gone. He didn't give her time to protest or agree, simply let himself out the door, turned the lock, and headed down the stairs, until footsteps faded into silence, leaving only the ragged rhythm of her own breathing. She tried the door, desperately, vainly, but the lock wouldn't budge.

She was alone in the small room, but Sandro's presence lingered like a seductive mist. She inhaled deeply, drawing in not the scent of a villa abandoned to the fate of time, but of a man who'd stepped out of her dreams and into a nightmare she'd never imagined would come to pass.

Frowning, Miranda put her key to the lock, then wandered to the other side of the room, where she sat on the old sleeping bag, pulling the threadbare fabric around her legs, not at all sure why she'd suddenly become so cold.

Or why she wanted to have something of Sandro as close as possible.

The backup. Sweet Mary, she thought he worked for her father. The absurdity of it would have made him laugh, if the stakes hadn't been so obscene. For now, Sandro figured, they were both better off if he let her continue believing the simple explanation.

His real identity didn't matter, he reminded himself as he kept to the shadows and made his way back toward the resort community. The nature of his ultimate goal didn't change the immediate objective. He had to keep the ambassador's gypsy daughter away from the general's men and arrange an exchange that didn't jeopardize her life or his cover.

And he had to do it fast, he thought as he pulled his mobile phone from his belt.

"*Cristo,*" Javier swore a few minutes later. "Are you out of your mind? Taking the girl wasn't part of the plan."

Sandro glanced covertly around the alley where he'd stopped to call his ISA partner. "Tell me about it," he muttered into the phone. He'd wanted to protect her, not take her. But obviously he'd been double-crossed. The informant who'd sold him the information about Miranda's whereabouts had obviously had more than one buyer.

The question was *who?*

Regardless, Sandro was stuck with a complication he couldn't afford. "I had no choice."

"We all have choices," Javier reminded.

"Yeah, you're right. I could have left her for the shooter." Just the thought had his blood running cold all over again.

"I would tell you to just leave her at the villa," Javier mused, "call someone from the embassy and let them retrieve her, but there's no telling who else is on Viktor's payroll. But you can't keep her either, amigo."

"You think I don't know that? But I can't let her go right now. She's safer with me than anywhere else."

"Do you realize how insane that sounds?"

He did. "Javi, I need you to find out what happened to the bodyguard, Hawk." If the poor bastard still lived, he might be Sandro's best chance for a quick handoff.

"Consider it done," Javier said, then lowered his voice. "But there's something else you need to know first. Viktor knows you have her."

Damn. Implications stabbed deep. In order to infiltrate his organization, Sandro had been working to win General Viktor Zhukov's trust for close to a year. Turning the general's coveted bargaining chip over to the United States government would destroy Sandro's credibility. Countless lives, including his own and Javi's, would be thrown into jeopardy.

"How the hell does he know already?"

"He's got eyes and ears everywhere. He's pleased and waiting for you to bring her in."

Sandro leaned his head against the stone wall. His shoulder burned like a son of a bitch, he had an untrained, frustrated woman on his hands, a ruthless criminal on his heels, and now years' worth of work threatened to blow up in his face. "Cristo."

A hard sound broke from Javier's throat. "I thought you might feel that way."

"Get word to Omega," Sandro said, thinking quickly. With international security on the line, arrangements needed to be made carefully. Discreetly. He could afford neither the risk to his cover nor the time of making plans himself. Calls could be traced, tapped, overheard. Any of those would be akin to signing his death warrant. There were appropriate channels and protocols, well-rehearsed methods designed to minimize risk.

Sandro's job was to keep straddling that line. If the general caught so much as a whiff that Sandro was working to turn his prize over to the United States government, he was a dead man. This time for real.

And the carefully engineered plan to avenge eight operatives and bring the general to justice would be set back immeasurably.

"Tell Omega what's going on," he instructed. "Have him notify Ambassador Carrington."

"I'll take care of it."

"And I'll await your call."

Javier muttered something under his breath. "I hope you know what the hell you're doing."

Sandro frowned. "So do I."

Javier Fernandez thumbed off his phone and threw a wad of cash on the small round table, quickly exiting the Stockholm café where he'd been grabbing a late lunch before Sandro's call. He had to get back to his hotel room, make those calls and figure out how the hell he was going to extract his comrade from a potentially explosive debacle. And he had to do it fast.

"What's the hurry, Fernandez?"

Javier glanced over his shoulder, realizing his mistake too late. Three men circled him. Three guns were trained on various parts of his body.

"I don't think you'll be taking care of anything, after all," one of them said in broken English. "The girl is ours."

"It's me. Open up."

Shuffling came from the other side of the door. "Sandro?"

"Expecting someone else?"

"How do I know you're alone?"

He heard something in her voice, a fear and uncertainty that hadn't been there before. Obviously, the time alone had allowed her imagination to kick into high gear.

"Sweetheart, I appreciate your caution, but you need to know something about me. I'm a trained professional. I'd die before I'd let someone follow me back here. Now open up."

Nothing. Sandro put his hand to the door, wondering if he'd made a serious mistake by trusting her. But he'd had no choice. Giving trust was the best way to receive it in return.

More than anything, he needed her trust.

He waited, silently, patiently, until the lock clicked and the door opened. The ambassador's gypsy daughter stood there, blond hair smoothed behind her ears, those fascinating green eyes darker than before, her expression somewhere between relief and alarm.

The sight damn near knocked the breath from his lungs.

Ignoring the reaction, trying to ignore *her,* Sandro strode into the small room and secured the door behind him. That morning, when he'd awakened in the old sleeping bag, the cramped quarters had seemed stale and dank, but after only a few hours of Miranda Carrington's presence, everything seemed brighter, fresher, more welcoming. Like sunshine.

"Everything okay?" he asked brusquely.

"Just dandy," she answered, making him realize the absurdity of his question.

He set down his briefcase, then several sacks of supplies he'd picked up at the Jumbo superstore. He didn't know how long he'd have to await instructions from Javier, but knew it was smarter to be prepared than sorry. They couldn't stay holed up in the villa forever. Soon, they'd have to venture into town. And when they did, he couldn't risk anyone recognizing them.

Grimly, he wondered how she would react to the steps they needed to take to conceal their identities.

"How's your shoulder?" she asked, watching him warily.

"I rinsed the wound in a public rest room—there's some bandage and ointment in one of those bags."

She rummaged through his purchases, pulling out the cheese and bread he'd bought for dinner, then the medical supplies. "Take off your shirt."

She issued the command matter-of-factly, but too long had passed since Sandro had found himself alone with a woman at all, much less the kind of woman who made a man forget about what needed to be done, evoking instead fantasies of all the wicked ways they could kill their time together.

"Bella," he said slowly, "A man could go his whole life and not hear words like that from a woman like you."

She pulled the knife from its sheath around her ankle and cut five even strips of medical tape. Eyeing the blade, she mused, "Do you think I'll need to lance your wound?"

He coughed out a laugh. "Not with that."

Never missing a beat, she reached for the ointment. "Maybe while I'm fixing you up you'll tell me what's really going on."

He owed her that much. "I said I would," he reminded, slipping out of his shirt. She watched him, making him too aware of the fact he was shucking off his clothes in front of her, like it was the most natural thing in the world. Not that he had a problem with nudity, because he didn't. He rather enjoyed it, actually. Especially in the company of a beautiful woman. But the room was small and her eyes were big, and other parts of his body wanted to feel her soft hands, as well. Not a good idea.

"Let's get this over with," he muttered.

She picked up his T-shirt from the day before, dampened it with bottled water, and gently smoothed the cloth over his shoulder. "Does that hurt?" she asked, leaning so close her hair teased his arms, the swell of her breasts his back.

He winced. "I can handle it," he bit out.

"Let me know if it gets too bad."

"Why?" he asked. "Will you put me out of my misery then?"

If she picked up his innuendo, she gave no indication. "I'll be gentle." Putting her left hand at his waist, she ran the cloth down his back. "Who was shooting at us?" she asked. "And why?"

Sandro closed his eyes and inhaled deeply. Her cool hands played over his body like silk, and even though his shoulder still stung, her touch came damn close to making him forget what had to be done. "Have you heard of Viktor Zhukov?"

Her fingers skimmed the tender spot in the center of his back, where a bullet had slammed against body armor, penetrating several layers. "He's a former general in the Soviet Red Army, right? Linked to the senseless slaughter of innocents and executions of several U.S. counterintelligence agents?"

ISA agents. Fathers with families, men with whom Sandro had broken bread and laughed, for whom he'd sworn vengeance. "Right."

Against his back, her hands stilled. "What does he have to do with me?"

Sandro opened his eyes, noting the lengthening shadows creeping across the room. "His son was arrested by the U.S. government," he started to explain, then broke off abruptly.

"What?" Miranda asked.

"Shh." He listened carefully, focusing beyond the sound of their ragged breathing for the noise he'd heard moments before.

"Sandro?"

He stood, reached for his briefcase. "Get in the bathroom."

Her eyes went dark. "What?"

"The bathroom," he mouthed, gesturing toward the small dark closet. "Now."

He saw the reluctance in her gaze, the return of the hated fear, but she didn't question him again, just quietly moved to the small room.

Sandro crept toward the locked door. His heart hammered viciously in his chest. Adrenaline rushed. He'd been careful, damn it. So damn careful. No one had followed him. He'd made sure of it.

But then he heard it again, the sound of a door opening. Only this time, he heard voices, as well. Muffled and in Portuguese, but deadly and dangerous all the same.

"You check upstairs," a man instructed. "I'll take the back. And remember, if you find them, Vellenti's had his chance. Only the girl leaves here alive."

Chapter 4

Very few times in Miranda's life had she been afraid. Uneasy, yes. Exposed and trapped, definitely. Her family's wealth and political prestige rendered simple luxuries most people took for granted, like privacy, impossible. The media's fascination with the Carringtons ensured someone was always watching her every move, breath, mistake. Her first kiss had been splashed on the front page of a tabloid. Her first drink. Her first heartbreak.

A book had been written about her sister's brief, tragic life.

But none of those intrusions had frightened her. There'd been only frustration and a blade of determination that nicked harder, deeper, with every invasion of her privacy. Her heart had bled, but rarely had it hammered in fear.

Like it did now.

Adrenaline surged like the tide rushing in all at once. Her pulse raced. Her blood ran cold. Curling her clammy fingers around the doorframe, she peered into the small room, her gaze riveted on Sandro. Shirtless, he stood in the lengthening shadows of late afternoon, completely still, completely at attention. In his hand he held the semiautomatic he'd quietly removed from his attaché case, his finger on the trigger.

Miranda forced herself to breathe slowly, deeply. In. Out. In. Out. Sandro was a careful man, the secret room well hidden. Chances were no one would find them. And if they did, Miranda knew beyond a shadow of doubt whoever walked through that door wouldn't live to tell about it.

Sandro wouldn't let them.

That thought both thrilled and horrified. She abhorred violence, had fought revulsion every time she'd visited the firing range and squeezed the trigger on the Lady Colt she'd bought to assure her father she could take care of herself. She'd learned to hit the target with unerring accuracy, but had secretly wondered if she'd be able to fire on a human being.

To end another's life.

Sandro, this mysterious man her father had sent to protect her, who could change from charmer to commando with quicksilver speed, would have no such compunction. He wouldn't hesitate. Instinct told her violence was second nature to him. The nasty scar slashing across his throat confirmed that. Without doubt, he was a man shaped and hardened by the kind of brutality most people saw only in movies and on the evening news.

She wondered if his scars ran deeper than the flesh.

For some crazy reason, she found herself hoping they did. Not that she wanted him to hurt, not this man who'd willingly put his body between hers and a bullet. But she didn't want to think him heartless. She didn't want to think he could fire his gun and stop a human heart without experiencing a flicker of sorrow for a life gone wrong. She didn't want to think him so calloused that he no longer felt anything.

She didn't want to think of the pain necessary to create such a hardened, impenetrable exterior.

An emotion she didn't understand scraped against a throat already raw. She squeezed her eyes shut, opened them a moment later. Sandro still stood there, still hadn't moved. Silence filled the room like helium stretching a balloon to the brink of exploding. Every beat of her heart seemed to echo with punishing clarity.

Or maybe that was his heart.

Maybe both.

Voices then, in a language she didn't understand. She didn't need to recognize the words, however, to hear the frustration. The anger. Danger.

Sandro moved his head a fraction of an inch. From where she stood, Miranda saw his eyes glittering behind a scraggle of dark hair.

The voices continued, growing more distant with every ragged breath she drew. As they faded, so did the tension riddling Sandro's body. His back still looked carved of dark, magnificent stone, but he didn't look coiled so tight, didn't look as lethal.

Still, she didn't speak, didn't dare. Not until he issued the all-clear.

Long moments passed, long moments during which her breathing leveled out and the thrumming of her heart gradually relaxed. Finally Sandro lowered his semiautomatic and turned to her. "You can come out now."

Careful not to make a sound, she eased into the shadows of the small room. "Are they gone?" she asked quietly.

He crossed to the dirty window and narrowed his eyes, his gaze fixed on some point in the distance. "For now."

Relief skittered through her. As a child she'd loved to play hide-and-seek, scampering through her grandfather's sprawling estate, slipping among the shadows of the basement or squeezing into obscure nooks and crannies, climbing the mammoth trees alongside the lake, but the stakes had been innocent and inconsequential, a candy bar or a wad of bubble gum.

After her sister's death, the fun and games had stopped forever.

"Who were they?" The voices could have belonged to anyone, she tried to convince herself. Tourists who'd lost their way. Locals who'd lost a dog. "What did they want?"

Sandro turned from the window, but remained drenched in shadows. "They're gone, Miranda. Just leave it at that."

His grim tone abruptly killed the fleeting hope that the men's appearance was nothing more than a coincidence.

"They wanted me, didn't they?" she asked, and felt the chill of the realization all the way through to her bones. "They were looking for me."

He started toward her. "They're not going to find you—"

She stuck out her arm, warning him to keep his distance. She didn't want him to touch her. Couldn't bear it. She might crumble then, all those battered walls she'd thrown up against a fear she didn't want to feel might just come tumbling down.

"I thought you said I'd be safe here!" The accusation tore out before she could stop it. "You said virtually no one knew about this room—"

He ignored the pathetic barrier of her arm and pulled her against his chest. "The house is no secret," he said against her hair. With one of his arms around her waist, he ran his free hand along her back. "But the room is. Even if I hadn't been here, they would never have found you, not unless you'd made enough racket to the wake the dead."

Miranda held herself very still, refusing to sink against the tempting warmth of his embrace. His shirt remained on the floor, leaving the side of her face in intimate contact with the wiry hair covering his chest. His heart beat slowly, calmly. Strongly. If she closed her eyes—

No. She wouldn't close her eyes, not to this man. He operated too efficiently in the shadows. In the darkness, he'd be lethal.

"Then how do *you* know?" she asked, struggling against his arms.

Surprisingly, he let her go. At least his arms did. With his gaze, he continued to hold her just as fiercely. "I went to school with the grandson of the last man to live here, die here. He told me."

She swallowed hard, tried to think. "He could have told someone else, then. He could have told those men."

He released her fully, the shadows of the room filling his eyes, as well. "Not unless they summoned him through a séance."

Miranda staggered back. The room was too small to put distance between her and Sandro, but as she looked at him standing there, inches might as well have been miles. Years. His dark eyes were bleak, lost, for the first time since she'd met him, not full of command or confidence, but sorrow and pain.

"I'm sorry," she whispered, and was.

"Me, too." Like a macabre slide show, he closed his eyes, opening them a moment later to reveal the agony completely gone, replaced by a ferocity that jolted through her like lightning.

Questions surfaced—what had happened to his friend? Had Sandro been there? Had he been hurt as well? Is that how he got the nasty scar across his throat? But instinct warned not to veer too deeply into his personal life. Instinct warned he'd retreat further, and for some crazy reason, she didn't want him pulling back from her, not now. Because of the threat, she told herself. Because as much as she craved freedom, she wasn't foolish or naive. She knew she couldn't hold her own against criminals armed with hatred and submachine guns. Whether she liked it or not, for the time being, she needed this man sent to protect her, whether he was one of her father's yes-men, or not.

She also needed answers.

"Why do they want me?" she asked, returning to the conversation they'd begun before the noise downstairs had sent her into the bathroom and transformed Sandro back into a commando. "What do I have to do with anything?"

"You, *bella*," he said without hesitation, "are the bargaining chip."

"The bargaining chip?"

He moved from the window, deeper into the shadows. Very little of the sun remained, only a few meager rays seeping through years of neglect and decline.

"Jorak Zhukov was arrested in the United States a few days ago," he told her, returning his semiautomatic to the attaché case. "His father, General Viktor Zhukov, wants him back, but knows there's no way in hell that's going to happen. Not unless he has something the United States wants more than they want him."

A chill cut through Miranda. She heard what he didn't say, understood what he'd left unsaid.

"I'm not that important," she protested.

Sandro looked up abruptly. "To your father, you are."

The words wove dangerously close to her heart, but rather than comforting like an embrace, they stung like the yellow jacket she'd kneeled on when she was eight years old. The insect had stung and stung, and she'd cried. And cried.

Her father had told her she needed to be more careful. If she didn't respect boundaries, she'd always end up hurt.

"There are those who believe nothing is stronger than a parent's love for their children," Sandro went on, having no way of knowing how badly his words scraped, or how bitterly her throat burned. "This is personal for Viktor," he said. "By making it personal to the ambassador to Ravakia, as well, he hopes to put himself in a stronger position. Your father is an influential man. Your grandfather was legendary. Your family is much loved." He stood, moved toward her. "All in all, it's a pretty smart move. You're the perfect target. A child for a child."

The thought chilled her. The Carringtons had already lost

a child. She didn't think her father could survive burying another.

Sandro closed the distance between them with three long strides, his big powerful body moving with a stunningly virile grace. And for a moment, a dangerous moment, she wanted him to pull her into his arms again, against that warm, reassuring chest, to tell her this really *was* one of her father's drills and if she just played along, the morning would come and with it her freedom.

But deep in her heart, she knew that wasn't going to happen.

"Everyone knows the United States doesn't negotiate with criminals," she said, backing away from Sandro. The wall stopped her before she could insert more than inches between them.

"You're right," he said. "America doesn't negotiate. That's why I was there this morning, to make sure you didn't become a pawn in a high-stakes game you're not the least bit equipped to handle."

She'd become that pawn, anyway, and the game extended far beyond rules of fair play.

She looked him in the eyes, determined to convey strength, when really she wanted to slide down against the increasingly cool wall. "Why didn't you just tell me this straight-up?"

It would have been easier that way; she would never have indulged the fleeting, dangerous fantasy that the tall dark-haired stranger had really wanted to take her picture.

You're not a woman for shadows.

"Would you have believed me?" he asked now.

"The truth is always better than lies."

"Not always, *bella,*" he murmured, then lifted a hand to her face. His touch was warm, gentle. Unbearably sad. "Sometimes, they're one and the same."

Her throat tightened. They stood body-to-body, the room darker by the second, the only sound that of their breathing. She looked up at him, at that mouth he'd pressed to hers in the alley. He'd only been trying to staunch the flow of her words, but the feel of his lips on hers had tapped into another flow, this more like a lazy river, a foolish, ill-fated river that now lapped against a papier-mâché dam.

Miranda could count on one hand the number of men with whom she'd wanted to share intimacies. For the most part, the boys and men with whom she'd had contact had been as stuffy, predictable, and uninteresting as geology textbooks.

That within only a matter of hours her father's new yesman had created the need to engage her other hand blew her mind.

"I'd better clean and bandage your shoulder," she said, ducking under his arm and returning to where the supplies lay strewn on the cold stone floor.

"I hardly feel a thing," Sandro said from behind her.

That's what she was afraid of. He was a man who followed orders, doing what needed to be done regardless of impact. He'd come on to her with the same efficiency with which he'd fired his briefcase gun. He'd kissed her with the same thoroughness as the shopping trip he'd made into town. No detail escaped his attention.

And other than the mention of his friend's death, he gave no indication that anything that had happened today fazed him one way or another.

Just another day on the job.

"So you'd rather let it fester and risk infection?" she asked pointedly.

He turned her to face him, having moved without making a sound. "Careful, *bella*. A man might think you care."

"You saved my life today," she said. Caring involved emotion. What she felt right now, this…longing, involved an entirely different area of her body. Because of the danger, she rationalized. She'd heard men and women whose lives had been in jeopardy responded by reaching out to each other to affirm life.

"No matter what else happens," she said, "nothing can erase that. I don't want to see you suffer."

Sandro winced. "It's a little late for that," he muttered.

Miranda blinked. His shoulder, she told herself. That was all he meant. "Then sit," she instructed. "And let me help."

That glimmer again, a speck of light in those dark, dark eyes. "How?" he asked, lowering himself to the floor. "With a kiss?"

She looked at him sitting there, one long, incredibly muscled leg stretched out before him, the other bent, his darkly tanned chest bare, that broad shoulder patiently awaiting her touch, and knew the real danger had yet to begin.

"You think that will make everything better?" she asked.

His smile faded. "Not a chance."

Going down on her knees, she picked up the bottle of antiseptic. The wound on his shoulder didn't look anywhere near as bad now that he'd rinsed away the blood, but it still needed treatment.

"What happens next?" she asked, trying to distract him from the sting about to follow. "Where do we go from here?"

He watched her squeeze the clear liquid onto cotton, as though she was preparing to brutalize him in some hideous manner.

"After you finish torturing me," he said evenly, "we eat and wait for total darkness. Then we head for Lisbon."

She looked up from the bandage she'd been preparing. "I thought you said we'd be safe here."

"I changed my mind."

Uncertainty nudged against caution. He said she was safe and she believed him, but she couldn't shake the feeling that there was more going on that he'd yet to share with her.

"If I didn't know better," she commented, "I'd think you were making this up as you go along."

He lifted a single dark brow. "Do you know better?"

No, she didn't. But rather than answering with words, she smiled and pressed the cotton to his shoulder.

His shout of pain gratified more than it should have. "I thought you said you didn't feel anything," she reminded, with all the innocence of a newborn kitten.

"And I thought you didn't want to see me suffer," he growled through clenched teeth.

She eased the cotton from his flesh and dribbled the antiseptic onto the wound.

"What was it you said about the truth and lies?" she asked breezily. "Sometimes they're one and the same."

"Fred and Ethel?"

Sandro closed the door to the small hotel room and crossed the well-worn carpet to secure the curtains. Flashing lights from the adjacent discotheque cut through the darkness, much as they had only two nights before, when Javier had first called with news of Miranda Carrington. The remainder of that night Sandro had paced, and planned.

Never had he imagined less than forty-eight hours later he'd be escorting the ambassador's daughter into a small, barely clean room that smelled like stale antiseptic and cheap perfume.

But he trusted Teresa at the front desk, and with a smile and a handful of escudos worth over a hundred American dollars, he could be assured of safety for a few hours.

"The clerk needed names for her records," he told Miranda. She stood with her back to the door, a turquoise scarf holding thick blond hair from her face, revealing the odd mix of fascination and dread shimmering in the green of her gypsy eyes. Her blouse was dirty, the peasantlike skirt torn. She looked more like a vagabond than a member of one of the most elite, beloved families in America.

Regret cut hard and fast, that he couldn't give her the same accommodations she'd no doubt enjoyed back in Cascais. A woman like her deserved finery, bright clean rooms with fluffy white bathrobes and strawberries awaiting near a bottle of champagne.

He had only shadows to offer.

"Couldn't you have been more creative?" she asked, finally moving deeper into the room. She set the supplies he'd purchased on the pitiful excuse for a dresser, then reached for the remote control and sat on the bed.

"What did you have in mind?" he asked, then immediately wished he hadn't. Not the right question to pose to a woman sitting on the side of a bed.

She looked up slowly, a curtain of hair falling back to reveal a grin that damn near knocked the breath from his lungs.

"How about...Boris and Natasha?" she suggested, lips twitching. "You look much more like a Boris to me."

Sandro just stared. Only moments before he'd wanted to slam his fist into the wall. Now with a few simple words, she had him damn close to laughing.

"Too exotic," he almost growled. He couldn't let the sight of her on that squeaky bed distract him. He couldn't forget who they were and why there were here. "We're traveling as tacky American tourists, not glamorous Russian spies."

Call me, Javier, he added silently. *Call, damn it!*

"Spies sounds much more exotic."

"Exotic is dangerous. My job is to keep you safe. As tourists, we can hide in public."

Miranda picked up one of the bags he'd dropped on the floor by the bed and pulled out a floppy straw hat. "So that's what this is all about? Looking like tourists?"

"The Jumbo doesn't offer the world's greatest selection."

She rummaged through the bag, pulling out brightly colored shirts and a few pairs of denim shorts. "I don't see any clothes in here for you."

He motioned toward a duffel bag sprawled near the

dresser, where a few shirts, sole remnants of the life he'd left behind, lay folded inside. "I had stuff at the villa."

He'd burned everything else. *Almost* everything, he corrected, slipping his hand into his pocket and curling his fingers around his only other link to the past.

"Oh." Frowning, Miranda dumped the rest of his purchases onto the frayed bedspread.

Sandro braced himself. When he'd visited the Jumbo, he'd anticipated spending the night at the villa. But after the unexpected visitors, he'd decided not to push his luck.

A moving target was always harder to find.

His decision to leave had nothing to do with the way the room that had served him well over the years had seemed to shrink with every minute they spent alone together, isolated from the rest of the world. They would be alone together here at the hotel, after all. And there was a bed here. Far more possibilities for his imagination to hang him out to dry.

"We'll want to strip these sheets and use the blankets I picked up before you go to sleep," he instructed.

She looked from him to the bed, where faint stains littered the spread. "Oh." Her nose wrinkled, but she rallied fabulously, as if she frequently found herself in hotels where the sheets could keep a DNA expert busy for weeks. "Where will you sleep?"

He heard no real alarm in her voice, only a mild curiosity. "Where do you want me to sleep?"

Another stupid question.

She hesitated. "Where…where do you think is safest?"

Again, her response surprised him. He'd seen uncertainty streak through her eyes, the awareness that the room held only the one bed and an old wooden chair, and that to offer her maximum protection, he needed to stay as close to her as possible. That would mean sleeping in the same small bed. He'd seen the moment of alarm, but rather than pitching a fit about how she wasn't about to let him into her bed, she'd bravely asked what arrangement would be safest.

"I'll drag the chair by the door," he said abruptly. "No one can get in through the window."

A flicker of relief. "You don't think anyone will find us here, do you?"

"No, I don't. But a man can never be too careful." And the last thing he needed was to crawl between two soft warm blankets, next to her soft warm body. That would be more than risky. That would be stupid. He had to remain alert, after all. Surrounded by all that softness and warmth, he might sleep too deeply.

Abruptly, Sandro turned and reached for another bag. Sleeping soundly while Miranda Carrington lay so close her unique scent of flowers and sunshine clouded his senses was as likely as waking in the morning, only to discover the past two days hadn't really happened. They'd only been a nightmare. His plan hadn't backfired. He hadn't ended up with Miranda Carrington, after all. The general wasn't waiting for Sandro to turn her over into his demented little hands. And he, Sandro, wasn't saying a prayer every time he looked into her startling gypsy eyes and saw possibilities he'd written off years before.

"How long are we going to be together?" she asked from behind him.

He turned toward her. "As briefly as I can help it. Why?"

She held up the toiletries he'd purchased. "Baby powder and lotion?" Next to her hand lay a bottle of plumeria shampoo.

"They were on sale," he explained lamely. It had been stupid and he knew it. He'd seen the toiletries on the end-aisle display, and they'd looked soft and feminine, alluring, like her. It was only a small thing, he'd reasoned with himself. Buying her a few luxury items didn't mean anything. It wasn't like he was going to insist on smoothing the lotion over her curves and down her legs. And he sure wasn't going to be close enough to enjoy the clean scent of the baby powder.

"Here," he said, dumping the second bag on the bed-spread. With luck, he would douse the damning sparkle in her eyes. "I wasn't sure which shade you'd like best, so I bought a few."

Three boxes of hair color fell around her, one jet black, another auburn, a third soft brown. Miranda stared a long moment before looking up at Sandro. "You want me to dye my hair?"

"I want you safe," he corrected. "And while blond is sexy as hell, it's also likely to draw extra attention here in Portugal, where pale hair and eyes are the exception, not the norm." He could still see her standing by the sea wall just that morning, the sun glimmering off that gorgeous hair of hers. She'd stood out like a swatch of light on a cloudy night. "So why don't you just sashay into that bathroom and have an organic experience. I can't have you turning heads everywhere you go."

"I see." Frowning, she looked down at the three boxes, her hand drifting toward the one with the soft brown color.

"Don't look so sad," he tried to tease. "It's not true what they say."

"What's not true?" she asked halfheartedly.

"About blondes. They really don't have more fun."

That got her attention. She looked up abruptly, her expression no longer wistful, but almost...stricken. "I don't care about fun."

She muttered the words defensively, as though he'd backed her into a corner and accused her of something heinous. Protective instincts surged. "What *do* you care about?"

Light from the discotheque kept flashing in through the windows, illuminating her face in one instant, casting her in shadow the next.

Sandro found he much preferred the light. The shadows made her look too sad. Too remote.

"You wouldn't understand," she whispered.

"Try me."

Outside, the familiar drone of European sirens wailed closer, but she didn't flinch, didn't look away. She just looked at him, through him, tempting him to twist around and see what she stared at, but he knew there was nothing behind him, just a cheap piece of artwork featuring a sunset over the ocean. Slowly, Miranda lifted her hands to the turquoise scarf holding the hair back from her face and tugged it loose. Then she handed him the brush he'd purchased and turned her back to him.

Unease snaked through him. "You want me to brush your hair?"

"Please."

The request seemed simple enough, but there was something intimate about a man brushing a woman's hair while sitting on the edge of a bed in a motel room. And Sandro didn't want intimacy. Not with the ambassador's daughter, not with anyone. Intimacy led to expectation and complication. Intimacy distracted. Intimacy killed.

But in all likelihood Javier would call with the sunrise. Sandro's time with Miranda would be short. She was asking him to brush her hair, not indulge in sensuous foreplay, not stretch out alongside her and learn every contour of her body, memorize the sound of her sighs, the feel of her legs wrapped around his.

There could be no harm.

With the same cold determination he'd used when lifting his gun and standing alongside the door to the secret room in the villa, Sandro put the brush to the hair spilling over her shoulders and gently tried to ease the bristles through the tangled strands. But couldn't.

"You can go harder," she said. "You won't hurt me."

A distorted sound broke from his throat. She had no idea what a man like him would do to a woman like her, just how many ways he *could* most certainly hurt her.

Just the thought twisted him up inside. "It's too tangled," he muttered. "I think you'd better take it at your own pace. I'm not sure how much you can handle."

For a change, she didn't argue. She just lifted her hand and closed it over his, then jerked down. Hard. The brush gave way, the force of movement slamming it hard against his thigh.

Her hair pooled around their joined hands.

Sandro stared at all that luscious blond hair spilling across his lap as though she'd been scalped. "What the hell?"

She twisted to face him, revealing a row of dark auburn braids framing each side of her face, joined at the base of her neck and trailing down her back.

She'd been wearing a wig.

"Hair color doesn't matter to me," she said quietly, but her voice broke on the words. Her eyes were huge, dark, liquid. "It never has. Freedom does. Anonymity. The ability to live my life, without the whole world watching."

Sandro didn't know what to say, wasn't sure he could say anything. He felt like a man who'd just waded in about ten feet over his head. With lead boots on his feet. "*Cristo,*" he swore softly.

"So if you want to dye my hair brown or red or blue for that matter," she went on, her voice growing stronger with every syllable, "fine. It's not the end of the world."

He'd hurt her, he realized. In insinuating she was the flighty, sex kitten the tabloids painted her to be, he'd clearly prodded a wound that cut straight to her core.

"If General Zhukov's men recognize me," she said before he could apologize, "what happens?"

"I'm not going to let that happen." That much, he *could* promise her.

"But if they do," she persisted. "If the worst came to pass…what would happen?"

With the aid of the flickering light from across the street, he studied the resilience glowing in her eyes, the determination. Strength he hadn't noticed before. "You'd be taken to the general."

"That's all?"

"No, that's not all."

"What else?"

"Damn it, Miranda," he all but growled, then surged off the bed and started to pace. "Don't make me spell it out!" *Don't make me think about it.* "Do you really want to hear what those depraved lunatics would do to a woman like you? Men who live their whole lives in shadows and alleys? Men who either have to pay or brutalize to have a woman underneath them?"

Her eyes were huge, dark, but she kept her chin high, her shoulders square. "Here," she said, reaching toward her ankle and coming back up with the knife she'd pulled on him in the alley. "We'd better not take any chances."

He stopped abruptly. "Here, what?"

"If changing my identity is important enough to color my hair," she said, working to unweave the tight braids, "you should cut it, as well."

"Miranda—"

Her gaze met his. "You said it yourself," she reminded. "This isn't a game. It isn't a drill. It's real." Nimble fingers quickly freed masses of thick auburn hair. "Cut it off."

The abject horror tightening through him made no sense. She was right, he knew. Long hair always drew attention. A shorter length was less likely to stand out. And he'd certainly performed grimmer tasks than cutting a woman's hair. But…

"I'm not taking a knife to you," he growled, then strode to his duffel bag and fumbled for a pair of scissors. They weren't sharp, but they would cut through her hair without requiring him to hack or saw, like he'd have to do with the knife.

A flick of his wrist bathed the room in lamplight, taking away the shadows he preferred, but destroying the growing intimacy, as well. Miranda watched him walk toward her, then turned her back to him when he sat on the edge of the mattress.

The simple, trusting gesture practically skewered him.

Thick, auburn hair tumbled down her back, sweet-smelling from some exotic shampoo, crimped from the braids. Over the years, Sandro had learned the best way to handle an unpleasant task was to just do it. Don't think. Don't dread. Just shut off emotion and execute. But cutting a woman's hair was not like cutting a man's throat. It should be easier, he knew, but when he raised the scissors, God help him, his hands started to shake.

Chapter 5

Sandro looked at all that gorgeous hair spilling over his hands and draped across his arm, and he just couldn't do it. He'd walked away from his life without looking back, turned his back on friends and family, held men while they died, caused more than one premature death himself, but he couldn't make his fingers lift the scissors to her hair.

"What's wrong?" Miranda asked, twisting to face him.

"I've never cut a woman's hair before." Didn't understand why the thought of doing so struck him as sacrilege.

"It's just like cutting anything else," she said, looking at him peculiarly. "And don't worry. It'll grow back."

But not in the brief time they'd be together. Every time he looked at her, he'd be reminded of the carefully constructed plan that had blown up in his face, forcing him to take this woman of sunshine into a world of shadows in which she didn't belong.

"In all likelihood this whole nightmare will be over tomorrow," he said, untangling his hands from her hair. "There's no point in doing something so permanent—"

"Sandro."

Her tone stopped the rambling stream of logic. "What?"

"Give me the scissors."

"The scissors?" he repeated lamely.

Frowning, she reached down to his lap and pulled them from his fingers. "I'm not going to force you to do something you don't want to do," she said impatiently, then opened the scissors and lifted them to the hair at her shoulder.

A swath of wavy auburn hair fell to his lap, landing in the palm of his hand. His fingers closed around it instinctively, protectively, ridiculously, because deep in his gut, Sandro couldn't quell the growing chill of inevitability.

Some damage, like the silky hair Miranda cut with such blatant disregard, could never be repaired.

Sandro aimed the remote at the old TV and jabbed viciously at the power button. He cranked the volume high, not wanting to hear the water rattling through the old pipes. He didn't want to think about the shower running in the next room, behind a door that didn't lock, the woman standing under the spray of water, behind a curtain that was more see-through than not. She would be naked, he knew. Beautiful.

And he really was a masochist.

Just the thought of her standing in the small white tub had his body hardening, which only served to heighten his frustration. Literally, and figuratively.

Earlier, he'd gathered ice from a machine down the hall. Now, he popped a cube into his mouth and sucked. Hard. Distractions weren't doing a damn bit of good.

Counting on the drone of CNN to douse thoughts he had no business thinking, he leaned against the headboard, stretched his legs and focused on the familiar anchor. But the news felt as stale as the musty hotel room and his thoughts returned to the bathroom, where Miranda had retreated after butchering her hair. She'd taken all three boxes of color with her, leaving him with no clue which she would choose.

Frustrated, he lifted the remote and began skimming channels. Several screens of static gave way to a clear picture, prompting him to pause. And groan. He heard the shower in stereo now, the one from the adjacent bathroom and the one on the television. A woman stood with her back against ceramic tile, while a man stood facing her, holding her hands stretched above her head. They were both naked. Water rained down on them, but the glazed look in the woman's eyes indicated she was completely oblivious to anything but the man. He had his mouth—

Sandro changed the channel abruptly, but not before his heart rate accelerated. He reached for more ice, chewed it this time. Closed his eyes. Opened them abruptly.

Water no longer rattled from the bathroom. A moment of silence gave way to the rattle of the curtain being pulled open. Then more silence. She would be drying off, he figured, then wondered if she'd use the lotion he'd bought for her.

Then cursed himself for wondering.

He could not afford to think of Miranda as anything more than an assignment. He sure as hell couldn't think of her as a beautiful woman. The danger she posed stemmed from far more than a smile that lit up the shadows and curves that made a man's fingers itch, extended deeper than the flesh. She was the kind of woman who could distract a man, blur his focus, make him forget.

And Sandro could never, ever let himself forget.

He'd made his choice long ago, a choice forged through brutality and cemented in blood. He was as committed to his decision as though he wore a gold band on his ring finger. And he'd never tolerated infidelity, not among his buddies, not between his parents. They'd never much seemed to care, but with each indulgent affair Sandro had discovered, something inside him had died a little further.

His mother and father had never been concerned with more than the pleasure of the moment.

Sandro was determined to be different. To honor commitments. To focus on the big picture, not the indulgence of the here and now.

Except with Miranda naked in the next room, the here and now seemed pretty damn appealing.

He rolled from the bed, picked up his semiautomatic, and crossed to the window, where he used the barrel to nudge the curtain aside. Across the street, the lights from the discotheque flashed relentlessly, promising escape. In the crowded confines of gyrating bodies and ever-flowing alcohol, a man didn't have to think about responsibility or staying alive. Didn't have to think about the kind of temptation that could damn, could instead indulge in the kind of temptation that carried no consequences.

"Sandro?"

He stiffened at the sound of her voice, turned abruptly. He hadn't even heard a door open. She stood in a puddle of light spilling from the bathroom, wearing nothing but a cloud of baby powder and the oversize Surf Portugal T-shirt he'd purchased for her at the Jumbo. She had a white towel wrapped around her head, hiding her newly colored hair and accentuating her eyes. Lamplight glinted off the lotion-drenched flesh of her neck and her arms and her legs.

Wrapping her arms around her middle, she moved her hands up and down her sides, inadvertently stretching the T-shirt tighter over her breasts. He saw no signs of a bra.

"It's cold in here," she said. "Can you crank up the heat?"

Swallowing hard, Sandro squelched the urge to replace her hands with his, to create warmth through a more holistic method, rather than the rinky space heater provided by the hotel.

Never in his life had he been so sure a colossal mistake loomed just around the corner.

Never in his life had he wanted to hear from Javier more.
Or less.

Never in his life had he so deeply regretted the lie he
lived, the truth he couldn't hide forever. She would even-
tually learn both, this woman of sunshine who'd given him
smiles and laughter and compassion even when her life lay
on the line, and then she would hate him. There would be
no more smiles, no more laughter. No more compassion.

He wouldn't deserve any.

Miranda's mouth went dry. She watched Sandro standing
there in the shadows, wearing nothing but a pair of well-
worn camouflage pants and a white undershirt that emphasized the darkness of his flesh, the strength of his chest. In
his hand, he held his semiautomatic, as though it served
some kind of impenetrable shield between him and the
world. In his eyes glittered a harshness she didn't understand, a look that screamed equal parts pain and pleasure.

Danger, was the first word that came to mind. Dangerous. Not just because he held a gun in one hand and her
life in the other, but because that brutal commando exterior
he'd perfected to an art form couldn't hide the glimmer of
compassion deep inside. He'd given her patience in the face
of fear and confusion. He'd bought her lotion and shampoo.
He'd been unable to cut her hair.

Standing there in the shower, naked with water sluicing
over her body, she'd been unable to forget the way his
hands had shook, the look of panic on his face. *Panic.* This
man who had not shown one ounce of fear or worry during
gunfight, or flight, or the impending discovery of their hiding spot, had shown true panic at the prospect of taking
scissors to her hair.

Her chest tightened at the memory.

She didn't want to consider why.

Nor did she want to consider why she'd felt so...antsy
while she showered. Maybe because she knew Sandro was
just a heartbeat away and the door didn't lock. Maybe be-

cause the shampoo and soap she smoothed over her body had been purchased by him. For her. Or maybe, just maybe, because when she closed her eyes, she could see him as vividly as though he'd joined her in the shower, could imagine the hands running over her body were not her own, but rather those strong, capable hands that had been unable to cut her hair.

Danger, she thought again. Dangerous.

He still hadn't moved, hadn't spoken. He just watched her, the light from across the street slashing in, momentarily rescuing him from the shadows, then returning him with brutal speed and precision. As the day had worn on, the whiskers covering his jaw had thickened, darkened, to the point now where they looked soft, rather than hard. Tempting, rather than menacing.

Something deep inside her started to tremble. "Sandro?" she said, looking from his eyes to the gun. Her heart started to pound. "Has something happened?"

He followed the direction of her gaze, abruptly lowered his weapon. "Just a precaution."

"Oh. Good." Again, she shivered. "Is there any way to heat things up?" she asked. "I mean, it's okay if we can't, I'm not complaining, but I just thought I'd ask."

"You mean the heater," he said.

"Yes. What else?" she asked, then her imagination took over.

He abandoned his post at the window and crossed to the rinky-looking unit. He moved with surprising grace for such a big man, not making a sound, barely disturbing air currents.

"This should help," he muttered, then fiddled with a knob. "You might want to try some socks, too."

She looked down at her bare feet. Little remained of the glitter polish she'd run across her nails the week before. "Good idea."

"I fixed up the bed for you," he said as she sat on the

mattress and pulled on a pair of plain white socks. "It's not much, but at least it's clean."

"Thanks," she said, looking up with a smile of gratitude.

But the hard look on his face warned he wanted no gratitude from her. He wanted nothing.

Silence then, broken only by the soccer match blaring from the black-and-white TV. *Goallll!*

Sandro dragged a chair to the door, and for some crazy reason Miranda felt even colder than before. Soon they would turn out the lights and she would crawl between the blankets he'd purchased so she didn't have to sleep on dirty sheets.

But before then, there was something she had to know.

"Sandro?" she asked, leaning forward to remove the towel from her hair. Then she worked at combing out the newly shoulder-length, cinnamon-brown locks.

Across the room, Sandro inspected the lock on the door for the umpteenth time. "Yeah?"

"How did you know about my tattoo?" The question spilled out in one breathless rush.

He stilled. Straightened. Turned to face her. "The tattoo?"

She nodded, forced a nonchalant smile. The tattoo wasn't a secret, had caused quite a scandal in her family. Her father had been furious, her mother distraught. Why, her mother said, didn't Miranda realize she'd never be able to wear a sleeveless gown without the whole world seeing the small dragonfly?

But she wasn't talking about the whole world here. She was talking about Sandro, a man she'd never met, never heard of. A man who knew something very personal.

"It doesn't matter," he said brusquely.

"It does to me." More than it should.

He resumed fiddling with the door. "I saw it in a picture," he said noncommittally.

"*What* picture?"

Again he stilled, again he glanced at her. But this time

he lifted his fingers to his mouth, drawing her attention to the stubble on his jaw, those lips far too sensuous for a man of such hard lines and stark angles. "Just a picture."

And she had her answer. Along with it came the same cold fingers of exposure she'd come to Europe hoping to escape.

He'd seen the tabloids.

Darkness still covered the land, but soon the sun would nudge against the eastern sky, lighting the land and stealing their cover. Sandro watched Miranda sleeping, envied her that ability to drop off so completely that not even the constant drone of sirens disturbed her. When was the last time he'd slept through the night without the aid of whiskey? When was the last time he'd awoken with his heart rate steady, his body dry?

When was the last time he'd watched the rhythmic rise and fall of a woman's chest while she slept, listened to the soft little sound of her breathing?

He hated to wake her. Hated to disturb her. Sometime during the night the blanket had slipped down over her shoulder, riding low along her waist. She slept on her side, with one leg stretched out, the other crooked up at an angle. She looked peaceful, her newly brown hair spilling across the pillow. Even the shoulder length looked provocative. He was tempted to lift a hand, to touch, to smooth the strands back from her cheek.

He really was a son of a bitch.

They weren't here for a lover's tryst. They were here because his plan had backfired and her life lay on the line. They were here because the general wanted her every bit as badly as Sandro did.

But for very different reasons.

"Miranda," he whispered, putting a hand to her shoulder. The sleeve had fallen back, allowing his fingers to skim the small dragonfly. "Time to wake up."

She moaned softly, then shifted against the mattress as

her eyes drifted open. They were heavy with sleep, unfocused, hazy like that mind-blowing moment when a man pushed inside a woman. A dreamy little smile curved her lips, as though waking in a strange bed with a strange man was a common occurrence for her.

Because the thought twisted his gut, he pushed it aside. "Miranda?"

"Hmm." She stretched, sighed. "Sleepy."

"I know, *bella*, but it's almost sunrise. We've got to go."

The haze shattered immediately, and her eyes came fully open. No longer glazed, but alert. Sharp. Heartbreakingly courageous. "Go where?"

"North."

She pushed the hair from her face. "North?"

"It's never a good idea to stay in one place for long. Until I receive word on how we're getting you out of the country, we keep moving." He'd hoped that information would have come by now, had tried to call Javier during the night. Nothing.

"Hawaii?" Miranda asked sleepily.

"Afraid not," he answered with a smile, then realized she was staring at his shirt. An array of retro surfboards floated against a melon-green background. "We're traveling as tacky tourists, remember? I'm Fred. You're Ethel."

She pushed up against her elbow. "You hardly strike me as a Hawaiian-shirt kind of guy."

But he had been. Once. In another lifetime. They'd all been. He and Roger and Gus. They'd had a contest to see who could procure the loudest, tackiest, most outrageous Hawaiian shirt. Some sported hula girls, others grass-skirt-clad Elvis Presleys, one boasted flamingos, another showcased woodies. They'd worn them all the time, everywhere.

Even when they died.

And now Sandro had them all.

Because even in death, he'd managed to live.

"I'm full of surprises," he muttered, then stood and

crossed the room. "Thirty minutes to sunrise," he said. "We need to be on the road before then."

The morning sun burned off the gray, bathing the land in shimmery strokes of yellow and peach. A heavy mist clung to the vegetation that tangled along the right side of the road, while off to the left, the Atlantic crashed mightily against ancient sea cliffs. No tourists yet, just an occasional bicyclist enjoying the last minutes of quiet before day seared away night.

They'd been driving for over an hour in the same car Sandro had used the night before. They'd hugged the shoreline, rather than taking one of the major roads, and gradually they'd left behind the sprawl of resort communities, hotels and restaurants, even a casino. Now as Miranda looked from side to side, she saw nothing but the wild beauty of land untamed.

"Are you okay?"

The question pierced the silence and had her glancing toward Sandro. He looked deceptively casual sitting there in the loud Hawaiian shirt, one hand draped over the wheel, the other in his lap, but the hard look in his eyes gave away his alertness. As did the gun resting between them.

"I'm fine," she said. "Why?"

He glanced at her. "You look a little…green."

She forced a smile, pressed a hand to her mouth. She hadn't realized her discomfort had been obvious. "Curvy roads always get me."

"Do you need me to pull over?"

She heard what he didn't ask. "I'm not going to be sick, no."

"Would fresh air help you feel better?"

She didn't understand his sudden concern. Since leaving Lisbon behind, he hadn't spoken, hadn't looked at her. A tension had settled between them, one she didn't understand. It was as though something had changed while she slept.

"Is it safe?"

He checked the rearview mirror. "I haven't seen another car in over half an hour. A brief stop shouldn't hurt."

She swallowed against the nausea. "That would be nice, then. Thanks."

He veered left and pulled the car onto the rocky area leading down to the ocean, easing to a stop behind a clump of overgrown oleander. He killed the engine then reached into the back seat, came back with a bottle of water. "This might help."

After he unscrewed the cap, she took the bottle from his battered hands and put it to her mouth. The liquid felt cool sliding down her throat, refreshing. "Thanks."

"You should have told me you get car sick. I could have taken another route." He looked toward the west, where huge swells gathered and crashed against the shore. "There's less traffic on this road—I thought you might like the view better."

An unfamiliar warmth flowed through her. "The road less traveled," she murmured.

Sandro turned toward her. "What?"

"'Two roads diverged in a wood,'" she said with a smile, "'and I took the one less traveled by.'"

"'And that has made all the difference,'" he surprised her by concluding.

She looked at him sitting there, eyes intent, jaw unshaven. He was in commando mode again, but the words of a poet fell from his mouth. She remembered thinking the same thing the day before, that though his dark hair and unshaven face lent him a look of danger, he had the mouth of a poet.

"Can we get out?"

He checked the phone clipped to his belt, then reached for his gun and curled his fingers around the butt. "For a few minutes."

A blast of cool ocean air hit her the second she opened the door. The wind was sharp, damp, chilling, and instantly she shivered. But it was better than being in that cramped front seat that seemed to shrink with each breath she drew.

Sandro came up beside her and put a hand to the small of her back, guided her away from the road, toward an outcropping overlooking the ocean. They made their way down a rocky path until they stood out of view from the road. Waves crashed below, relentless. Beautiful. The spray shot up like a mist to tease them, driving home that this was real and not some bizarre dream.

Miranda pulled in a deep breath, felt the cool air spread through her. Behind them the sun climbed the sky, leaving a blue so vivid, so sharp, Miranda longed to run back to the car and grab her camera, snap a picture. A photographer's sky, she called it, the kind of stunning backdrop that lent pictures a crispness rarely found.

They stood in silence, the only sound that of the waves battering the sea cliff, a few gulls dipping and diving for breakfast. Hard to believe just the day before she'd been running for her life.

"How long have you worked for my father?" she asked, glancing up at Sandro.

The sharp wind ruffled hair that looked a few weeks past due for a cut, but other than that he stood completely still. His gaze was fixed somewhere on the horizon.

"Five years," he said, then looked directly into her eyes. A ghost of a smile fought with the scowl of seconds before. "Five years since I took the road less traveled."

Miranda blinked. There was something in his voice she didn't understand, a note of regret, a tinge of sorrow.

"And you?" he asked.

Her heart started to pound. Hard. She didn't like talking about herself, had long since learned the consequence of revealing too much, only to read a distorted version in some magazine or newspaper article at some point down the road.

"What about me?" she asked cautiously.

"How long have you taken your own path?"

She thought about not answering him. She thought about

lying. But the way he was looking at her, those midnight eyes all narrow and concentrated, his unshaven jaw set and his lips slightly parted, turned her defenses useless. When he put his mind to it, the man could probably coerce a nun to give up her habit.

"For as long as I can remember," she answered honestly.

"I can't imagine that going over well in your family."

Her breath caught. Never before had one of her father's men made a comment that could in any way be construed as passing judgment on Peter Carrington. She looked at Sandro standing there with the vivid blue ocean at his back and the sun at his face, and wondered how it was possible to still see shadows. The incongruity nagged at her, like working a puzzle and finding two pieces that at first seemed to fit...but didn't.

"People don't choose who they are," she said, watching a seagull dive toward the churning water. "Lots of people try to pretend, to fit into tidy preconceived notions of how they're supposed to act, how they fit into the world." After Kristina's death, her sister Elizabeth had retreated into that category. "But to me, that's like selling yourself out. You are who you are."

Sandro lifted a hand to ease a tangle of newly brown hair from her face. "And who are *you*, Miranda Carrington?"

Her throat tightened. For a crazy moment she wanted to close her eyes and savor the feel of his fingers against her cheek. Standing there on the edge of the world it was tempting to believe that she was just a woman, and he was just a man. That's why she'd become Astrid Van Dyke, after all. To be just a woman and, perhaps, to meet just a man. A man who didn't want anything from her. Who didn't care about her family or her name. A man who wanted only to be with her, and she with him.

Sandro was not that man. He held a semiautomatic in his hand. He worked for her father. He wouldn't even tell her his last name.

"I'm just a woman," she said, startled by the thickness to her voice. "Just a woman trying to live her life." A woman whose heart had no business hammering so crazily, a woman who knew better than being attracted to the yesman her father had sent to protect her.

But was.

"Who are you?" she asked, lifting her chin. "Who are you *really?*"

His smile faded, his hand fell away. "I'm just a man trying to do the right thing."

He made it sound simple, but in his muttered words she heard a struggle she didn't understand. And maybe that was it. She was used to her father's men being like robots, displaying no personality, no emotion.

"You're not like the others," she told him.

"What others?"

"The other men my father has sent to shadow me. The other agents. They always treated me like a disobedient child."

A distorted sound broke from his throat. Frowning, he broke eye contact and quite openly surveyed the length of her body.

"You're not a child, *bella*. I'd have to be deaf, dumb, and blind not to notice that."

And she'd have to be made of cold hard stone not to feel the heat of his gaze.

"I'm not sure my father realizes that," she said, ignoring her reaction to him. Soon they would part. Maybe in only a matter of hours. They were as different as shadow and light, she longing to try out her own wings, he content to take orders from others. No matter how tempting it was to ignore caution and explore the attraction between them, she had only to think of her sister Elizabeth, and of Hawk, to drive home how devastating that kind of carelessness could be.

She winced at the memory of Hawk going down, refused to think of it quite yet. She'd have to tell Elizabeth…

"I'm twenty-eight years old," she said, looking over the ocean. The blue stretched on forever, fading in color as it melted into the horizon. "Many women are married and raising a couple of kids by my age. But I feel like my life has just begun. I've gone to college, gotten a couple of degrees, worked for the Carrington Foundation, but…"

"But what?"

It was difficult to put into words. "When I was a little girl, my mother had matching outfits made for me and my sisters. Mom took us everywhere like that, in velvets and lace and silk. She thought it was the image people wanted to see of the Carrington family, nice and tidy, pristine." Her mother had commissioned countless photographs and even a painting of her girls dressed in everything from matching red velvet to frilly pink.

After Kristina's death, those pictures had brought both smiles and tears.

"But Mom never understood playing dress-up didn't change who we were inside." Kris had been the best and the brightest, Ellie the peacekeeper, Miranda the free spirit. "We could be made to dress alike, but we weren't alike. All the clothes in the world can't change who someone is, deep inside. That's the way I feel about my life, so far. I've done the so-called right things, but none of them have rung true for me. None of them have felt right."

"And that's why you became Astrid Van Dyke?" Sandro asked quietly.

The observation pierced deep, bringing with it an ancient ache. Whereas many of her friends had dreamed of big fancy weddings and sprawling houses in the country, Miranda had always dreamed of one thing, and one thing only. Freedom.

Longing for a normal life, she'd lifted her chin and pasted on a smile, protecting the thirst to live that fluttered inside her like a butterfly trying to escape a mason jar.

"I love my family with all my heart," she said, looking at Sandro. Once, she'd been bitter. With time, acceptance had set in. "But growing up a Carrington was complicated, especially after my sister Kristina died. There were expectations. Requirements. Restrictions. People would say my family had the world at our fingertips, but it's a world I knew nothing about. That's why I became Astrid. To experience the world outside the Carrington safety net. To see new places and meet new people, to taste different foods and hear new music."

"And have you?"

"These past few months have been the best of my life, everything I ever dreamed, and more. That's why I started taking pictures along the way." To record and capture, to share with others upon her return. To make a difference, in her own way. "The world's an incredibly big place, beautiful in so many ways, but horrible in others. I think it's important to see beyond our own boundaries, our blinders."

Sandro frowned. "Sometimes, *bella,* boundaries and blinders are in place for a reason."

The words were gentle, but they pummeled like stones. "Now you sound like my father."

"And that disappoints you?"

"He means well, I know that. He loves me, but he's never understood me. Just because I don't want to go into law or politics like everyone else in my family doesn't mean I'm a failure. I have goals just like everyone else. Dreams."

Sandro's eyes darkened. He stepped closer, his body blocking the wind blowing off the ocean. "What does a woman like you dream of, Miranda? What do you see when you lie in the dark and close your eyes?"

Her throat closed up on her. Her dreams had always been simple, tame. Until last night. Sleep had eluded her there in the dark hotel room, forcing her to watch Sandro pace the small room, gun in hand. But when she'd finally dropped off, he'd been waiting for her in that darkness, too.

But he hadn't been pacing.

"Miranda?" he asked now, his voice barely registering

above the roar of the ocean. His hands were on her shoulders. "What is it? What's wrong?"

Swallowing hard, she looked up and met eyes as dark and mercurial as midnight. And then she stepped over the edge.

"Last night I dreamed of you."

Chapter 6

A cool wind whipped off the ocean and tangled Miranda's hair. There was color to her cheeks, fire to her eyes. She had her chin tilted, her shoulders squared. Behind her, the incoming tide turned the waves crashing against the cliff increasingly violent.

Sandro had never seen a more provocative sight.

Or one more dangerous.

Everything about her screamed defiance, that tough facade she tacked up so effectively, and yet, for the first time, vulnerability seeped through.

It was the vulnerability that alarmed him.

"You dreamed of me?" he asked, clearing his throat. The hoarse rasp had nothing to do with the explosion that had permanently damaged his vocal chords five years before. His imagination held that right, the immediate images of what kind of role he might have in Miranda Carrington's dreams.

She pushed the hair from her face, just as he'd done a

few minutes before. "Nightmare might be a better description."

He swore softly, instinctively turning to scan the rocky area behind them. Few cars traveled the road, and Sandro knew even if someone did see them, his loud Hawaiian shirt and her blue smock-top would label them as nothing more than tourists. But caution demanded they keep moving.

"I'm not going to let anything happen to you," he said, returning his attention to her.

She looked at the gun in his hand. "I believe you."

"Then why the nightmare?"

"Not all nightmares have to do with violence," she said, and her eyes met his. "There are other things that scare people."

"Yes," he agreed slowly, "there are." Fate and destiny and inevitability, men like General Zhukov and the minions who carried out his dirty work. Small hotel rooms and squeaky beds and noisy showers, soft skin and luminous green eyes capable of drowning a man. Smiles and laughter and promises. Tears.

Choices.

"Come on," he almost growled, "we should head back." He turned to leave, but she put a hand to his forearm.

"What happens next, Sandro? Where do we go from here?"

The question stopped him cold. There were many places he wanted to go, only a few he could. "We've got another few hours of driving ahead of us."

"That's all?" she asked softly.

If he was lucky. "That's enough."

The road wound away from the beach and up a mountain, curving, climbing, narrowing. Every now and then a tour bus teetered past them at an alarming speed on the way to some unknown destination. There was more vegetation here, the trees taller, the undergrowth thicker. Semitropical flowers in vibrant shades of yellow and orange and red added splashes of color.

Sandro drove relentlessly, hour after hour, stopping only once to allow Miranda a breath of fresh air. He took her on a short walk through the woods, where what looked to be a crumbling stone turret rose from the middle of a small pond, guarded by two black swans. The second Miranda rounded the corner, she understood why he'd suggested she take her camera.

"It's beautiful," she whispered, then broke from him and hurried to the side of the murky water. Tangled vines fought their way up the crumbling, moss-covered stones and clung to the sides of the round structure. Not much sun cut through the dense vegetation, but the few rays that seeped through created a haunting study of shadow and light.

"What is it?" she asked, raising her camera.

Sandro joined her. "The locals say it's magical."

She adjusted her aperture setting. "It looks lost."

"Lost?"

"Lonely," she clarified, going down on a knee and trying to find the angle that best captured the play of shadow and light. "Like someone plucked it from the side of a castle and dropped it here in the middle of nowhere."

The theory made no sense, but she could think of no other reason for the structure to be in the middle of the small pond.

"Maybe someone built it right there," Sandro said. His voice was quiet, thoughtful. "Maybe it was a prison of some sorts."

"Or maybe an escape," Miranda mused. The structure had what looked to be a door and several rectangular holes that could have been windows toward the top. The romantic in her imagined some lovely maiden, escaping an oppressive castle and coming down to her reflecting pond, where she could be alone with herself.

Or a lover.

Smiling at the thought, Miranda snapped several shots, then stood and held her breath, waiting for the two graceful swans to converge in front of the crumbling stone.

She'd never seen a black swan before.

The air was cooler here beneath the thick canopy of trees, quieter. No sounds permeated from the road, only the occasional rustle of the wind or wail of a bird.

At her side Sandro stood with one hand in his pocket, the other holding his semiautomatic. Whereas she'd managed to find a swath of sunlight in which to stand, only a few inches away, he stood in the shadows he seemed to favor. His gaze was distant, focused on some point across the small body of water.

Miranda's breath caught. Her heart started to thrum low and deep. Slowly, she turned her camera toward him, not wanting to disturb the stillness.

"What the hell are you doing?" He had the camera out of her hands and into his own before she realized he'd even moved.

She stared at him, felt herself step backward. "I was just taking your picture," she told him, unnerved by his swift and near-violent reaction. From the fierce glitter in his eyes, if she hadn't known better, she would have thought she'd pulled a gun on him. "A picture, Sandro, that's all."

"I don't do pictures." He turned and headed back toward the road. "Come on, let's go. Sightseeing's over."

The hurt came swift and unexpected. She watched him stride away, didn't understand how or why the calm had shattered.

"Are you coming?" he barked over his shoulder.

"I don't do commands," she bit out, mimicking his curt words of moments before. It was all she could do not to put her hands on her hips.

He stopped abruptly, but didn't turn. He looked up toward the sky in what appeared to be silent prayer, then down at his feet. Only then did he turn to face her. "I don't do pictures and you don't do commands. Considering you're a photographer and I'm a soldier, I'm not sure where that leaves us.''

For some insane reason, she smiled. ''Stuck in the middle of nowhere, it looks like.''

The mouth that had been a forbidding line only moments before slowly cracked into a grin. He hooked the strap of her camera over his shoulder, then extended his hand. ''Please, then. Please come back to the car with me.''

Miranda looked at him standing there, that kooky Hawaiian shirt covering his chest and the lethal weapon in his hand, with the smile of a little boy and the midnight eyes of a fully grown man, and realized the danger facing her stemmed from far more than just a demented general with a thirst for revenge.

Sandro, the man sent to protect her, might well be the one to do her in.

''Wow.''

Miranda stepped into the semidarkened building, where seemingly endless rows of huge oak barrels lay on their sides, lining the walls. The air was cooler here, slightly moist. Musty. Almost forgotten. Stonework covered the floor, thick wooden beams stretched the length of the ceiling.

''What is this place?'' she asked, but when she turned, Sandro had moved away from her. Gun in hand, he kept his back to the wall and moved without making sound, weaving between the massive casks. He turned toward her with a finger to his mouth, clearly commanding her to be quiet.

She could do that. Had, in fact, been doing that ever since they left the pond with the swans. Sandro had barely spoken to her, becoming more and more like one of her father's men with each mile they drove.

Hours had passed, the curving mountain road giving way to a verdant valley, where late-afternoon sun shimmered down on gnarled olive trees and endless rows of grapes.

There they turned off the two-lane road and onto what could scarcely be called more than a dirt path.

Quinta de Madeira, the sign had read, and Miranda's mouth had instantly started to water. The Madeira label boasted the finest *vhinos* in all of Portugal. *Tinto,* just as she preferred.

"We're buying wine?" she'd asked, confused, to which Sandro had barely cut her a glance.

"No, we're spending the night."

After about five minutes they'd reached a fork in the road, one path leading toward an ancient but well-preserved stone farmhouse, the other toward what looked to be storage buildings.

"Friends of yours?" she'd asked.

But acting more like Hawk by the second, Sandro had answered with only a few barked words. "Close enough."

The path leading from the house brought them to a gravel parking lot where, just beyond, a whitewashed stone building with no windows and only one door awaited. The wraparound porch seemed like an afterthought, the rocking chairs like window dressing.

They parked behind the building, in what Miranda could only guess had once been a shed or a garage. The falling-down structure wouldn't provide much shelter from the elements, but she figured it would keep the car out of view.

The lengthening shadows of late afternoon greeted them, the temperature already dropping in anticipation of nightfall. After retrieving several knapsacks from the car, Sandro paused before stepping into the opening, gun in hand, and surveyed the surrounding area. Miranda had pushed up on her toes for an inspection of her own, seeing nothing but a hillside terraced with endless rows of grapes. Somewhere, a dog barked rambunctiously, but other than that, the only sound had been that of their breathing.

"Where is everyone?"

"Eating dinner," he'd answered simply. "This building is only used on the weekends. That gives us two days."

Two days. After the frenetic pace of the past twenty-four hours, two days sounded like an eternity.

Now they stood inside the cavernous room that Sandro had explained doubled as a reception hall. On weekends, the Madeiro family rented the facility for weddings and cocktail parties, reunions, once even to a romantic, who hoped the intimate setting would increase the chances of his girlfriend saying yes to a very important question. But during the week, the wine cellar stood empty, save for the enormous casks of wine.

"All clear."

The rough-hewn words echoed through the cavernous room, kicking Miranda's heart into overdrive. She spun to find Sandro standing in the shadow of one of the oak barrels, his midnight eyes trained on her. He'd lowered the gun, but his body still looked alert, primed, ready to spring into action at the slightest provocation.

"We'll be safe here for the night," he said.

Emotion chose that moment to pour in from all directions. Caught off guard, she lifted a hand to her suddenly tight throat, where her pulse hammered crazily. It was the word, she knew.

Safe.

"Will we?" Her voice was thick, strained. "Is that even possible, Sandro? Is anywhere really safe?"

His gaze darkened. "What's that supposed to mean?"

It was a damn good question. She moved deeper into the maze of wine casks, the chill deepening with each step she took. The barrels were at least double her height, and for a crazy moment, she imagined one of her sisters' Barbie dolls coming to life and roaming through the Carrington country estate. The new world would surely fascinate, but danger would hide in every shadow, around every corner.

"When I was a little girl…" she said, but didn't turn to face Sandro. She didn't want to see him. Didn't want to see those midnight eyes which had been remote ever since leaving the stone turret. Didn't want to feel the stab of longing, the crazy desire to feel him pull her into his arms and hold her tight. He was her father's man, that was all. He was here to protect her body, not her heart, and sure as hell not her soul.

That was her responsibility.

"When I was a little girl," she said again, her voice thicker than before, "I would crawl into my grandfather's lap and he would tell me stories." The memory brought a rush of warmth. If she closed her eyes, she could still smell the aroma of his pipe.

"He had the most wonderful voice, deep and booming, but soothing all the same. And when he told stories, his eyes twinkled. Sometimes my mother would scold him for speaking so openly of war and famine and violence, saying he was going to give me bad dreams." She paused, lifted a hand to one of the casks. "But his stories always had happy endings. The bad guys always got punished, and the hero and the heroine always lived happily ever after." Her throat tightened. "And I never had bad dreams," she said, stroking the soft, cool wood. "I always felt safe, because Grandpa taught me that good could triumph over evil."

"You don't feel safe anymore?"

She shivered. He'd done it again, moved without making a whisper of sound. He stood behind her now, so close the warmth of his words had brushed the back of her neck.

Lifting her chin and forcing a smile, she turned toward him. "The world is different now. I know people who died simply because they were at the wrong place, at the wrong time. I attended a funeral for a friend from boarding school whose only crime was showing up for work one morning." Hot moisture burned the backs of her eyes. She longed for those carefree days of youth, when the greatest danger stemmed from rickety cellar stairs or high-up tree branches forbidden by her parents.

That world was gone now.

"Nowhere is really safe," she whispered, "not if fate is against you."

Kristina's death had driven home that lesson loud and clear.

Sandro frowned. His eyes weren't cold anymore, weren't remote. They were as warm as the hand he laid against the side of her face. "You're safe with me."

She swallowed hard. "Safe is a relative term."

"Not in my book."

Not in her father's, either. That was the problem. Men like Sandro tackled problems by finding solutions, never realizing their fabulously well-thought-out, fabulously executed plans could wreak an equally dangerous havoc.

"A bird in a cage is safe, too, isn't it?" she challenged. "Fed everyday, given water and light. The cat can't get in. The temperature is always just right."

A faint smile played at the corners of Sandro's mouth. "Sounds pretty cushy to me."

"But what happens when the house catches fire and the bird can't get out of its cage? Can't fly away?"

Against her cheek, his fingers tensed. "Is that why you were so intent to roam Europe without your father's men around to protect you? Because you felt like a bird in a cage?"

She stepped from his touch, knowing she'd revealed more than she should have. "You're a complete stranger," she pointed out, lifting a hand to her shoulder. "But you know about my tattoo. *That's* why I came to Europe."

"To hide," he muttered darkly.

"To live," she corrected. There was a big difference. "To get away from people who pose as friends or lovers, when all they really want is the next big story."

He swore softly. "Ouch."

"When a man kisses me, Sandro, I want to know that he's kissing *me,* not just an assignment. When he tells me he wants me, I want to know that he wants *me,* not just a story, that his words reflect desire, not ambition." She paused, met Sandro's eyes. "When I give myself to a man,

I want to know that lies aren't crawling into bed with us. Is that so very wrong?"

A moment passed before he answered. "No," he said quietly. "It's not so very wrong at all."

She stepped closer. "Sandro—"

"We'll set up toward the back," he said, turning from her. "There's a rest room along the wall. You can freshen up there." Then he was gone, melting into the shadows while something deep inside Miranda silently shattered.

Midnight pushed closer, but sleep remained elusive. Miranda slipped from the pallet Sandro had made for her, tired of pretending she could just close her eyes and nod off. Too much adrenaline streamed through her. Too much...uncertainty. She'd never been one to run or hide from her problems, even though Sandro thought that's why she'd come to Europe.

Even now, hours later, his words, his abrupt departure, stung. She'd foolishly opened to him, shared a little piece of herself, only to have him walk away. He'd barely spoken over their dinner of cheese and bread, muttered only a few curt words as he'd made a pallet for her and told her to get some sleep.

Apparently he'd forgotten their little showdown earlier that day at the reflecting pond.

She wished she could. She wished she could forget the way he'd looked standing there, so very still, as out of place and forsaken as the stone turret. She wished she could forget the way his fingers had felt against her face, his mouth against hers. The way her heart revved and stalled whenever he stood too close. Whenever she heard his voice. Whenever she looked into those eyes like chips of midnight ice and saw the shadows of a struggle she didn't understand.

But she couldn't do any of those things.

There was a stillness to the musty room, a quiet so deep and pure she figured Sandro must have allowed himself to sleep. Restless, she stood and stretched, lifted a hand to an oak barrel. The wood was smooth and cool, almost magical. The wine resting inside would be red, she knew, and her mouth watered. It wouldn't take much to tap into one of the barrels and let the *vhino* trickle down her throat. The thought made her smile.

Danger lurked in the darkness beyond the cellar, but the huge casks lent the room an intimate feel, especially now that night had fallen and the only light stemmed from candles.

Running her hand along the big barrel, Miranda wandered toward the center aisle.

Then froze. She just barely managed not to gasp.

Sandro didn't sleep. He sat with his back against one of the giant casks, the flickering play of candlelight emphasizing the unforgiving line of his jaw and the sharp angles of his cheekbones, the brutal intensity of his eyes. His knees were slightly bent, his head bowed. In his hand, he held a viciously sharp knife.

Her heart kicked hard against her ribs. She'd grown used to seeing him with the semiautomatic in hand, but the knife caught her by surprise. So did the knowledge of how skillfully he could wield it.

Turn around the voice of caution whispered, but curiosity nudged closer. Questions scurried through her like the mice she hoped did not reside in the wine cellar. Sandro, this man who turned into a commando if the breeze so much as blew the wrong way, seemed oblivious to her presence. His concentration belonged to the knife he jabbed against the palm of his other hand.

His expression bordered on reverent.

A sense of the forbidden shimmied through Miranda, as though she was eight years old again, sneaking downstairs on Christmas Eve, eager to learn the secrets of Santa Claus. But she wasn't a little girl anymore, and the man she watched from the shadows had nothing to do with childhood mischief.

She eased closer anyway, stilled the second she caught sight of his left hand. Or, more precisely, the object in his palm.

He looked up abruptly. "Miranda."

Her breath caught. Whittling. The dangerous man with the briefcase that turned into a gun was sitting quietly on the cold stone floor, diligently, deliberately, painstakingly, turning something plain into something beautiful.

"Don't stop," she said, moving to stand beside him.

"You should be sleeping."

"So should you."

The shadow crossed his gaze so briefly, she wondered if she'd seen it at all. "Couldn't."

"Me, neither." Most people grew more comfortable with each other as time passed, but Sandro seemed increasingly uncomfortable around her. Determined to bridge the widening chasm, she slid down alongside him. "What are you making?"

"Nothing special," he said with a quick flick of the blade. "Just experimenting."

She leaned closer, noting the pile of wood shavings against the stone floor. "Seems like more than an experiment to me."

"Maybe."

Fascination whispered louder. Just when she thought she had a handle on the man, he went and proved she didn't. "You hardly strike me as a whittling kind of man."

He nicked the knife against the wood, carving out a little indentation. "Why not? Patience and precision is about all it takes. That, and a little imagination."

Miranda didn't want to think about his imagination. Hers was dangerous enough. "It's just a man in your line of work—"

"Spends a lot of nights alone," he finished for her. "Even girlie magazines get old after a while."

The image formed before she could stop it, prompting

her to say a silent prayer of thanks she'd found Sandro with a knife, and not a centerfold.

"How does a man get into your line of work?" she asked. Dark humor had underscored his words, but she'd heard something else, as well. Something she desperately wanted to understand.

He shrugged. "Fate, maybe. Destiny. Who knows."

In other words, he wasn't going to tell her. She sat quietly for a moment, biting the inside of her mouth, watching him work. The block of wood gave away none of his secrets, though, no hint of what lay ahead. "Did you teach yourself?"

"I didn't go to bodyguard school, if that's what you're asking."

"No," she clarified. "To whittle."

Against the wood, his knife stilled. "No."

Miranda bit back a sound of frustration deep in her throat. She wanted to bang her hands against the barrier he'd erected between them, but knew she would find only air.

His walls weren't of stone or flesh, but something deeper, far less tangible.

Silence rushed in from all directions, but rather than breaking it with another question, she let it hang between them. Let it thicken. Let it deepen.

Slowly, Sandro began working again, using the blade to round the edge of the wood. He executed a series of quick, precise strokes, followed by one long glide. Miranda wouldn't have thought such big hands could perform such delicate maneuvers, but his fingers were sure and nimble, and he wielded the knife like an extension of himself.

"When I was a kid," he finally said, "I always wanted a dog."

Miranda wrapped her arms around her knees, tried not to shiver. There was a chill to the cavernous room, a cold that bled from the walls and seeped from the stone. She fought it, didn't want Sandro to see her tremble, didn't want to shatter the moment. He wasn't a man to talk of himself. She wanted every second he would give her.

"All my friends had dogs," he was saying in a voice so remote, she wondered if he realized he spoke aloud, or if the cover of darkness hid what she sensed he would consider an unpardonable sin.

"Gus had one he'd trained to play Frisbee, and the three of us would go at it for hours." He flipped the wooden block in his hands and began carving the underside. "Molly never got tired, she just ran and ran, always wanted to play. To please."

A smile slipped from Miranda's heart. "Sounds like my dog Huntress."

He turned to look at her, sent her pulse skittering. The inches between them had seemed like plenty of distance when she slid down against the barrel. But now, with those intense dark eyes focused fully on her, she could see the candlelight flicker in his pupils, feel the rush of his breathing. All she had to do was lift her hand, and she would discover if the whiskers on his jaw were as soft as they looked.

"One day I was walking home from baseball practice," he said, and Miranda couldn't help but notice the way his mouth formed the words. Heat flashed through her as she remembered those lips against hers, those dangerous, thrilling moments when he'd broken off her cry for help and sent her world spinning.

Miranda jerked herself back from the memory, forced herself to concentrate on his story, not his mouth.

"There was this terrible screech behind me. I turned around just as a big black Mercedes skidded to a stop inches from the most pathetic, mangy dog I'd ever seen. The driver of the car honked and shouted, then swerved and kept going. But the dog never moved. It was almost like he'd wanted the car to hit him."

Miranda cringed. "Was he okay?"

Very gently, Sandro culled out a small circular section

of wood. "He was starving, losing his fur to mange, covered with fleas. And when I reached out to touch him, he winced and went down low, like he thought I was going to hit him."

Another chill, this one deeper, closer to the heart. "He was abused."

"I got down on my knees and coaxed him out of the road," Sandro said. "Took him home with me. He was a lab. Yellow. About forty pounds, instead of eighty. You could literally count his ribs just looking at him. My parents were in Europe, so I took care of him myself, feeding him several small meals a day, dipping him, playing with him."

Miranda sat very still, trusting herself to neither move, nor speak. There was something unfathomable about those fragile hours when the rest of the world slept, when defenses lowered and the truth bled through. That's when lies crumbled, she'd learned, as though with the land gone dark, no one could see you bleed. It was as though the sun generated the fortresses that kept people tough, and as twilight gave way to night, illusions faded, leaving only the bare bones of the truth.

It was that truth she wanted, the part of Sandro he kept hidden from the world.

"Did he like Frisbee, too?" she asked.

"Not at first. He was so malnourished he could barely run. I'd throw the Frisbee and he'd take off, but after only a few steps his paws would buckle and he'd go down."

"Poor guy."

"He got better," Sandro said, and Miranda heard the smile in his voice before she saw it on his face. "He wanted to please so damn bad, I could see it in his eyes." Sandro eased the knife along the edge of the block. "After the fleas were gone, I let him inside. He followed me from room to room, sat at my feet while I ate dinner, slept with me, you name it."

Her throat tightened. Sandro spoke of happy times, but there was sorrow in his voice. She looked at him sitting in the shadows against the oak barrel, at the play of the candlelight against the planes of his face, the tightness of his jaw and the hard line of his mouth, and for a crazy minute, she wanted to lay her hand on his leg, touch him, pull him out of the past and back to her.

"What happened?" she asked instead. "What happened to the dog?"

And what did this story have to do with whittling?

Sandro's hands stilled. "My parents came home from Europe."

"They didn't like him?"

He stabbed the knife viciously against the wood. "Pets don't belong in or around the house, Mother said. They might break a lamp or a crystal vase. Get the furniture or carpet dirty. Or God forbid, lick one of her friends."

Miranda braced herself, but said nothing.

"I came home from school one day and Virgil, that's what I named him, was gone. Just gone. My mother had been having a garden party, and she said he must have found a way out of the backyard. But I knew he would never leave me like that." Sandro turned to look at her again, his eyes darker than before. "Two days later my grandfather and I found him at the pound, just a few hours before they were going to put him down. The guy there said my mother had brought him in, said he was a stray."

Nothing, not wisdom nor restraint nor caution, could have kept Miranda from reaching out then, settling her hand against his thigh. His muscle contracted beneath her palm, tightened. "Why would your mom do that?"

A hard sound broke from Sandro's throat. "Thinking beyond the moment, beyond herself, was never her forte. She'd had a hard childhood. Marrying into my father's world was like a dream come true. She had this image of who she was supposed to be and the life she was supposed to lead, and willful children and dirty dogs didn't fit into it."

"Your father's world?" Miranda asked.

"His family came to the U.S. from Italy in the fifties and ended up doing pretty well for themselves. About the most work he and my mom had to do was hosting parties and planning trips."

"Oh." She knew about growing up in a financially secure family, and she knew about growing up among suffocating rules, but she couldn't relate to parents more interested in themselves than anything else. Her philanthropic parents were the exact opposite. Her mother always had a cause, her father an agenda.

"Gramps was different," Sandro said. "He never understood the woman his daughter became." He paused, let out a rough breath. "He took Virgil home with him, let him live in his backyard. That way, I could see him as often as possible."

A cheer rose up within Miranda. She hated the thought of Sandro and the dog he'd rescued from death being separated. Even more, she hated the thought that there'd been no one in his childhood who'd cared about what dwelled in his heart. "Did he live close?"

"Close enough." His eyes met hers, the cool air suddenly warmer. Seconds dragged by. She tried to breathe normally, but there was nothing normal about the way Sandro looked at her. They sat too close. She could feel the heat of his body, the burn of his gaze.

Something deep inside her responded, fluttering instantly, valiantly. She would never have imagined a musty wine cellar could feel so unbearably intimate, but there, surrounded by the giant casks of sleeping wine, the world beyond barely seemed to exist. For the first time she could remember, even since assuming the identity of Astrid Van Dyke, she didn't feel like the ambassador's daughter. She didn't feel like a Carrington. She felt like just a woman, alone with just a man.

The realization tightened her throat, sent her heart strumming low and deep.

Finally Sandro moved. She saw him lift his hand, felt

herself brace in anticipation of his touch. Instead, he reached down to retrieve something from the pocket of his loose-fitting camouflage pants. And when he extended his hand toward her and uncurled his fingers, she cringed at the jagged cuts from when he'd taken the knife from her.

The object in his palm stalled her breath.

Chapter 7

Miranda just stared.

There in the darkness, on the run from men who wanted to use her as a pawn, with the hour sometime past midnight, she was again thrown back to the magical Christmas Eves of her youth, when she'd eagerly torn open packages from her grandfather.

He'd had an offbeat sense of gift-giving, one year giving her a polished rock collection, another year an assortment of pressed four-leaf clovers he'd found in his yard, still another giving her a framed series of cartoons he'd cut from the paper. But each year, it was his gifts that touched her the deepest, because she'd known they came from his heart, not some generic department store.

It hardly seemed possible that a man she'd known for less than forty-eight hours, who was more stranger than friend, mystery than confidante, could give her such a gift. But with deep certainty, Miranda knew that even though Sandro had turned his back on her confession earlier that evening, in showing her the wooden statue in his hand, the dog he carried in his pocket, he was showing her something of himself.

And that was a gift.

"It's beautiful," she said, reaching over to run her fingers along the smooth, clearly well-worn wood. It was very similar to the statue she'd found him carving.

A faint smile played at the corners of his mouth. "It's Virgil," he said. "All the way down to the slightly crooked tail, which the vet said had been repeatedly broken." Pausing, he pressed the dog into her hands. "My grandfather carved him so I'd always have him with me, even when we were apart."

And now, more than twenty years later, the lonely little boy had become a battle-scarred man, but he still carried the statue with him. "Your grandfather sounds like a wonderful man."

"He was."

Her heart snagged on the use of past tense.

"While you were curled up in your grandfather's lap listening to stories," Sandro added, "I was probably on the porch with mine, learning how to whittle."

There was a soft glow to his eyes now, a light she recognized as memory. "The two of you must have been close."

"He was the best."

There it was again. Past tense.

"The rest of your family?" she ventured, pretty sure she knew the answer. Even when he'd come on to her by the ocean, she'd sensed an isolation to him, a wall between himself and the world as tangible as the dark sunglasses he'd worn. Instinct warned there weren't many he'd truly allowed close to him.

"I was an only child."

Was. When he spoke of his family, he used the past tense.

"Is there someone special waiting for you, Sandro?" she asked, returning Virgil to his owner. "A dog, maybe?"

He stared down at the dog in his hand. "What?"

"I was wondering if you have a dog, if somewhere a four-legged friend is waiting for his daddy to come home." For some crazy reason, she hoped there was.

"No."

The finality of that one word chilled more deeply than the floor, the walls. "Why not? Don't you still want one?"

Abruptly, he returned Virgil to his pocket. "A man in my line of work learns not to want what he can't have. There's no faster way to lose your edge, to make a mistake that could get people killed."

And just like that, the commando was back.

Miranda shivered. A smart woman would accept the finality of his words and return to her pallet, shut her eyes, dream of the moment she could walk unabashedly in the sunshine without worrying about some lunatic who wanted to turn her into a pawn. A smart woman would leave the wounded animal in his dark little den, not try to lure him out. A smart woman would ignore the ache in her chest, the tightness of her throat.

"What happened to that little boy, Sandro? The one who went after what he wanted, even when it looked impossible? How did he grow up to turn into a yes-man?"

The knife clattered to the stone floor. "A yes-man?"

Miranda swallowed hard. His tone, the hard look in his eyes, told her he hadn't appreciated her choice of words. But she neither liked nor understood how a man such as Sandro could abandon his hopes and his dreams, the core of himself, to crawl into the back seat of someone else's life.

"One of my father's men," she clarified, "someone who takes orders, rather than making his own decisions, carving his own path."

The lines around his mouth hardened. "You make it sound black or white."

"Isn't it? You're letting my father dictate what you do

and don't do, just like your mother wouldn't let you have a dog.''

Wincing, he swore softly and stood, turned his back to her.

Miranda pushed to her feet, ignoring the sharp pain in her right leg, which had fallen brutally asleep. No way was she letting Sandro shut her out again, walk away, pretend.

"Are you really going to stand here and tell me there's nothing in this world that you want? That everything in your life is exactly the way you want it to be? That you don't still want a dog, a living, breathing companion to—''

He spun toward her. "I'm not telling you any such thing,'' he practically growled. In the glow of the candlelight he looked combat-ready, eyes on fire, hands curled into fists. "I want plenty, *bella,* trust me. When it's right, neither hell nor high water gets in my way. But when it's wrong…'' He hesitated, letting the word linger between them. "When it's wrong, I do whatever it takes to resist.''

Miranda stepped toward him, prompting him to step back. "What then?'' she asked, smiling slyly when she realized an oak barrel prevented him from retreating. "What do you want?''

He didn't try to sidestep her like she'd expected. "You sure you want me to answer that?'' he asked very softly.

Her mouth went dry. The momentary thrill of backing him into a corner gave way to the realization that he'd skillfully, deliberately, managed to turn the tables. She was the one now poised between the bluff she was trying to call and the dare glimmering in his smoky gaze.

Heat streaked through her. Caution demanded she turn and walk away, but Miranda had never been much on caution. Life offered no guarantees. After tomorrow, she might never see this man again. These hours together in the wine cellar might be all they had.

"Yes,'' she said, simultaneously taking a leap of faith and bracing herself. "Yes.''

* * *

Sandro swore silently. The shadows had always been his friends, but the way they played across Miranda's face made him itch to throw on every light he could find. Her skin looked softer, her gypsy eyes even more provocative. The soft brown hair played against her cheekbones and curved beneath the chin she'd lifted in clear, utter, foolish defiance.

The stupidity of his mistake, his miscalculation, burned.

He'd meant to back her into a corner, not himself. He'd meant to send her scurrying to her cozy pallet, not to instigate a game his body burned to finish. Clearly Miranda Carrington had never learned what happened when you played with fire.

He had.

Silence gathered, exposing the minutest of sounds, the thrumming of his heart, the blood roaring through his veins, the scratch of a tree limb outside, the drip of a leaky pipe. But the ambassador's daughter didn't look away, didn't so much as blink. She just looked up at him with those devastatingly slumberous eyes of hers, daring him to answer her question.

What did he want?

His body tightened brutally at the answer. He wanted to erase the past fifteen minutes. He wanted to take back the story of Virgil, to wipe her fingerprints from the statue in his pocket. He wanted to trample the intimacy gathering between them, the desire to put his mouth to hers, to drink her in as greedily as he'd once consumed the Medeira label.

But all of those wants were equally impossible. She was a woman of sunshine. He was a man of the shadows. She'd made it obscenely clear she longed to live her life without her every step, smile, word being scrutinized. He'd walked away from his life the first chance he got, turning his back on the personal freedom she craved. As soon as Javier made contact, Sandro would turn her over and never see her again.

Making more memories than absolutely necessary made about as much sense as telling her about Virgil.

"Well?" she asked, and he knew he really had no choice.

Very slowly, very deliberately, he put a hand to her waist and pulled her against the hard planes of his body. He saw her eyes widen at the contact, at the discovery of truths his body couldn't hide. With his other hand, he cupped her face, skimmed his thumb along her bottom lip.

The sexy little hitch to her breathing almost did him in.

"I want plenty," he murmured, his voice deliberately thick and low. He slid the hand at her waist to cup her bottom, and tried not to groan. Candlelight flickered cruelly across her face, revealing the thin veneer of bravery in her gaze, the vulnerability leaking through.

Precision had always been Sandro's calling card, not cruelty. But now he had no choice. "Did you know you sleep with your lips parted?"

Her eyes flared, but she said nothing.

"You do," he said. "And ever since last night...hell, ever since you kissed me so hotly in the alley, I've wanted to take your mouth again, to feel you open for me, accept me, take me deep, give me the same ride you gave the man in that picture."

In his arms, she went deathly still. In her gaze, confidence splintered into cold shards. "W-what?"

"You know," he forced himself to continue. "The man in that tabloid picture." Self-contempt backed up in his throat. "I looked it up on the Internet the night I learned the general was going after you, and wondered if you'd be as willing as you were in the picture, if the ambassador's daughter could really make a man weak with nothing more than a kiss." Cruelly, he added a laugh. "My partner Javier said I didn't stand a chance."

She stood so still that had she not spoken, he wouldn't have been sure she breathed. "You and your partner talked about me?"

The question was little more than a broken whisper, making it harder to force a smile. "He was jealous, said I didn't deserve the chance to live out his wet dream."

She came alive then, beautifully, horribly. Shock flashed hotly in her eyes. Color surged to her cheeks. Her mouth fell open. She struggled against him, ripping free of his arms and staggering back.

"You asked," he reminded, hating himself more than he'd imagined humanly possible. "Don't worry, *bella*," he added. "Like I said, I know we don't always get what we want."

He didn't expect the sudden rush of tears flooding her eyes, not from this fiery, defiant woman. He didn't expect to see tiny pieces of her unravel right before his eyes.

"I was wrong about you," she whispered.

The urge to yank back his words almost sent him to his knees. Instead, he shrugged. "Most people are."

"I thought you were different," she went on, hurt and disillusionment glowing in her eyes. "I thought you had a heart. But you're just as cold and indifferent as all the others." She turned then, walked away. Just like he'd intended.

But it didn't feel anywhere near as good as he'd hoped.

Sandro watched her disappear between two rows of oak barrels. His heart pounded hard. His lungs couldn't take in enough oxygen. Coldness slammed in from all directions, chilling him on the inside, battering him from the outside.

And he couldn't take it. Couldn't just stand there and let her slip into the shadows, not the woman who belonged in the sunshine. He couldn't let her hurt like that. Never in his life had success left such an obscene taste in his mouth.

He went after her, found her just around the corner. She stood next to one of the huge casks of wine with her back to him, arms hugged around her middle.

Leave her alone, the voice of preservation whispered, but Sandro could no more turn his back on her than he could take back the heartless words he'd told to crush the intimacy growing between them. Words he hadn't meant. Lies. He'd only wanted to put some distance between them, dampen the attraction that threatened to burn out of control.

Three long strides eliminated the distance between them. No power on earth could have stopped him from doing what he did next, from putting a hand to her shoulder, turning her to face him. With his index finger, he gently brushed at the moisture beneath her eyes. "I'm sorry."

"Don't be."

"Impossible," he said. "I don't want to hurt you."

"You mean you don't want to hurt the ambassador's daughter."

The jab dug deep. "You're not the ambassador's daughter to me, Miranda. You're a beautiful, spirited woman." He hesitated, replaced lies with truth. "You're Astrid."

She said nothing at first, just looked at him. Through him. Her eyes were dry now, overly bright, even in the darkness. The sole candle revealed the color gone from her cheeks, replaced by an unnatural paleness.

"When I was growing up," she said, her voice oddly remote, "we had a live-in housekeeper named Luciana. She was this wonderful Brazilian woman with two daughters, one a year older than me, one a year younger, and in the evenings, she'd play Brazilian folk music in the little house out back and teach her girls to dance. One night she caught me looking in the window and invited me inside. I never even hesitated, even though my parents were hosting a garden party I was supposed to be attending. I went inside Luciana's small house, and there in her barely furnished den she taught me to dance."

Sandro tensed. His hand remained against the side of her face, but his fingers had drifted back into her soft brown hair. He knew he should sever the contact. But couldn't.

Didn't want to.

"Did your parents find you?" he asked.

"No," she said with a tight smile. "A reporter did. Mitsy Maynor. She'd slipped free of the party and was wandering the grounds, looking for something more exciting. She hit pay dirt when she found me. The next morning, we were eating breakfast when my mother opened the paper to read the write-up on her party, only to see a picture of me dancing with the hired help.''

He smiled at the image. ''Ouch.''

''I used to lie in bed at night and wish I was one of Luciana's daughters,'' she admitted, revealing just how deep her desire for freedom, anonymity, ran. ''That I could grow up without a camera in my face, without people cataloguing and analyzing every move I made. Every experiment. Every mistake.''

The recrimination hit with unerring accuracy. ''Without jackasses like me thinking they know you, when they don't,'' he finished for her.

She pulled his hand from her face. ''I just want to live a normal life,'' she said simply. ''Is that really so very wrong?''

The longing in her eyes, her voice, twisted him up inside. ''No,'' he said. ''Just dangerous.''

In more ways than she realized.

''But that's just it,'' she said, angling her chin. The color rushed back to her cheeks, the life to her eyes. ''*Life* is dangerous, not just for me, but for everyone. And that's all I really wanted. To be like everyone else. To slip into a crowd and not be mobbed. To dance in the street and not be splattered across the front of every tabloid. To embrace my friends without speculation as to my sexual orientation.''

Sandro braced himself, tried to hold himself back, but felt himself going over the edge anyway. ''There are some things more important than dancing in the street, *bella*.''

She looked up and met his eyes. ''Like what?''

He might live to be an old man like his grandfather, or maybe just another year, another day. A man in his line of work never fully knew. He did his job as best as he could, taking every precaution imaginable, and then some. Mistakes were unacceptable, because mistakes got people killed.

Miranda was a mistake. He knew that. He accepted that. But for the first time in five long years, he couldn't find the right countermaneuver. He felt himself move, felt himself draw her close. Felt the heat shoot through him. Felt himself stiffen.

Felt the long freefall begin.

"Like dancing in a wine cellar," he murmured against the clean smell of her hair.

She didn't move against him like he wanted, didn't curl her arms around his waist. "Sandro—"

"There's no tabloid photographers waiting in the shadows," he whispered. "Only me."

"There's no music."

That, he thought grimly, was a bald-faced lie.

He pulled back far enough to see her face. "Not all music comes from radios and compact discs, *bella*. Listen," he instructed, pausing to let the purr of the wind and the whisper of the candles prove his point. "Don't you hear it?"

Her eyes took on a slow glow. "Drums?"

He took her hand and drew it to his chest, pressed her palm to the soft cotton of his shirt, felt the heat clear down to his bones. "The next best thing."

A smile of pure sunshine touched her lips and slayed the last of his common sense. "Staccato," she whispered. "Just like mine."

The words seeped through him like a benediction. He could do nothing but draw her against his body, curling one arm around her lower back, the other around her shoulders. She didn't pull away as he'd dreaded but half expected, didn't stiffen. She went liquid in his embrace, sinuous, wrapping her arms around his body much as he'd done hers. They began to sway then, moving in unison with the rhythm of the night.

Sandro closed his eyes, savoring the way she felt in his

NO POSTAGE
NECESSARY
IF MAILED
IN THE
UNITED STATES

BUSINESS REPLY MAIL
FIRST-CLASS MAIL   PERMIT NO. 717-003   BUFFALO, NY

POSTAGE WILL BE PAID BY ADDRESSEE

SILHOUETTE READER SERVICE
3010 WALDEN AVE
PO BOX 1867
BUFFALO NY 14240-9952

Get FREE BOOKS and a FREE GIFT when you play the...

LAS VEGAS GAME

Just scratch off the gold box with a coin. Then check below to see the gifts you get!

YES! I have scratched off the gold Box. Please send me my **2 FREE BOOKS** and **gift for which I qualify**. I understand that I am under no obligation to purchase any books as explained on the back of this card.

345 SDL DUYH   245 SDL DUYX

FIRST NAME	LAST NAME

ADDRESS

APT.#	CITY

STATE/PROV.   ZIP/POSTAL CODE

(S-IM-03/03)

Visit us online at
www.eHarlequin.com

7	7	7	Worth TWO FREE BOOKS plus a BONUS Mystery Gift!
🍒	🍒	🍒	Worth TWO FREE BOOKS!
🔔	🔔	☘	TRY AGAIN!

Offer limited to one per household and not valid to current Silhouette Intimate Moments® subscribers. All orders subject to approval.

arms. Like holding sunshine, he thought ridiculously, heat and radiance, beauty. The rays warmed the chill of the shadows, brought light where he'd become accustomed to darkness. She was so strong and brave and courageous, it surprised him to feel how slender she was, drove home how vulnerable she really was.

The need to keep her safe tangled with other needs, needs that had nothing to do with safety, and everything to do with desire. He wanted to taste her lips again. To feel her taste him back. He wanted to lose himself in her innocence, her spark, to intoxicate her senses with the desire pounding through him.

He wanted to lay her down between the rows of resting wine, strip away the barriers between them, make her his.

Lead us not into temptation.

The prayer from his childhood echoed relentlessly through him, but he couldn't bring himself to pull away. Instead he savored the feel of her in his arms, the way she rested her head against his chest. Something so wrong shouldn't feel so right. He told himself to step back, even as his hands began sliding, urging her closer. They molded together perfectly, making it impossible for her not to realize how badly he wanted her.

Still, she didn't pull away. She inhaled deeply, tightened her hold on him. He chanced a glance down at her face, saw her eyes closed, a contented smile curving her lips.

And his heart damn near stopped.

With brutal detail he remembered their moments by the reflecting pond, how beautiful she'd looked standing there in the puddle of sunshine, with the crumbling stone turret behind her, the swans gliding across the water. He remembered the enchantment on her face, the sense of adventure, the intimacy he'd skillfully destroyed when she'd tried to take his picture.

He'd wanted to crush her in his arms, not crush her.

But there could be no pictures, just as there could be no intimacy. There could be nothing real and tangible stemming from their time together. It was a mistake in the first place, a mistake they would both have to forget.

Pictures, the intimacy his body hungered for, would make that impossible. They could have only these moments in the shadows, memories that would fade without leaving permanent scars.

Instinctively, he knew she already bore too many of those.

Outside, the wind whispered louder, sending a branch strumming against the side of the wine cellar. A few splatters against the roof indicated a nearby storm. She stilled then, looked up at him. The little candle had almost burned itself out, but its valiant flicker provided enough light to see desire glowing in the green of her eyes.

It was like standing before an executioner with no hope of a pardon in sight.

Deliver us from evil, he thought desperately, but realized the prayer couldn't help him. The need to put his mouth to hers was dangerous, but it wasn't evil. The desire to taste her, drink her in, was purity in its most unabashed form.

The moment stretched to the breaking point. Pull away, Sandro told himself, but could no more let go than he could rip his heart from his chest. He slid a hand over her shoulders to tangle in her hair, then did the only thing he could.

Miranda put a hand to Sandro's chest and stopped him before his mouth could touch hers. The fever in his midnight eyes burned through her, but she couldn't indulge it. Not until she knew for sure.

"Who, Sandro? Who do you want to kiss?"

Tangled in her hair, his fingers tensed. And a languorous smile curved his lips. "The woman who's doing her best to drive me insane."

"But who am I?" she persisted, and saw the moment he realized what she asked.

"You're you," he whispered. "Not a Carrington, not the

ambassador's daughter, but a beautiful woman who needs no name.''

That was all it took. She melted there in his arms, sliding her hand from his chest to curve around his neck and urge him to her.

He needed no urging. On a groan his mouth found hers. Whereas in the alley she'd tried to shut him out, this time she opened for him, inviting him in, hungering to taste the same passion she'd tasted the day before. This kiss was different, though. Deeper. Almost…seeking. His mouth moved against hers as though searching for something lost. Something precious. Miranda felt his need deep in her bones, and responded instinctively. There was a tarnished nobility to this man of the shadows, a thread of regret beneath the swagger and hard muscle. She didn't know why he unsettled her so, only knew she wanted to bring him light. Help him find what was missing.

He slid a hand to her hips, where he slipped around to cup her bottom. She felt the hardness of his body against hers, the bulge against his pants that made it impossible to pretend this was just a simple, innocent kiss. There was nothing simple or innocent about the interplay of their mouths. Carnal was the only word to describe the little nips, the way he sucked her bottom lip, the way he seemed to be absorbing her inside of him.

But she didn't want to be inside of him. She wanted him inside of her.

The thought jarred her, thrilled her. She felt as though they'd tapped into the casks and drank greedily, as though wine now flowed through her veins, thick and rich, heady, intoxicating. How long since she'd been held with such possession, kissed with such delicious thoroughness?

Never, she knew. Never.

The fact that one of her father's men would be her first, her bodyguard of all people, shocked her clear down to the toes his kiss sent curling. She'd never understood how Elizabeth had let herself become involved with Hawk, but if this same fire had burned for her, even fractionally, she understood the wrenching sobs she'd heard from her sister's room after Hawk asked for a transfer overseas.

The sense of foreboding slammed in from nowhere and chilled Miranda to the bone. She fought it, intent on Sandro, the moment, the way he backed her against a cask. His mouth cruised down her neck, toward her chest, where he lifted a hand to gently tease her nipple.

She didn't mean to tense, but knew she had when his mouth stilled against her collarbone. They hung that way a heartbeat, body to body, heart to heart. In his kiss she'd found warmth, but the damp chill of the night pushed closer now.

"Don't stop," she whispered.

"I have to."

"No, you don't," she said, pushing up to brush her lips over his.

He took her shoulders and stepped from her, holding her at arm's distance. His eyes were dark, ravaged. His breathing was shallow. "If I don't," he practically growled, "I won't until I have you naked and under me, and I can't let that happen."

Miranda wasn't sure how she stayed standing. "And what's so bad about that?" Just the thought had her wet and wanting.

Or maybe she owed that to the kiss.

He swore softly. "Some lines," he said tightly, "can never be crossed."

Lines. Rules. Protocol. They were the stock and trade of her family's world. She'd always hated them, found them as restricting as a straitjacket. "You wanted to kiss me," she reminded, trying to keep the hurt from her voice.

The waning light of the candle emphasized the tight line of his jaw. "I want to do a lot more than kiss you, *bella*. But I've already told you a man in my line of work has to think about more than what his body wants."

His body. The crude dismissal of the passion between them stung.

"Call me selfish," she said, stripping the hurt from her voice. "But I've always believed if you don't go after what you want, then you're selling yourself short."

His expression gentled. "You're not selfish, Miranda. Just innocent."

There it was again, that tarnished nobility. "Innocent?" She was hardly a babe in the woods.

"You've never had your life blow up in your face," he said. "A fact for which I'm grateful."

Her throat tightened. The man always said more with what he didn't say, than what he did. "And you, Sandro? Have you had your life blow up in your face?"

The ache in her chest said that he had.

"I don't like to dwell in the past," he said as the candle at their feet flickered out. "My life has made me the man I am today, and it's that man who's going to make sure nothing bad happens to you. That's all that matters."

She wished to God she could believe that.

"Go to sleep," he whispered, releasing her. She heard his footsteps moving away from her. "With any luck, to-morrow is the day your nightmare ends."

Not all nightmares came under the cover of darkness. And not all could be vanquished. Some never ended. They lingered, Sandro knew, even in the brightest of light. Vivid images playing like a movie through the mind, over and over.

The boom always came first, loud, jarring. Then the hor-rific screams, contorted beyond the point of sounding hu-man. Flailing bodies flung through the air. Glass shattered, sliced.

Then came the blood.

Always, always, the blood.

So much of it, pouring from his body, the bodies around

him, turning into a river running down the cobblestone sidewalk.

Sandro swore viciously, demanded the nightmare go away. The hated images belonged to the past, not the present. He'd grown used to them penetrating his sleep, but he refused to let them encroach upon wakefulness. He had a job to do, couldn't afford the distraction.

But he lifted a hand to his neck anyway, his fingers idly tracing the scar across his throat. Sometimes, he'd swear he could still feel the pulsing pain, the searing, the blood draining from his body. Who would have guessed the elderly woman with the white crocheted shawl had been an army nurse back in World War II? Who could have predicted it was to be her quick thinking, her handiwork with a napkin, that saved his life?

When so many others died.

The doctors said plastic surgery could remove the scar. His family had wanted that. They'd wanted to erase the incident, eliminate all traces of the horror. But what they hadn't understood was that while external scars could fade or be removed, those on the inside never went away.

Sandro had refused to pretend otherwise.

Miranda would be different. Her nightmare would end. He would make it so. She would go back to her life, go back to the freedom she craved. He would make sure she never paced the darkness, refusing sleep because of the nightmare she knew awaited her. He would ensure she never awoke bathed in a cold sweat, with a scream burning in her throat. He would make sure she had no scars, not of the body, nor the spirit.

If she'd spent one more second pressed to his body, there would have been scars.

He watched her now, curled peacefully on the pallet. The candles surrounding her had flickered out, leaving the only light stemming from the one in his hand. Shadows played beneath her eyes and in the hollow of her cheeks, along her mouth, down to her neck. He wanted to trace his finger along that same path. He burned to use his mouth, like he had before.

And like before, he knew she would let him.

He'd felt that in her response to him, the warm fluidity. He'd felt her breasts pressed into him, felt the way her hands had eagerly run along his body, possessive, exploring, pressing his hips against her. She had, no doubt, discovered the response he couldn't hide.

Just the thought had him painfully hard. Again.

Because torture wasn't his schtick, he turned from her, stalked to the end of the row and picked up his knife. He wanted to stab the blade into one of the casks and watch the red wine bleed, to open his mouth and let it trickle down his throat. He wanted to taste.

He needed to forget.

But of course he couldn't, wouldn't, do any of that. He couldn't risk losing his edge for even one sliver of one second. He'd come close enough just holding Miranda in his arms.

There was a spark to her, a glimmer, he didn't want to dim. She reminded him of the dragonfly tattooed on her arm, vibrant and colorful, full of life and an innocence he didn't want to shatter. She was pure sunshine, a rebel with a cause, a free spirit determined to make her way in a world of rigid rules, restrictive obligations and suffocating protocols.

Forgive us our trespasses…

Taking advantage of her would be unforgivable. Because even though he'd felt the willingness in her, he'd seen the vulnerability, the hurt, shimmering in those wild gypsy eyes of hers. He'd indulged in affairs before, affairs of the flesh. But Miranda made him think of more than flesh, more than the moment. She made him think of tomorrow.

Tomorrow was a gift, a luxury, he could neither afford nor offer.

The ache in his chest caught him by surprise. He fingered the scar at his throat again, turned to look at her sleeping in the shadows. He wanted to return to her, to ease down alongside her, mold his body to hers. He wanted to slide his hands along her curves and feel the heat of her body. He wanted to hear those sexy little sighs, to taste freedom.

Lead us not into temptation, Sandro thought again, but this time he realized the truth. Miranda Carrington was more than temptation. She represented that crucial piece of himself he'd lost in a crowded open-air café five years before. She made him feel alive, he realized. Painfully, dangerously, seductively alive.

More alive than he'd felt since the cold night the news of his tragic, violent death broke to the world.

Javier's message came just before dawn.
TONIGHT. ORUM.

Chapter 8

Sandro stared at his mobile phone for a long time, his eyes going dry and the words blurring. He was the kind of man who prided himself on working efficiently and relentlessly to turn goals into reality. And until just five minutes ago, he'd been cursing Javier for taking so damn long to make arrangements.

Now, the end to this nightmare blessedly in sight, something deep inside him twisted.

Anticipation, he told himself. Relief.

Not dread.

Javi's text message was vague, but Sandro knew that was by design. Whatever went down tonight had to appear like a rescue mission, which meant to protect his cover, Sandro couldn't look prepared. There had to be an element of surprise. Navy Seals, maybe. Army Rangers. Other, less known special forces operatives. They would converge upon him and Miranda at an undisclosed time, in an undisclosed manner.

And they would rescue her.

From him.

The thought turned everything inside him ice-cold.

Already, he could see the look in her eyes when she connected the dots and realized the magnitude of the lies he'd told. Not real lies, of course. He really was trying to protect her. And he'd never *said* he worked for her father, even if he had led her to believe that.

He knew she would make no distinction.

He didn't want her, too, either. He didn't want her thinking about him after tonight. He didn't want her trying to figure out why a man who kept a carved statue of his childhood dog in his pocket had crawled into bed with a criminal on the FBI's ten-most-wanted list. He didn't want her pondering details he shouldn't have mentioned, ferreting out secrets that could not only destroy his mission, but also place countless lives in jeopardy.

He didn't want any of that, but the alternative, the hate she would feel toward him, didn't make him feel any better.

Feelings, however, didn't enter the equation. He was a highly trained operative, and this was just another mission. The next few hours would be critical. He had to be casual, play it cool. He couldn't let her sense the anxiety already coiling through him. He would need his Kevlar, he figured, just like the day of the original kidnapping. Shots could easily be fired tonight. He could be hit.

But somehow, he didn't care. It was a risk he had to take.

For her.

For Miranda.

"Do you believe those children really saw the Virgin Mary?"

Sandro shrugged. "It's not for me to say."

Standing near the middle of a wide, crowded esplanade, Miranda glanced toward the celebrated basilica, where pilgrims from all walks of life flocked toward the shrine built on the site where three young farm children reported seeing apparitions of the Holy Mother in 1917.

There was a serenity to the pristine site, even though limestone and concrete had replaced rocky slopes and gnarled olive trees. Two curved galleries flanked a massive white church that almost seemed to glow against a back-drop of pure blue sky. From somewhere unseen, inside the sanctuary maybe, the innocent voices of a children's choir echoed through the esplanade.

People were everywhere, men and women, young and old, prosperous and penniless. A few of the extreme devout made their way down the long, red-carpeted walkway lead-ing to the holy site on their knees. One older woman looked so frail, a considerably younger man walked beside her with his hands on her shoulders as she inched her way toward the shrine.

Such was the power of belief.

Miranda had grown up Methodist, but the reverence em-bracing the plaza extended beyond religious affiliation.

"It's...breathtaking," she said.

"So are apparitions, I'd imagine."

Frustrated by the distance she'd sensed from Sandro all day, she turned toward him. And just like that first day, she felt her breath catch. Sunglasses again concealed his eyes, but tight lines fanning out from the corners of his mouth gave away the tension she sensed churning behind those dark lenses.

She just didn't understand why.

Because of last night, or something else? Something worse than almost making love.

"So you *do* believe," she stated with a little smile. For some reason, she liked the thought of tough, gun-toting Sandro believing in intangibles, things that could neither be seen nor heard, touched nor smelled, but that were real and powerful all the same.

"I never said that, *bella.*" His jaw tightened as he stared beyond her toward the throng of believers clustered around a fountain of holy water. Many cupped their hands and drank greedily. "*They* believe. That's all that matters."

The early afternoon sun shone brightly from a sky so clear and blue it barely looked real. Yet Miranda shivered. Forsaken, she thought again. Now that the word had taken root in her psyche, she couldn't shake it. People milled about everywhere, but Sandro seemed to stand alone, like a 3-D image against a pencil-sketch background, larger than the life around him.

Miranda felt her lips twist at the foolishly romantic thought. Of course the man stood out. He was almost a head taller than anyone else around, he wore dark sunglasses and a silly banana-yellow Hawaiian shirt dotted by surfboards in every color imaginable, and he held a sleek, severe-looking attaché case in his left hand.

That was really a gun.

With inky black hair slightly long and rumpled by the warm breeze and the increasingly thick whiskers shadowing his jaw, he looked somewhere between a beach bum and a hit man.

Forsaken.

"What do you mean that's all that matters?" she asked, frowning.

He shoved his free hand deep into his pocket, hesitating a moment before answering. "If these people believe drinking water from that fountain or burning some cheap wax candle or saying the rosary before the altar will cure their illnesses or heal their broken hearts, grant them some sort of forgiveness, then who am I to say otherwise? Faith comes from the heart. We each have to make, to believe in, our own path."

The sudden sense of foreboding made no sense. Nor did the tightness in her chest. Sandro, this enigmatic man her father had sent to protect her, who'd been willing to take a bullet for her, was unlike anyone she'd ever met. He lived in the world of rules and protocol she'd grown to hate, but he spoke of faith and free will and fidelity like they were akin to the Holy Grail.

"Why do you work for my father?" she asked before she could talk herself out of it.

"I'm doing what I need to do."

"Which is what?" she persisted.

He turned to her then, surprised her by lifting a hand to tuck a flyaway strand of light brown hair behind her ear. It was the first time he'd touched her all day.

"Right now," he said, "it seems to be playing twenty questions with a beautiful woman."

She looked at the faint smile tugging at the mouth which had kissed her so thoroughly the night before, felt the heat sing to every nerve ending. She wanted to feel his mouth on hers again, to taste the ferocity of his kiss, to feel the hard planes of his body.

Some, she remembered, much harder than others.

She still didn't understand why he'd pulled away. As she'd lain there wrapped in blankets that did little to mute the chill of the stone floor, trying to find sleep, she'd seen him pacing among the huge oak barrels, knife in hand. She'd wanted to go to him, but had known he'd only reject her again.

Then this morning, there'd been...nothing. She'd used the rest room to change into another tacky outfit, this one a near-unimaginable combination of aqua and orange polyester, and when she'd come out, not even the floppy straw hat or out-of-style sunglasses had evoked a reaction from him.

"You've got evasion down to an art form, don't you?" she asked, fighting the urge to yank the dark sunglasses from his face and see his eyes.

"It's a skill that comes in handy in my line of work."

The words were matter-of-fact, but Miranda found little matter-of-fact about his chosen profession. At least, not for a man like him. "You could have been killed, Sandro. This path you're following, is it really so important that you're willing to die for causes that have nothing to do with you?"

Like Hawk had done.

The memory chilled her. Did Elizabeth already know? Did anybody? She hated thinking of how her sister would react. Elizabeth was strong and polished and poised, and she insisted Hawk meant nothing more to her than a forbidden fling with a sexy bodyguard, but Miranda knew her sister had given Hawk Monroe a piece of her soul she could never get back.

"Risks are part of the job," Sandro said simply.

Her throat tightened. "You really don't care, do you?"

"I care," he said quietly. "But what I do is worth the risk. It's like you said. *Life* is dangerous. Only a coward chooses the path of least resistance."

A smile slipped from her heart to her lips. "You really take that road-less-traveled stuff to heart, don't you?"

Through those dark sunglasses, he held her gaze a moment before answering. "Are you sure you never thought about becoming a cop or a shrink?"

"Never a cop," she answered, then paused. Around her, devotion and capitalism clashed almost violently, believers emptying their pockets to purchase wax figurines and souvenir trinkets manufactured in Taiwan. Barely a week before, she would have been nearly dizzy from aiming her camera in every direction, but today, she'd only snapped a few requisite shots. The carnival-like atmosphere that once would have intrigued was nothing compared to the man standing beside her.

The man to whom she'd soon say goodbye.

"Have you heard anything, Sandro?" She couldn't shake the cold feeling of dread. "Do you know when they're coming for me?"

He frowned. "Not much longer," he said, then startled her by reaching for her hand. "Let's go get some ice cream."

In other words, end of subject. The fingers he laced with

hers were warm, however, the palm of his hand callused, the physical contact oddly reassuring.

Maybe Fatima really was a place of miracles.

"Actually," she mused, "I was hoping for a bubble bath."

"Honeysuckle?"

Sandro stabbed his hands deep into his pockets and tried not to look at the small white tub. "It was all they had."

Miranda just stared at him. She'd finally taken off the ridiculous hat and sunglasses he'd purchased to disguise her beauty, but had succeeded only in making her look more like a gypsy. The light brown hair suited her, making those exotic eyes of hers look greener, her mouth like berries.

"You bought me bubble bath?" she said for the third time. "That's the stop we had to make?"

"Just don't stay in so long you wrinkle," he said ambivalently. She didn't need to know about the other purchase. She would find out, of course. Later. After everything was said and done. But she would already hate him then. One more deception would hardly make a difference.

For a moment, she said nothing, just looked from him to the bottle in her hand, the baby powder and lotion and shampoo sitting on the counter of the small bathroom. After the ice-cream debacle, they'd left Fatima behind, traveling to the town of Orum, where tonight Miranda would be rescued.

From him.

She had no idea. At least, he didn't think she did. He'd been playing it cool, telling her only that the small wooden house was another in his network of secure locations, and that at least for the night, they could enjoy the creature comforts of warmth, a table to eat at, a mattress on which to sleep, and…a bubble bath.

"This is…" She turned back to him and beamed a smile so bright, so honest, it sliced to the bone. "Thank you," she said simply.

She might as well have told him to go to hell. "You're welcome."

An awkward silence descended as Miranda looked at him expectantly, and he tried not to think about her sinking into a steaming tub of bubbles. Naked.

"I'll give you some privacy," he practically growled, then walked away before he did something foolish like pull her into his arms and put his mouth to hers, see if he could still taste the mint-chip ice cream he'd watched her lick from the cone. What the hell had he been thinking? He might as well have been watching her audition for a starring role in a porn flick.

But that was the problem, he knew. When it came to Miranda, he had a damn hard time thinking. Other parts of his body tended to take over.

He didn't want to think about which parts.

Instead, he closed the door to the bathroom, but never heard her click the little lock. He kept walking, determined not to think about her sliding out of those tacky clothes and into the steaming water.

Just the aborted thought had him groaning out loud.

Impatience trampled through him, but for the next few hours, there was little he could do. As far as Miranda could know, tonight was nothing special. He'd thought about giving her a heads up, had *wanted* to clue her in so the operation wouldn't frighten her, but protecting his cover necessitated extracting Miranda from him as though he'd kidnapped her, not protected her. If she suspected he knew the cavalry was coming, she was too smart not to question how a criminal had learned of the mission, and why he'd done nothing to stop it.

And that was a risk he could not take.

They'd both be better off if she slept through the entire operation.

He lived in a violent world, populated by men who didn't think twice about hurting innocents to further their own causes. The general's reach was far, and deep. He had followers everywhere, even in America. He could easily disguise someone as a reporter, even someone interested in purchasing her pictures, to scout out what had really happened when the ambassador's daughter vanished from the world stage for a few tumultuous days. And though he trusted Miranda wouldn't knowingly say anything to compromise his cover, his life, he also knew she wasn't a trained liar. And the general's men *were* trained observers. They'd see the flicker in her eyes, the dilation of her pupils. They'd hear the hesitation in her voice, notice the flush to her neck. And if they suspected, for even one threadbare second, that she knew more than she was saying, they had ways to make her talk.

Heinous ways that made Sandro want to stab his paring knife into the safe house's ratty sofa.

He would never put Miranda in that position. Never. It was his battle, his life, and he would fight it by himself.

For Gus, and for Roger.

Penance, he knew, didn't always come from confessionals or burnt offerings. Real penance came from the soul.

The sun dipped lower against the western horizon, inviting the shadows of early evening to spill across the dirty, hardwood floor. Sandro went to the kitchen and pulled his other purchase from his pocket, eyed the small bottle grimly, then made one last precaution to protect Miranda from what was about to go down. When he returned to the main room, he stared out at a few storm clouds gathering against the twilight horizon, refusing to think about Miranda naked in a tub of steaming bubbles.

"Your turn."

He spun around in one smooth move, gun in hand.

"Whoa," Miranda said with a damningly impish smile. She lifted her hands into the air. "I didn't do it."

Oh, but she did. She stood there in the oversize Surf Portugal shirt he'd bought her to sleep in, her hair piled behind her head, leaving a few stray tendrils to drip down and play at the corners of her mouth. Her eyes twinkled. Her skin was scrubbed clean. Her feet were bare.

"Never sneak up on an armed man," he barked, lowering his gun. Self-recrimination sank like a rock in his gut. "Don't you realize what I could have done to you?"

If she heard the edge to his voice, she ignored it. "You haven't done anything to or with me, Sandro, except keep me safe. Why would I think that's going to change now?"

He looked at her standing in the shadows and hoped like hell the cavalry charged in soon. "Every man has his limits."

"Yours must be far and deep, then," she said with a completely straight face, and it was all Sandro could do not to eliminate the distance between them and crush her in his arms. He didn't understand how she made him want to smile, when he knew damn good and well in only a few hours she would despise him.

With a casualness that belied the frustration tightening through him, he started toward her. To reach the bathroom, he had to pass her. "The doors are locked," he said, "the windows secure. No one can get in."

"You got that right," she agreed, her smile turning rueful. "At least not yet."

Not once in his thirty-two years had Sandro expected to see the day he didn't want a beautiful woman to want him. Just a few more hours, he told himself. *Just a few more godforsaken hours.*

"Yell if you need me," he said, moving past her.

"And you'll come?" she asked glibly. "That's all it takes?"

He didn't stop, didn't turn around, just kept walking toward the small bathroom, one deliberate step at a time. He refused to run like a coward, even though he needed to feel the cold water raining down on him with the same intensity his body hungered to feel her moving beneath him and above him, with him.

Hell, who was he trying to kid? It wasn't just his body that hungered for her and he damn well knew it.

"Sandro."

He stopped, let her voice slam into him like a bullet. "What?"

"It doesn't have to be this way."

He closed his eyes, inhaled deeply. Exhaled raggedly. Knew better than turning to face her, exposing himself to those bewitching eyes. Even from the shadows, he would see the green. "You don't have a damn clue what you're saying, Miranda."

"And I suppose you do?" she asked, and he could tell she was moving toward him.

"Damn straight I do." He stepped into the bathroom and closed the door behind him.

Unlike her, he clicked the lock.

Irony sluiced in from all directions. He wasn't a monk. Far from it. Granted, he hadn't been with a woman in too many months to count, but that didn't mean the desire wasn't there, the need. Lately, it had only been the opportunity lacking.

Now, the desire and the need and the opportunity had presented themselves to him in a tidy, heaven-sent package. Miranda Carrington was a grown woman. His job was to protect her life, not her virtue. There was no rule in the ISA operations manual that said he couldn't make love to a beautiful woman who made it abundantly clear that's what she wanted.

Sandro shucked his clothes, stepped into the cool white bathtub and turned on the shower, all cold. Water rained down on his shoulders like icy daggers, but he barely flinched. He savored, actually. Because while there was no ordinance in ISA regulations that prevented him from having Miranda hot and naked and twined around him, the rule did exist. Despite some of the choices he'd made, despite the way he was raised, the example set by his philandering parents, he knew right from wrong.

And making love to Miranda would be very, very wrong.

Soon, she would think him a liar, a criminal. Soon, she would hate him. He refused to saddle her with memories of intimacies between them, intimacies that would turn her stomach in only a matter of hours. She didn't deserve that, no matter how badly they burned for each other right now. Soon, desire would be washed out by deceit.

The scream damn near stopped his heart. It was low and throaty and shocked. Scared. "Sandro!"

He ripped open the shower curtain and grabbed his gun, his pants. The locked door barely slowed him. He tore it open and ran down the hall. "Miranda!"

Nothing. No more screams, only a silence as cold and still as a graveyard. *Cristo,* he thought savagely. It was starting already. They'd come for her.

The reality of events he himself had set into motion caught him grossly unprepared. He hadn't had a chance to take that one last precaution, the one that would protect her from the brunt of the ugliness.

"Miranda!"

She could be gone already, he knew. Special ops worked quietly and efficiently.

"Stop struggling," growled a guttural voice in broken English, and Sandro's blood ran cold. The broken English wasn't right. He spun toward the kitchen, where he heard something loud crash to the floor.

Nothing prepared him for the sight awaiting him. The cavalry had not arrived.

The general's lieutenant had.

Chapter 9

"Expecting someone else?" Petros Racca asked mildly.

Sandro thumbed off the safety and lifted his semiautomatic toward the man who held Miranda pressed to his filthy body. She thrashed against him, her eyes wild, her struggles bringing the oversize T-shirt high on her thighs.

"Take your hands off her," he commanded in the deadly quiet voice he'd used when he'd pressed his hand to a cold tombstone and vowed to bring down the man who'd murdered his friends, his ideals. "You know how itchy my trigger finger can be."

The wiry man with a long dark ponytail flashed a rotted-tooth grin. "I see you came dressed for the occasion."

Gun steady in one hand, Sandro fought viciously to pull the camouflage pants over still-wet legs. Inevitability slashed in from all directions. He'd known Miranda's illusions about him would shatter tonight, but not like this.

Sweet Mary, not like this.

He had no choice, however. Around General Zhukov's former go-to man, a dangerous criminal who'd been trying for months to reclaim Viktor's favor, Sandro could be no other than the merciless killer they thought him to be.

Even if doing so destroyed the light in Miranda's eyes.

"Let her go," he growled, yanking up his zipper, despite his commando state. For one of the few times in his life, he hated the ruthless efficiency his work required. "The girl is *mine*."

"You had your chance," Petros smirked, snaking a hand along Miranda's stomach and sending a black rage drilling through Sandro. She winced, but no fear shone in her gaze, just the silent determination he'd come to treasure.

"What is it they say in America?" Petros went on. "Something about possession being nine-tenths of the law?" He backed around the small wooden table and toward the door which hung open, letting splatters of rain blow into the kitchen. "I am afraid your time has expired, *amigo*. The general grows impatient to get his hands on the prize. If you cannot deliver, I will."

Sandro saw Miranda's eyes go wide, dark. Her face go pale.

Saw the blurry moment of confusion.

Saw the truth dawn with all the vivid finality of a mushroom cloud signifying the transformation of oasis to wasteland.

Saw illusions shatter.

Saw the horror, the pain. The betrayal.

Saw, and bled, but just like with Roger and Gus, could do nothing to prevent. Or protect.

Everything inside of Miranda went very still. Deadly still. Even her heart.

The prize?

She stared wildly at Sandro, the man who looked like an edgy rock star but carried a statue of his boyhood dog in his pocket, the chameleon who transformed from Casanova to commando in the blink of an eye, who spoke like a poet but wielded a briefcase that turned into a submachine gun, and deep inside, felt something real and vital and irreplaceable go stone-cold. Because in that instant, she knew.

God help her, she knew.

For a moment, everything went white. Glaring, blinding white. Then color exploded, stark shades of red and black, exposing the sharp edge of every lie Sandro had told her.

And that she'd naively believed.

Shock and horror twisted viciously, paralyzing her with the sting of the truth. What she'd thought to be real and powerful had been an act. He'd been playing her, pushing her buttons with skillful precision. He didn't work for her father, but for the general he told her about, the man who wanted to use her as a bargaining chip in a game of cat and mouse.

She came to life, ripped viciously and irrevocably from a dangerous dream.

"You son of a bitch!" she erupted, thrashing wildly against the man who'd sneaked up on her while she lay on the couch, listening to the water rattle through the pipes and trying not to think about Sandro standing naked under the spray. The man's arms were thin but strong, and he reeked of sweat and wine and danger.

Sandro was across the small kitchen in a heartbeat. She heard the low roar tear from his throat before she saw him kick out his leg, his foot landing hard against the other man's chest. Her captor released her, went sprawling.

Miranda broke for the freedom beyond the open door, but Sandro intercepted her, his hands closing around her arms like manacles.

"Take your hands off me!" she shouted, twisting violently.

He held steady. "That's not what you said last night, *anima mia.*"

The endearment burned.

"Your love like hell," she rasped. Betrayal slashed brutally, gave her strength. "You lied to me!"

"I never lied to you," he said. His eyes were flat and

his tone mild, but he pulled her firmly against his body. "I just didn't correct you when you jumped to the wrong conclusions."

Hurt and betrayal welled like blood from a gut wound. She swung her elbows and slammed her foot against his shin, but his hold on her never wavered. He had her arms pressed against her sides with disgusting ease. Her fingers itched to close around the hilt of her knife, but like a fool, she'd left it in her purse, not figuring to need the weapon tonight.

She'd had other ways of passing time on her mind.

"Quite a little hellcat, ya?" the other man slurred, dragging himself off the dirty floor. "Is she always so…how is it you say? Energetic?"

Miranda didn't stop to think. She spat at the vile man.

He laughed.

Sandro swore. "Calm down," he ground out. "This isn't a schoolyard and you're not in the third grade."

If she could have slapped him, she would have.

"How the hell did you find us?" Sandro growled.

The wiry little man grinned. "You were smart to let Javier do legwork, *amigo,* but not smart enough. You cannot really believe I'd let you two have all glory, do you? Technology is both friend and bitch. All messages can be intercepted."

"Cristo," Sandro muttered, then bit out something low and savage, but not in a language Miranda recognized. Anger, however, needed no translation. He was coldly furious. She felt it in every rigid plane of his mostly naked body, saw it in the fierce glitter that had returned to his eyes.

The other man narrowed his gaze. "I track you for days," he said in heavily accented English. Miranda wondered why. "I am not coming away empty-handed this time."

Miranda felt Sandro tense. He spoke again, still in a language she didn't understand.

The other man, who Sandro referred to as Petros,

laughed. "That is right," he said, still speaking in English. He obviously wanted her to realize fully what was going on, even though Sandro clearly wanted to protect as many of his secrets as he could. "If I had not been in Cascais to clean up your sloppiness, you would never have gotten your hands on her in the first place."

He was the other shooter, she realized sickly. This dirty little man with whom Sandro had some kind of affiliation was the man who'd killed Hawk.

"You won't get away with this," she hissed, jabbing an elbow into Sandro's stomach. She might as well have jabbed a brick wall. "My father will hunt you both down like the dogs you are. He'll find you, and he'll make you pay."

Petros was grinning again, but Sandro remained in soldier mode. "Your father won't find us unless I want him to," he said darkly. "And I can't really see that happening, can you?"

She glared at him, fought the hurt and rage scratching at her throat. She could do nothing about the jagged tearing deep inside. How could one man enter the bathroom, yet another emerge?

How had she not seen this coming? "You disgust me," she said through clenched teeth and shattered ideals.

The shadow crossed his dark gaze so quickly she wondered if she'd seen it at all. "That changes nothing, *anima mia.* I told you before. I'm doing what I have to do, whether you like it or not."

She lifted her chin, refused to let tears fall. "Go to hell."

His mouth curved cruelly. "Yes, I think I just might."

Petros started toward them, but Sandro lifted his gun and stopped him cold. "I told you," he said with deathly quietness. "She's mine."

"She's the general's," Petros corrected.

Sandro's hold on her tightened, one of his arms coiled around her waist. "Not until I turn her over."

"*We,* amigo. *We* will turn her over, or one of us will not leave here alive."

For the first time, Miranda realized Petros carried a gun, as well. It was a sleek little black outfit pointed directly at her heart.

Sandro shifted her behind his body and backed toward the hallway. His dark hair was damp, the warm skin of his shoulders smelled of honeysuckle and betrayal.

Thank God he'd pulled on pants.

"There's no need for that," he was saying in a voice so empty she hardly recognized it as his. "As long as I get what I want, I don't really give a damn what happens afterwards."

Miranda stiffened, felt her skin crawl. Her throat closed up on her. Surely Sandro didn't mean the words the way they sounded.

Petros's smile turned lewd, and his beady little eyes took on a fever. "Make sure she still has some…energy for me, that is all I ask."

Revulsion coursed through Miranda. She struggled against Sandro's hold, but he was like a robot, holding her securely and ignoring her heartbreak. Even with her pressed to his back, his strength far surpassed hers. Frustration had her sinking her teeth into the warm flesh of his shoulder.

A hard sound broke from Sandro's throat. "Hold your horses," he muttered darkly. "They'll be plenty of time for biting later." Then he nodded toward the chipped Formica counter. "Help yourself to the *vhino,* Petros. It should help pass the time."

The other man swaggered over, picked up the bottle, and swigged deeply. "Just don't take too long. I grow impatient."

"I'll take as long as I want to," Sandro said as if he hadn't a care in the world, then turned toward Miranda and hustled her from the kitchen and toward the darkened room at the end of the hall, where the only bed in the house awaited. She went willingly, knowing if she was to catch him off guard she had to make him think she'd given up.

"I know you're scared," he said as they entered the bedroom. He flicked on the light, closed and locked the door. "But—"

She spun around and jabbed two knuckles against his windpipe as hard as she could, then broke for the window she'd opened for fresh air.

Outside, the wind blew wildly, a few splatters of rain slashing into the room. She didn't care. She climbed through anyway, was halfway to freedom when his hands closed around her.

"Let go of me!" she screamed, but he didn't listen. Still coughing violently, he pulled her back into the room and, with one hand, slammed the window shut.

"What the hell did you do that for?" he asked in a voice even more hoarse than usual.

She refused to feel remorse. "Take your hands off me," she bit out.

Surprisingly, he did. "How many times do I have to tell you I'm not going to hurt you?"

"You expect me to believe *anything* you told me?" she asked, backing toward the dresser, where her purse waited. "You played me for a fool."

"Things aren't always what they seem," he said tightly. "I did what I had to do."

And she was going to do what she had to do, despite the jagged emotions tearing around inside her. Fear and betrayal barely scratched the surface. She'd trusted this man, not just with her life, but with that part of herself she kept tucked away from the rest of the world. She'd shared her dreams with him. Worse, she'd let him infiltrate those dreams. Shape them. Now she realized what a dangerous mistake she'd made.

With pretenses stripped away, with seduction no longer an option to earn her compliance, that left only force.

He stood there beside the bed in the glare of a single,

unprotected lightbulb, his damp hair shoved back from his face to reveal the glitter in those black, black eyes, the hard lines of his face, the whiskers that darkened his jaw to the color of his soul. He wore only the camouflage pants he'd yanked on in the kitchen, not bothering to fasten the button. Nasty white lines streaked against the hard, tanned flesh of his chest and arms, a silent testimony to brute strength and a life of violence.

"Who are you?" she demanded, narrowing her eyes. Everything inside her was cold, but she refused to shiver. "Who are you *really?*"

He watched her steadily, but never moved. "I've already told you that, *bella*. Nothing has changed since then."

"You've told me lies," she said as lightning flashed, briefly illuminating the room. Thunder added the punctuation. "Is Sandro even your name, or is that some kind of alias?"

"I would think you of all people know names don't matter. They're just labels. It's what inside that counts."

She inched closer to the dresser, working to keep her face as blank and emotionless as his. But rage burned hot, defiance hotter. He was actually trying to use her quest to escape the Carrington name to explain his lies.

"Tell me what's inside you then," she challenged, wishing he'd chosen anywhere other than beside the bed to stand. "Tell me what you think justifies your actions."

Something dangerously close to disappointment flickered through his gaze. "You haven't figured that out yet?"

The words were smoky, their intent clear. "Seduction won't work anymore, Sandro."

"If I recall," he said with a sardonic curl of his lips, "most of the seducing came from you."

The low blow landed with unerring accuracy. She didn't hesitate. She grabbed her purse, pulled out her knife, wrapped both hands around the hilt and thrust it toward him.

"Call me a romantic fool," she said with cold precision,

"but I actually thought I cared about you. I believed your lies. The bit about your grandfather and the abandoned dog was especially good. If you get out of this alive, you might want to try Hollywood."

He sighed, eyeing the knife. "*Bella, bella, bella.* Do we have to go down this road again? Don't you realize if I'd wanted to hurt you, I would have by now?"

The pain was swift and immediate, the truth scalding the backs of her eyes with tears she would never let fall. Chin high, she refused to let him know how brutally he'd already hurt her.

Because in truth, she was the one who'd set herself up for the fall.

"I'm too valuable to hurt," she said instead. "I'm the *prize*, remember? The perfect target."

He frowned, an odd glow coming into his eyes. "You're also a terrible liar."

"What's that supposed to mean?"

"There are many ways to hurt, *bella*. Not all of them are physical."

"You haven't hurt me," she said defiantly.

"I haven't hurt your body," he amended. "I didn't crawl all over you at the hotel or the winery like I could have. I didn't use the cuffs in my bag. I didn't tie you up, rough you up."

She narrowed her eyes, fought the emotion stabbing into her throat. "No, you didn't do any of that," she said thickly, holding the knife toward him. Her mind raced for a plan. There was no way she could get out the window or the door without disabling him first. "You're just going to turn me over to a bloodthirsty man who wants to use me to get his son back." Just the thought sent horror convulsing through her. "It won't work," she vowed. "The United States will neither cower nor barter. If you turn me over to that man, all you'll be doing is sacrificing me to some ridiculous cause."

He stepped toward her, his hands curling into fists.

"General Zhukov isn't going to hurt you, not your body, nor your spirit."

Miranda swallowed hard. Primed on the balls of his feet, Sandro looked like a boxer ready to pounce, and she was the only opponent in sight.

"If you believe that," she said as steadily as the rain now pouring from the sky, "you're a fool in addition to a liar." Just the thought of the amoral man made her blood run cold. She'd once read he'd cut off part of his pinkie merely to show his men pain meant nothing.

The planes of Sandro's face tightened, his eyes burned with an intensity that sent her heart hammering wildly, but he didn't take another step toward her. He seemed to be physically restraining himself, an animal at the end of a chain that would not break.

"Miranda, please," he said in that sandpaper voice of his. "Listen to me. There's not much time. I've got to get you away from Petros. He's a very dangerous man."

She gaped at him, felt her eyes flare. "And what are you? The Pied Piper?"

"I've told you who I am," he said, and took another step toward her, this one slow, purely predatory. "I'm the man who's not going to let anything bad happen to you. But Petros doesn't share my…philosophy. He's a wild card I didn't plan on."

She cut her eyes at him. "Gee, what a shame."

"Give me the knife, Miranda."

"Tell me there's been some kind of horrible mistake," she offered, pausing when another flash of lightning cut across the darkness. Thunder rumbled more quickly, the storm ever closer. "Tell me I don't understand what's going on here. Tell me this is just a nightmare and soon I'll wake up."

"I can't tell you any of that, *bella.*" The remorse in his voice sounded real, but she knew better than trusting illusions. This man was a trained liar, probably a killer. He worked for a ruthless man responsible for the deaths of eight elite U.S. undercover operatives.

"Put down the knife," he instructed. "Don't make this harder than it already is."

"Why not?" she asked a little wildly. With every step he took toward her, the room seemed to shrink. She could barely see the window beyond his shoulders. She could barely breathe without drawing in the cloying scent of honeysuckle and betrayal.

She couldn't let herself care.

She couldn't let him win, either, not when doing so would cost her family so dearly. Better to end it all here, then to put them through the horror of knowing General Viktor Zhukov had possession of her.

"How's it going to get harder?" she challenged. "What will you do, shoot me?" A maniacal little laugh broke from her throat. "The general wouldn't like that much, would he? With his *prize* dead, how would he get his son back?"

Sandro winced. "I'm not going to kill you."

Miranda tightened her grip on the knife, but her palms had started to sweat. And if she quit concentrating for even one second, her hands might start to shake. He wouldn't kill her, she believed that. Not intentionally, anyway. But images flashed through her mind as lethally as the lightning outside, of all the things he could do to her now that he no longer had to pretend. Things that would not involve death. At least not physical death.

There were far, far worse deaths than those of the body.

"Just damage me?" she asked snidely. "Rough me up?"

He swore under his breath. "You don't believe that."

"I don't believe anything right now," she bit out, backing away from his steady advance. He could be on her in two strides, but he didn't seem in any hurry to pounce. She wanted to rush him, to thrust the knife into his black heart and run from the room, but knew he'd have her weapon out of her hands before she made contact.

All she was really buying now was time.

"I don't believe how easily I fell for your lies, that I ever trusted you, let you touch me. I don't believe I'm going to get out of this unharmed, either, so why prolong the inevitable? Why not get it all over with here and now?" She wasn't sure where the taunt came from, but once started, found she couldn't stop the flow. "Why wait for that disgusting little man out there or the general to do the dirty work? You started this—don't tell me you don't have the guts to look me in the eye and finish it."

He stood so still he looked more stone than man. "The knife, Miranda."

She had nowhere to run, nowhere to hide, but squared her shoulders anyway. "No."

Sandro moved so quickly he had the knife clattering to the cold wood floor before she had a chance to react. Unlike the day in the alley when he'd grabbed the blade with his hand, this time he took hold of her wrist, twisting just enough for her fingers to open.

Miranda gasped, but he granted no reprieve, backing her against the wall and pinning her there with his body. "It's not smart to play with fire, *bella*."

"Don't touch me!" she shouted, pushing against the hard heat of his chest.

He caught her wrists and held them in one hand, raised them to the wall above her head. "Thatta girl," he encouraged, his smile grim, his eyes bleak. "Now let him hear you scream."

Miranda blinked at him. "W-what?"

His breathing was ragged now, strained. "Petros thinks I'm giving you the ride of your life right now," he explained. "Best not to disappoint him."

The heat from Sandro's body warmed her flesh, but the cold filth of his words sank through to her bones. "You're disgusting," she whispered, wondering how she could have been so completely wrong about this man.

"Be that as it may, if Petros thinks I'm going easy on

you back here, he'll get suspicious. Best to make him think that I'm forcing you, that you despise me.''

''I do despise you.''

Something hot and dangerous flashed in the midnight of his eyes. ''Then let it rip, sweetheart. Now is not the time for holding back.''

''Stop it!'' she cried out, thrashing against him. She went to raise her knee toward his groin, but he held her too close. All she could do was stomp down on his bare feet.

He showed no reaction, no signs of pain. He was all robot again. ''Good, good,'' he encouraged. ''Now scream for me.''

The memory hit Miranda without warning, had her cursing herself a fool all over again.

When I make a woman scream, it doesn't have a damn thing to do with a knife.

''I'll never scream for you,'' she vowed.

''Then scream for yourself, *bella*. Scream for the freedom you so desperately crave.''

She lost it then, the restraint that had held her together like glue. She struggled against the hand manacling her wrists, broke his grip and landed her palms against his chest. ''You bastard,'' she cried, pushing against him with her shoulder. ''You bastard!''

''Perfect,'' he said, neither fighting nor resisting. He just stood there, accepting one blow after another. ''Don't stop now.''

The tears started then, turning quickly into sobs. She gulped in huge breaths of air, but her body continued to starve. She kept at him anyway, pummeling him with fists and fury and shoving at him with her palms, battering him with all the useless intensity of the waves they'd seen crashing against the ancient cliffs, until finally he gathered her against the warm flesh of his chest and simply held her.

Which only broke her heart further.

''I'll never forgive you for this,'' she whispered, trying valiantly not to sound as shattered as she felt.

"I know," he whispered with an aching tenderness that sounded so real she almost thought she could reach out and touch it. "But I'm not in this for your forgiveness," he added, running his hands in a soothing gesture along her back. "Besides, just a few more days and you'll never see me again."

The fact should have brought her comfort.

It didn't.

She'd made a terrible mistake, one whose consequences she'd only begun to face. To survive, she had to be strong, cut off all feeling as completely and ruthlessly as Sandro did. There was no point in struggling against him now. Her time would come later, at a moment of her choosing.

She would never let him turn her over to the general.

"Better?" he asked against her hair.

She lifted her chin, didn't bother wiping the tears from her eyes. "It takes more than a few lies to break me."

He smiled then, a smile that looked as real and warm as the tenderness she'd heard in his voice. Whoever this man really was, he was as talented at lying as he was at everything else.

"Hey, Petros," he called over her shoulder, then continued in what sounded like a Slavic language.

Her heart start to race all over again. Panic and dread crowded out the moment of insanity. "What?" she demanded. Dear God, he couldn't really be turning her over to that vile little man. "What are you saying?"

A sliver of panic cut through the question.

"Hang on," he whispered, then waited. But above the fading patter of rain, no sound came from the other side of the house.

Chapter 10

"Get your things," Sandro instructed, pulling away but keeping one of her hands in his.

Miranda grabbed her purse and the bag with her clothes, but when she looked to where her knife had landed, she found only a threadbare rug mangled on the dirty hardwood floor.

"You won't be needing that," Sandro said. He pulled on a olive T-shirt, then traded the hand that held hers and stuck his other arm through the sleeve.

"Petros?" he called again.

Again, no answer came.

"Is he gone?" she asked.

"Doubtful."

"Then what?"

"Come on," he said, leading her into the darkened hall. She didn't want to follow, but he left her no choice.

The storm had just about passed, leaving a dark stillness in its wake. They passed the bathroom, where bubble bath, shampoo and stupid dreams remained, as well as the goofy floppy hat he'd bought for her.

The pang of loss only strengthened her resolve.

The kitchen was as empty as the bottle of wine on the table. In the main room, they found Petros on the sofa. His breathing was deep and regular, a faint rumble from his throat.

Sandro stared at the inert form, his hands balled into fists. "Touch her again, you son of a bitch, and you're a dead man."

The vicious words went through Miranda like lightning. Her heart staggered and stalled. There was a ferocity to Sandro that had not been there before, a raw possessiveness that both frightened and...fascinated. She'd never been around that kind of intensity before, like iron heated to the point it glowed like red-hot coals.

Petros was oblivious. Out cold, he didn't move a muscle.

Questions jammed through Miranda, but before she could squeeze the words past her impossibly tight throat, Sandro tugged her toward the back door. And as much as she knew better than trusting the man who had kidnapped her, she wanted to risk remaining near the sleeping Petros even less.

Five minutes later they were in the old car, tearing into the night. The substandard roads were slick, the air surprisingly balmy.

"Why did you do that?" she asked. She told herself not to be afraid, that he wouldn't hurt her, but the chill seeped into her blood and snaked around her bones. "Why did you just leave him there like that?"

Sandro kept his hands curled around the wheel, his eyes on the road. "Maybe he was right, after all," he muttered. "Maybe I want you, the glory, all for myself."

Sandro found no glory in what had just gone down. Destroying was part of what undercover special operatives did. Misleading. Calculating. And until tonight, he'd always reveled in the masquerade, savored the collection of false-hood upon falsehood, all building to the apprehension of dangerous criminals who threatened freedom everywhere.

But Miranda was not a criminal, and she posed no threat to freedom anywhere.

Except maybe deep inside, in a place he'd thought blown to irreparable bits one impossibly blue afternoon five years before.

He clenched the steering wheel tighter, stared straight ahead, saw only the truth. The ominously quiet, ominously still woman seated next to him, staring out the passenger window as the old car bumped down the roadway, was an innocent. Because of no other reason than her last name, she was caught up in a high-stakes game that had nothing to do with her personally, but threatened everything she held dear. Striking out at a Carrington was as much a head-line grabber, as much of an attack on an American icon, as blowing up the Golden Gate Bridge or finding a way to erase the faces from Mount Rushmore.

That's all I really want, she'd said that night in the wine cellar. *To be like everyone else. To dance in the street and not be splattered across the front of every tabloid.*

But Miranda Carrington, this woman who cherished personal freedom above all else, was *not* like everyone else. There could be no anonymity for a woman with gypsy eyes and a sense of adventure and excitement that radiated from her like a diamond against a sea of black velvet. Just like there could be no glory in the actions he'd taken back at the safe house.

No, he thought again, blinking against the grainy dryness of his eyes. No glory. No satisfaction of a job meticulously planned and executed. No pleasure in stripping the light from Miranda's eyes, replacing it with the stark hollow of betrayal. No sense of accomplishment in hearing the rasp to her voice, feeling the sting of her words. No success in the fact that she believed him and Petros to be in the same league.

No glory in the fact she believed the lie.

He'd been close. So damn close to extracting her from Portugal with minimal damage. He had the raw fury under control now, but deep inside the knowledge that he'd either been set up or ambushed continued to rage. He was a careful man. Twice now, however, Petros claimed to have been only a step behind.

A hard sound broke from Sandro's throat.

Petros would be more than a step behind this time.

"Where are we going?" Miranda asked for the fourth time.

And for the fourth time, he told her only "South."

She said nothing else, just as she'd said nothing each of the three times before. She merely continued to look away from him.

She was way too calm. Shock, he wondered, or cunning? Her silence could easily conceal plotting, just like that day in Cascais, when she'd claimed to be Astrid Van Dyke.

They'd been in the car for nearly an hour. Petros would probably sleep a while longer, but not the whole night through. If Sandro had known that lowlife would be the one drinking the wine, not Miranda, he would have mixed in the whole damn bottle of sleeping pills, not just a few tablets. He'd only meant to ensure Miranda slept while the worst of the so-called rescue mission went down, to spare her that brutal moment of discovery.

None of that mattered. She knew. She knew the lie, could never know the truth, how closely the two were related. All he could do was damage control. It mattered only that she lived.

And, he amended, that General Viktor Zhukov met a certain lady named Justice.

Frustration wound deeper. There had been no rescue tonight. Only a trap. And Javier... *Cristo,* let him still be alive. Petros was a dangerous wild card. He'd lost the general's favor after a botched assignment five months before, and since then he'd been desperately trying to prove himself to his former leader. Apparently, he thought Miranda Carrington looked like his meal ticket. His arrival on the scene could easily have created a bloodbath.

No way in hell was Sandro risking Miranda's blood.

Or her body.

Clenching his jaw, he cursed the fat raindrops splattering the windshield. For a man who lived his life in the shadows, he had a peculiar lack of tolerance for being in the dark.

Sandro grabbed the mobile phone from the seat between his legs and jabbed the familiar series of numbers for the fifth time in an hour. And for the fifth time, he listened impatiently to the high shrill of a ring unanswered.

"Damn it, Javier," he bit out. "Where the hell are you?"

His partner's voice came across the line then, a recorded message inviting his fans and followers to leave a message. Sandro scowled at his friend's warped sense of humor, but a bad feeling sunk low in his gut. He wanted to talk to the man, not a machine, but left with no choice, he barked out a few nondescript words, meaningful to Javier, innocuous to others.

"Change of plans, mate. Unexpected visitors. Need to reschedule."

Miranda turned to look at him. "Who's Javier?"

Her voice was flat, empty, just like her expression. "He's my compatriot," he told her, turning the car onto a narrow, one-lane road leading between two rows of towering trees.

She wrinkled her perfect little nose. "Your *what?*"

"My comrade," he clarified matter-of-factly. "My partner. He's making arrangements to get you out of the country without—" he broke off the words abruptly, regrouped "—without the wrong people finding us."

"By wrong people, you mean border patrol and whoever else it is that looks for kidnapped American citizens? Like the CIA?"

"Among other people," he answered vaguely. More often than not, that's all it took. People's imaginations filled in the blanks with unrivaled creativity and flair.

He knew this woman who'd once looked at him with mischief sparking in her eyes would be no different. He'd dulled that light for now, but deep inside, beneath that damningly sexy Surf Portugal T-shirt which rode entirely too high on her firm thighs, her spirit still burned bright. Of that, he had no doubt. She'd said it herself.

It takes more than a few lies to break me.

God, he hoped so. He could hardly remember anything he'd ever wanted more.

Swearing softly, he clicked on the radio, cranked up the volume. Out of the corner of his eye, he would have sworn he saw Miranda's lips twitch, but when he looked at her, her expression was as unreadable as the night beyond.

"I take it something went wrong tonight?" she surprised him by asking.

As far as understatements went, she'd hit the proverbial nail on the head. "You could say so."

She turned down the inspiring combination of Euro dance rhythm and static. "What?"

"It doesn't matter," he said, returning the volume to a level half of where it had been before.

"It does to me." This time, she turned the radio off.

Sharply honed survival instincts told him to ignore her request. Keep driving, keep looking ahead. But the man who already missed the light in her eyes couldn't do that, saw no reason to torture her. She'd been through enough. He didn't need to play brute now that Petros wasn't around. He could toss a few nuggets of truth, let her fill in the blanks.

"You were supposed to be escorted out of Portugal tonight," he told her. True.

She absorbed the words like a blow. "By whom?"

"Men I trust." Men who would give their life for his. And hers.

"You don't trust Petros?"

His hands tightened around the steering wheel. If Miranda hadn't screamed. If he hadn't heard her. If he'd been only a fraction of a minute later getting to the kitchen…

"Petros Racca is an amoral piece of scum," he ground out, "with no regard for human life."

Miranda frowned. "And what are you?"

This time it was Sandro's turn to absorb the impact of her words. And they hit hard. He knew he should accept her scorn and contempt, her hatred. It was safer that way. He'd complete his mission and escort her to safety, and then they would never see each other again. Piece of cake. End of story.

But Sandro couldn't leave it at that. He looked at her sitting next to him and winced at the betrayal and confusion in her eyes. But it was the horror that ripped at him like claws. They could have no future, but at the very least, she deserved to know she hadn't almost had sex with a man of evil and manipulation. They were just on opposite sides, that was all. They adhered to different ideals, hungered for different futures.

That's what he needed her to see, to understand.

"I'm just a man doing my job," he told her quietly. *Honestly.* "I'm the man who, despite what you heard back there, is not going to let a game that has *nothing* to do with you blow up in your face." He paused, struggled for the right words. Struggled even harder to breathe levelly. "I'm a man you'll be wise to forget about by the time you celebrate another birthday."

The night was dark, the rain again falling, but he saw the shadow cross her face. "My birthday is next month."

He looked back toward the road. "Like I said."

Behind them, lightning flashed, thunder rumbling seconds later. For the moment, they'd outrun the storm. But clouds continued to obscure the horizon, and Sandro knew with absolute certainty all hell would break lose again. Soon.

"How can you be so sure?" Miranda sounded angry

now. Frustrated. "How can you know this game won't blow up in my face? Are you going to be there with me every second of every day? Are you going to stop the general if he gets a taste for bloodlust? Are you going to convince the Americans not to send in a special forces mission that could go hideously wrong?"

All of that. Everything. And more. "I'm going to do whatever it takes."

He didn't know if his answer satisfied her, scared her, or just left nothing further to say, but she said nothing in response. She just stared straight ahead. About fifteen miles down the road lay the quiet centuries-old village where they would ditch the car and continue their journey by other means. If he didn't hear from Javier by sunrise, it would be time to abandon protocol and do exactly what he promised her he would.

Whatever it took.

"You're wrong, you know."

Her voice was soft now, hoarse. Strained. And it damn near made him bleed. "About what?"

"Forgetting about you." She turned to look at him, practically drilled holes through his heart with her gaze. "I'll never forget what a good liar you are."

Actually, he silently corrected, she'd never even know.

God help him, he wanted to yank the car off the road and throw it in Park, pull her into his arms and put his mouth to hers, show her what was real.

"Use the memory then," he said instead. His jaw ached from how tightly he'd been clenching it. "After all this is over, when you're home safe and sound, use the memory to keep you strong."

Her eyes flared, but she said nothing.

And Sandro counted his blessings. All his life he'd been drawn to help, not wound. Deliberately hurting Miranda was twisting him up inside in cruel ways he'd never imagined possible.

"Eat something," he told her. "It's been a long time since that ice cream in Fatima."

A freaking lifetime.

"I'm not hungry."

"You need to keep your strength up," he countered. "There's granola and bottled water in my bag."

Sighing, she unfastened her seat belt and crawled toward the back seat, forcing Sandro to keep his eyes on the road and not the sight of her crouched between the two seats.

"What do you want?" she asked.

Sandro swallowed hard, but the saliva did nothing to put out the ridiculous fire in his gut. Or lower. "Nothing. Thanks."

A few bumps in the road later she returned to her seat with a bottle of water. She unscrewed the lid and drank deeply, then again turned to face him. This time her expression was oddly seeking. And if he looked, which he tried not to, he would have sworn he saw a sheen of moisture glistening in her eyes.

"Was everything just a means to an end, Sandro? Was it all a lie?"

It took every ounce of strength he had to keep his foot on the gas pedal and not slam on the brakes. To keep his hands on the wheel and not reaching for her. To keep the soldier, the commando, in charge. He kept his expression carefully blank, but beneath the surface, emotion boiled.

And for the first and only time in five years, he hated his job, the shadows and the sacrifices, the lies.

The truth.

"No," he bit out, because he could stomach nothing else. "It wasn't all a lie."

That much, at least, she deserved to know.

That much would not get her killed.

He saw her eyes widen fractionally, saw the flicker of vulnerability. "What then? What was real?"

He hesitated only a moment before answering. "I really did have a dog named Virgil."

*   *   *

"Walk?" Miranda looked from the car Sandro had parked behind a stash of bushes to the sleeping village around her. She didn't see a single light, much less a hotel. "Where to?"

Sandro slung his knapsack over his shoulder and reached for his attaché case. "Somewhere Petros Racca won't find us."

"He's out cold," she reminded.

"He won't be all night." Sandro slammed the door shut. "Now come on. We need to make camp before the storm catches us."

Lightning illuminated the sky, not the violent slashes and streaks of before, but flickers that reminded her of someone turning a light switch on, then off. On. Then off. The thunder was more like a gentle rolling now, as opposed to the heart-stopping booms of before.

Miranda shivered anyway. The cool breeze, she told herself, not the tall man with the eyes like chips of black ice, standing so close she felt the tension radiating from his big body. The man who'd lied to her.

The man she'd wanted to take into her body the night before.

She looked at him now, the flashes of lightning revealing the hard line of the mouth that had kissed her with a hunger and intensity she'd never experienced, the increasingly thick whiskers on his jaw. She noted the blatant strength of a finely tuned male body, one she could neither overpower nor outrun. He would be on her in a heartbeat if she tried to escape him, and now that he no longer had to pretend to be her bodyguard, she would be at his mercy. He could do…anything.

And God help her, she wouldn't be able to stop him.

Last night, she hadn't wanted to.

That one thought both shamed her and gave her strength. She would not let this man win. She would let him think she was playing by his rules, but the game would be all hers.

And she would come out on top.

"Camp?" she asked. It was cold and damp outside, the storm bound to break again. "Where?"

"You'll see." He crossed the muddy ground separating them, took her hand and started toward the thickly wooded area just beyond. "It's not too far."

That was a lie. They walked, and they walked, and they walked some more. Miranda looked around alertly, trying to memorize their every turn, but thorough man that he was, Sandro kept erasing their tracks and creating diversions, making it impossible for anyone to follow.

Or retrace their steps.

The night was darker beneath the canopy of the trees, cooler, occasional raindrops falling from the branches overhead. The smell of mud and decay surrounded them, forcing Miranda to fight the chill sinking into her bones. She didn't want to shiver. Didn't want Sandro to have the satisfaction of knowing her physical discomfort.

He stopped abruptly, swore under his breath.

Miranda's heart and her guard leapt to simultaneous attention. "What? What is it?"

The lightning barely made it through the branches, but enough crept through to reveal the impatience snapping in his eyes. Showing his distrust of her by keeping her hand anchored in his, he slid the knapsack down his shoulder to the blanket of leaves, yanked it open, fished around inside.

Miranda's pulse started to race. She glanced around wildly, saw nothing. Couldn't imagine what had him so on edge.

"Here," he growled, rising to his full height. In his free hand, he held the yellow Hawaiian shirt he'd worn earlier that day. "Put this on."

She gaped at the shirt. "No."

"Damn it, you're shivering, Miranda. Now isn't the time for playing Joan of Arc."

Shivering. He'd realized she was shivering, and he was offering her his shirt.

She stared at the garment, refused to see him that afternoon in Fatima sitting across the small round table and watching her eat an ice-cream cone like it was the most fascinating event he'd ever seen in his life. His eyes had practically glowed. At the time, a thrill had rushed through her. Because she'd thought the glow meant hunger.

Now she knew the only hunger he felt was to turn her over to Viktor Zhukov, the bloodthirsty general who thought nothing of rape and murder.

But he was offering her his shirt, and she was so very chilled. "Fine," she said, refusing to let gratitude soften her voice. She took the garment that was big enough to be a dress for her and stuck her arms defiantly through the sleeves.

The sense of warmth was immediate, shocking. Damning. It washed over her and through her, mingling with the lingering scent of man to send her senses into meltdown.

"Are you just going to stare at me all night," she asked angrily, "or are we going to make camp before the storm hits?"

His expression softened. "Take no prisoners, eh, Miranda?" He laughed then, soft, quiet. "Let's hit it then."

Just like that they were off, him practically dragging her along the uneven, muddy path through the woods. The hand that held hers was warm and moist, strong. His fingers laced through hers in a grip she would never break. Hard to believe just last night she'd found his touch imminently reassuring.

She didn't want to consider how she found the slide of palm to palm, the twining of fingers, now.

Instead, she stalked along beside him, his long legs eating up the muddy path much more quickly than hers. She held herself together, determined not to let emotion, the hurt and the betrayal, the bitter disappointment, bleed through.

She had to be as merciless as he was. Survival left no room for compassion.

But he had shown her compassion, pointed out some quiet little voice deep inside. A voice she'd been working hard to ignore ever since Sandro had helped her escape from Petros.

Why did you just leave him there like that? she'd asked, a blade of hope burgeoning deep in her bones.

Maybe I want you, the glory, all for myself, Sandro had answered, squashing that hope with a few muttered words.

She needed to believe him, Miranda told herself. She couldn't let herself imagine that he was really trying to protect her from that vile little man, no matter what he'd sworn about not letting the general hurt her. She couldn't afford to remember the rush that had gone through her.

Freedom. That was all she could think about, escaping this man who was willing to sacrifice her in the name of a struggle that had nothing to do with her.

She almost wept when she saw the clearing. Hope surged. Through the darkness she couldn't see much, just the densely wooded area opening to a gently sloping patch of land. Then she rounded the bend, and through the flickering lightning, the castle stole her breath.

Tall, dark and stark, the ruins jutted up against the night sky like a picture straight out of a coffee-table book. Multiple turrets and parapets, big, dark, gaping holes that had to be windows, an imposing outer wall.

"Oh, my God," she murmured, then saw the river. The water was dark, angry, and it raced along on all sides of the castle.

And she knew. God help her, she knew. "Where are we?" she asked anyway.

Sandro led her to the muddy riverbank, where a rowboat sat tied to a wooden post. "Hotel California."

Once, the misplaced humor would have made her laugh. Now it came damn close to making her cry. Because she knew what he had in mind. She'd read about this castle on an island in the middle of the river, read about the tourist outfit that ferried visitors to the unbearably romantic ruins by day. It was a small operation, only one boat.

A boat Sandro was commandeering.

A boat she would have to commandeer in turn.

"We should be able to catch a few hours sleep here," Sandro said. "If we're gone by sunrise, no one will be the wiser."

And with only the one boat, no one would be able to cross the swollen river to reach them. The man thought of everything.

She eyed the dark, swirling water, the flimsy-looking paddles lying across the floor of the pitiful excuse for a boat, and fought the rapid-fire pounding of her heart. No way could she let him take her to that island.

"This can't be a good idea, Sandro. You hardly slept last night. Maybe we can just…break into the shack," she said in a moment of pure inspiration. Not twenty feet away a small metal building stood dark and apparently empty, probably where tour company employees sheltered themselves from rain.

"The river's not that bad," he said, efficiently untying the rope that held the rowboat in place. "And anyway, I don't need much sleep."

"What do you need?" The question broke free before she could stop it, and Sandro looked up sharply, the lightning casting his face in a fascinating play of shadows.

You. She would have sworn she saw the one word pass through his smoky gaze.

"Right now," he practically growled, "I need you to cooperate, Miranda."

Not *bella.*

Had that been a lie, too?

She swallowed hard, fought the stab of hurt. She had to get away from this man; it was as simple as that. And, she added silently, dipping her hand into her pocket, she'd have to do it tonight. Her icy cold fingers closed around the object she'd found in Sandro's duffel bag while looking for granola and water.

Yes. Tonight.

She refused to acknowledge the sharp pang freezing through her chest.

In minutes he had the boat that reminded her of a Boy Scout project dragged toward the river. She sat when he instructed her to, quietly, silently biding her time. He put one foot in and pushed off with the other, propelling them into the current.

The small vessel rocked and swayed violently, and for a horrible moment, she thought they would capsize. But Sandro quickly had the oars in hand and steadied them. She watched him silently row, tried not to notice his arms. They were big and powerful and they flexed with each stroke of the oars. The T-shirt he'd pulled on at the so-called safe house was olive and a little too tight, outlining the contours of his back. The muscles there, too, rippled. If she'd seen him on the street like this, or in a movie, in that T-shirt and the camouflage pants he'd dragged up his long legs— *after running naked from the shower, dear God*—she would have thought him an American commando. Not an Eastern European criminal.

It had never occurred to her that men of such diametrically opposed ideals would dress the same.

Miranda squeezed her eyes shut, tried to think of anything but the way he'd looked tearing into the kitchen, stark naked and dripping wet. At the time, she'd thought him her bodyguard. At the time, she'd still ached for his kisses. And more. She'd been nearly blind with fear, but even through that dark place she'd all but gasped at what a magnificent sight Sandro made wet and nude.

With a gun in his hand.

The little boat stopped moving, and Miranda abruptly opened her eyes. Sandro had turned to her, was looking at her peculiarly. "Miranda? You okay?"

She felt the cry rise in her throat, felt the wild desire to propel herself at him and pound her fists against his chest, to knock him into the cold, angry water.

"Do you really want me to answer that?" she asked more thickly than she intended.

His lips twisted in a cruel parody of a smile. "You think I'm an amoral piece of scum who lied to you and now I'm dragging you off to some forgotten castle as my prisoner to finish what we started last night. You're trying to figure out if you grab an oar fast enough, if you can crack my skull open before I have you over my shoulder and inside the master bedchamber."

She felt her eyes flare, her heart stagger, didn't understand the hurt. "Close enough," she muttered.

He stood, reached for her hand. "I know you're scared," he said, helping her to the little wooden dock. "But whether you believe me or not, I'm not going to let anything happen to you."

Miranda glanced skyward, where the occasional splatter of rain was giving way to a steady drizzle. "What I think doesn't really matter, Sandro, does it?"

A hard sound broke from his throat. "You'd be surprised."

She let the comment go, let him lead her inside the stone walls of the surprisingly intact castle. He pulled a lighter from his pocket and used the flame to guide them through cool dark passageways, until they reached a large room. Miranda stopped when he did, squinted to discern detail from shadow.

There was nothing to discern, just a packed dirt floor and stone walls. And the enormous opening against the far wall. "A fireplace?"

He tugged her toward it. "I'll build a small fire. It's the next best thing to—"

Body heat. He didn't say it. But she heard it. Thought it. Felt it.

"To an electric blanket," he finished, then glanced down

at his wrist. "I'd say we've got five hours before sunrise. We'll need to be on the move before then."

Miranda nodded. "And what of Petros?"

Sandro gathered several sticks from around the large room, then knelt before the fireplace so tall he could have stood inside.

"Petros won't find us," he told her. "And if he does, which he won't, it's a mistake he'll never make again."

Chapter 11

Touch her again, you son of a bitch, and you're a dead man.

Once, the vow would have thrilled her. Now it terrified. Because she knew the words weren't empty or overly dramatic. They were cold and simple fact.

She shivered, reminded how violently her world had shifted in only a matter of hours. No, not shifted. Shifted was too soft a word. Too subtle and gentle. Her world hadn't shifted, it had…shattered.

Miranda swallowed hard and surveyed the room, reinforced her resolve. "Are you going to sleep, too?" she asked as casually as she could. *Please, God, say yes.*

He twisted toward her, gave her a grim smile. "I won't be much good for you if I don't."

She kept her expression wiped clean, but inside, felt a burst of hope. With Sandro sleeping—

"I'm sorry, Miranda, but I can't let you do that," he said, standing and striding across the room in seemingly one move, grabbing his knapsack and tearing open the front pocket. Her expression must not have been as blank as she thought, she realized as Sandro pulled two shiny bracelets from the bag.

Alarm exploded through her in a dizzying rush of light. "What are those for?" she asked, but of course she knew.

He cut her a look. "What do you think they're for?"

Miranda couldn't stop staring at the handcuffs. Her mind raced wildly, images conjuring all by themselves. Sandro and handcuffs. Alone in a castle. No one to hear her scream.

In pain or in pleasure.

"Jesus, Miranda," Sandro swore softly. He started toward her, bringing the cold stone walls of the room with him and freezing the oxygen in her chest, but then stopped abruptly, almost violently. His hands clenched into tight fists. "How many times do I have to tell you I'm not going to hurt you?"

Her heart staggered, hard. God, she wanted to believe him. When he looked at her like he did now, with his eyes so hot, so desperate they seemed lit from the inside out, the lies and the betrayal fell away, leaving only the intense draw she'd felt from the beginning, the longing that tightened her chest like a vise, the aching that stabbed into her throat and overrode defenses.

Everything had changed, she knew, *she knew,* but her body didn't care. She wanted him to run his hands over her like he had before, until no trace of Petros's filth remained. She wanted him to put his mouth to hers and give her back her illusions. She wanted him to crush her in his arms and hold her, just hold her so the nightmare couldn't push any closer.

But that wasn't going to happen.

Because *he* was the nightmare, the worst-case scenario her father had warned her and Elizabeth about repeatedly.

"Then what?" she forced herself to ask.

A ghost of a smile replaced the frown. "Come on, *bella,* who are you trying to kid? I know you. The second I close my eyes, you'll be on your feet and running for the boat. And I can't let you do that.''

She blinked several times. ''Can you blame me?''

He hesitated only a moment before answering. ''No,'' he said in that hoarse voice of his, the one scarred by the sharp object which had slashed across his throat.

Instinct told her he harbored more than physical scars.

''I can't.'' Grim-faced, he crossed to the fireplace and resumed his work.

Miranda took advantage of his distraction and knelt before the knapsack. ''Ready for some water?''

His back to her, he put his lighter to the makeshift pile of kindling. ''That'd be great.''

Watching him out of the corner of her eye, she leaned over and quickly twisted off the lid, then slid her hand into the pocket of the shorts she'd pulled on back at the house and pinched the little white grains she'd been steadily grinding since she'd found the sleeping pills while looking for granola. Just as quickly, she dropped the granules into the bottled water, closed the lid, and started toward him, deliberately stumbling and sending the bottle careening across the hard dirty floor. That was the closest she could come to shaking the contents without drawing his suspicion.

''You okay?'' he asked, pushing to his feet.

She feigned embarrassment. ''Fine, just tired.''

He studied her a moment before going after his water, then unscrewed the lid and put the bottle to his mouth. One long swallow and almost half the liquid was gone. She saw the brutal slash across his throat bob as the water slid down, saw the fledgling firelight glint off the sheen of moisture on his lips.

''You must be thirsty,'' she said.

He shoved a hand through the swath of dark hair that had fallen across his forehead. ''Thirsty, hungry, tired as hell, not to mention wedged between the mother of all rocks and the papa of all hard places.'' He paused, finished off the water, then settled down in front of the fire and stretched out his long legs, patted the hard ground beside him.

"Come get warm," he said.

She blinked, felt her heart thrum in anticipation. Everything inside her felt tight, strained, like a rubber band stretched to the breaking point. And she desperately feared that if she snapped, she'd spring straight back toward Sandro.

"You don't act like a kidnapper," she practically growled.

Please.

His lips twitched. "Would you feel better if I was mean to you?"

No. She'd feel better if every time she looked at him, her heart didn't slam against her ribs. If every time she heard his voice, her breath didn't jam in her throat. If every time she thought of the way he'd held her in the wine cellar, how badly she'd wanted to make love with him, her eyes didn't fill.

Let It Happen.

She moved jerkily across the room, putting as much distance between them as he would allow. "You don't want to know what would make me feel better, trust me."

Fast.

Sandro watched her like she was an exotic dancer peeling off her clothes one garment at a time. He actually smiled, damn it. Faintly. Appreciatively. "Anyone ever told you you're beautiful when you're agitated?"

His voice was thicker, almost slurred, his eyes heavy. And something deep inside Miranda started to bleed. She didn't want to be beautiful for him. She didn't want to be anything for him. And she didn't want him to be anything for her, either.

Not even a memory.

Heart pounding mercilessly, she watched him watch her, watched him blink, watched the tight lines of his body gradually relax. She kept walking back and forth, doing her best to imitate an amulet swinging hypnotically on a chain, and finally his eyes drifted shut, and his body slumped to the ground.

And Miranda sprang into action. She rushed to his side, dropped to her knees. "Sandro?"

"*Bella?*" he muttered, reaching for her.

She shivered when his big hand found the exposed flesh of her thigh. She hadn't realized how cold she'd become until the heat of his palm seared into her. "I'm here," she whispered.

"Y-y-ou're c-cold. L-lie with...m-me."

Her throat tightened. And for a moment longing poured through her like floodwaters rushing from a broken dam to wipe out an unsuspecting valley. She wanted to do as he asked. Lie with him. Feel the heavy weight of his arm draped over her, his breath against her flesh, the rhythm of his heart. The rhythm they'd danced to. She wanted him to be just a man, her just a woman. She wanted the freedom she'd found only in his arms.

Her eyes filled, but she swiped back the tears. "Sandro?"

Nothing. No slurred words, no movement of his fingers against her thigh.

Robotically, she reached for his duffel bag and fished around inside, finding the precious mobile phone and the car keys. From his briefcase she helped herself to his semi-automatic and the small handgun he kept as backup. She didn't plan on using the weapons herself, but if he came after her, she couldn't bear the thought of facing Sandro with a gun in his hand.

She started to leave then, but the firelight glinted on a shiny surface, forcing Miranda to go very still. She knew what she had to do. No matter how badly she didn't want to, no matter how coldly furious he would be with her, she had to put those cuffs on him. Otherwise he would come after her.

She blinked at the ridiculous moisture clouding her vision and with the detached precision she'd learned from him, searched his bag for the keys.

Instead she found Virgil.

This time, the moisture spilled over, no matter how violently she blinked.

I really did have a dog named Virgil.

And he'd loved him. That much was undeniably clear. No matter what else had gone down in Sandro's life, he'd once been a boy who had loved a dog. A dog who'd bestowed upon him the same unconditional love as his grandfather. Unconditional love Miranda instinctively knew he'd not found anywhere else.

But something had gone horribly wrong in the life of that young boy who'd nursed a sickly, abandoned, unloved dog back to health. Something inside *him* had broken, and no one had been there to fix it, fix the man he'd become.

Forsaken.

Miranda squelched the foolish thought that maybe *she* could be the one to make a difference in his life and forced herself to continue searching the bag. Locating the keys, she returned to Sandro, ignoring the way he looked sleeping, his dark hair falling against his forehead. He looked almost…at peace.

Longing stabbed in again, sharper than before. Betrayal bled through, as cold and irrevocable as death. She'd let down her guard with this man. She'd danced with him, put her head to his chest and lost herself in the feel of his arms around her, his body pressed to hers, the two of them moving as one. She'd listened to his heart thrum. She'd let the heat of his body warm her. She'd marveled at the feel of his mouth moving against hers, kisses that alternated between excruciating tenderness and mind-numbing passion.

She'd wanted to be naked with him. She'd wanted to touch every inch of him, to have him touch every inch of her. She'd wanted to feel him over her and underneath her, inside her. She'd wanted to make herself his. She'd felt free with him. For the first time in her life, she'd felt beautifully, exquisitely, gorgeously free.

But all along, she'd been a prisoner.

And all along he'd wanted only to play her for a fool. It had been a game for him, an act, a skillful way of maneuvering her where he wanted her, as putty in his hands.

She touched his shoulder anyway, where a bullet had grazed him back on that first day. Then she skimmed her finger along his cheek and the whiskers shadowing his jaw, fought the crazy desire to touch his mouth. With hers.

To kiss her kidnapper goodbye.

Crazy.

The rubber band was about to break, she knew, snap clean in two. She forced herself to act quickly and without emotion, bringing the cuffs to his wrists and closing the jaws around his big bones. They fit snugly, manacles digging into flesh.

She couldn't let herself care.

Pocketing the key, she pushed to her feet and ran from the warmth of the fire, toward the chill of the gaping stone doorway.

Freedom lay just beyond, she knew.

Not in his arms.

Miranda jabbed the paddle into the water, saying a silent prayer when she connected with the muddy bank below the surface. The current had knocked her downriver, but here, at last, she was making her way toward shore. Her arms stung from exertion, her muscles no match for the violent pace of the water. She pulled the boat toward the oar, almost wept when she felt the bump against solid ground.

Soon, she would reach the car. And freedom.

Onshore, Miranda took only a moment to orient herself. First, she would follow the river back to the castle. She hated the extra time that would involve, but if she stood a chance of finding the car, she had to start from familiar territory.

Rain fell harder now, steady sheets plastering her hair and her clothes to her body, but she didn't care. She ran. Over broken tree limbs and washed-ashore debris, through mud and puddles. Didn't care. Only ran.

The phone, she remembered with a jolt. She had Sandro's phone. She could call the embassy, her father.

Excitement coursed through her as she fished into her bag for the small black phone. And when her fingers closed around it, the punch of relief almost knocked the breath from her lungs. She hurried along the shore, trying desperately to figure out which button turned the phone on. She pushed them all, but nothing happened. Finally she stopped, waited for lightning. Saw the on button. Pushed.

But nothing happened.

"No," she whispered, but when she turned the phone over, she saw that the battery had been removed. No doubt by Sandro the thorough. No doubt to ensure she couldn't outsmart him.

But she had, she reminded herself. She'd gotten away. She'd used his deceit against him. She could only imagine how he'd planned to use the sleeping pills against her.

Frustrated, she dropped the useless instrument to the riverbank and pushed on, until the otherworldly outline of the castle came into view. Lightning flashed, casting the ruins in silhouette.

Somewhere inside that crumbling stone wall, Sandro slept.

Alone.

Forsaken.

She turned abruptly and headed into the woods.

Someone was knocking at the door. No, they were pounding. Loudly. Furiously.

Go away, Sandro thought, but then instinct kicked through the blanket of fuzziness and he bolted upright. Not knocking. But thunder. Rumbling not through a house or a hotel room, but the old castle.

He blinked against the dryness of his eyes, brought the stone room into focus. It was cold now, dark, the paltry fire long gone.

Miranda.

He lunged to his feet and spun around, searching the room. Finding nothing.

"Miranda!" He listened for a response, heard only his voice echo through the castle walls. And he knew. God help him, he knew.

She was gone.

On the floor, his knapsack lay open, contents spilled around it. Sandro reached down to inventory what she'd taken, only then realizing she'd done more than just run. She'd tried to incapacitate him. His own handcuffs bound his wrists. And before he even sorted through his bag, he knew the sleeping pills were gone. So were the keys, the phone, the handgun. And when he looked to the right, there by the corner of the fireplace, he saw his attaché case open, his semiautomatic missing.

And his blood ran cold.

Adrenaline spewed through him. He had to find her, find her fast. He found a rock first, smashed the handcuffs against the sharp edge. Over. And over.

But nothing happened.

Swearing, no time to waste, he gathered his things and ran outside, not surprised to find the boat gone.

And this time, it was his bones that felt the chill.

The river was angry tonight, swirling and fast. He'd had to fight the current on the way over. Miranda…

Cristo.

He quickly searched the perimeter of the small island, but found no flotation devices. When he saw the plank of wood, he knew he had only one choice. His bound wrists would prevent him from using his arms to swim, but with his hands holding onto the wood, at least he could keep himself afloat while he kicked. Fifty yards. He could do that. He grabbed the plank, ran to the dock area, and dove into the dark swirling water.

Icy needles stung every inch of his body. The brutally strong current knocked him downstream, but he fought back, kicking hard, fighting for breath but getting mouthfuls of river water instead. He refused to think about Miranda in a similar struggle, but found his eyes scanning the wide river anyway, looking for any sign of the small rowboat. Finding none.

Thirty yards to go. More lightning. Thunder rumbling.

Twenty yards to go. A branch careening downriver, slashing his leg.

Ten yards. Five. Then shore. His feet sank in the mud the second he planted them. Shaking the hair from his face, he turned upstream and ran along the riverbank. And when at last he reached the dock area, he almost went to his knees.

Because there in the mud leading into the woods lay a single set of tracks.

Miranda broke through the clearing and said a silent prayer of thanks. She'd been running for a seeming eternity, the rain having long since destroyed any tracks Sandro hadn't erased in the first place. All the trails looked alike, old trees and clinging vines, and they'd all led in seeming circles.

Still, she'd run.

And now, she'd found the clearing where they'd begun. She rushed to the overgrown bushes, behind which waited the no-nonsense car. Almost deliriously, she jabbed the key in the lock and turned. Or at least tried to. Nothing happened. The key didn't turn in the lock. She tried again and again, same result.

On a cry of frustration she squeezed the handle, stunned when the door fell open.

Sandro hadn't secured the locks.

She climbed inside, then closed and locked the door

against the driving rain, shoved the hair from her face, took a moment to breathe. She would get out of here, find a phone. That was her first priority. Call her father. Let him know she was alive and safe. Find out where to go for help.

Shaking, she slid the key into the ignition and turned.

But just like with the door, nothing happened.

Miranda twisted her wrist as hard as she could, but the key remained jammed in place.

And in that moment she knew. She pulled it free and pushed on the overhead light, stared blankly as she realized that the keys she'd pulled from Sandro's bag were *not* the keys to the car.

Miranda blinked back the rush of tears and rested her head against the steering wheel. So close. She'd been so close.

It was a moment before the tap on the window registered as more than the pinging of rain. She sat there very still, fighting an inevitability that couldn't be outrun. She didn't want to open her eyes. She didn't want to see him standing there. She didn't want to see the cold fury in his eyes.

She didn't want to accept that freedom had slipped through her fingers yet again.

Throat tight, she lifted her head and turned toward the incessant tapping. She saw the gun first, felt her heart flat-out stop.

Because it was not Sandro who stood there in the rain.

It was Petros.

"Miranda!" Sandro ran through the tangled undergrowth and tore at the vines hanging from the trees. "Goddamn it, Miranda, answer me!"

Only the thunder answered, roaring low and deep.

Sandro pushed on, refused to let himself think of every fate that could have befallen her. In all likelihood, she was back at the car, furious at the precautions he'd taken, but safe and sound and out of the rain. She would glare at him, maybe launch herself at him again.

He'd be hard-pressed not to kiss her senseless.

He liked that thought, that of kissing Miranda senseless, so he used it to make himself run faster. The clearing was just ahead. He saw the bushes, ran toward them.

Stopped dead in his tracks.

The beat-up old car remained exactly where he'd parked it, and clearly Miranda had found it as well. But she didn't sit inside like he'd hoped. The two front doors hung open. And the windows had been shot out.

Sandro staggered forward, saw the tracks leading to the car, found the ones leading from the car. *Two* sets of tracks.

A cold rage stabbed in from somewhere dark and primal, and he took off at a dead run.

"Come out, come out, wherever you are."

Lewd laughter filled the abandoned old church, and crouched down behind the altar, Miranda shivered. Petros sounded darkly pleased with himself, forcing her to wonder inanely if his imitation of Jack Nicholson in *The Shining* was intentional.

Adrenaline crashed through her, keeping her heart racing long after her ankle had twisted out from under her. She'd half limped, half dragged herself from the rain and into the church.

"I hear you breathing," he announced, the words echoing through the damp chamber. "Heavily. For me, ya?"

Miranda pressed her back to the cold stone wall and held Sandro's gun in her violently shaking hands. Petros would find her soon. She would have only seconds to pull the trigger.

Footsteps shuffled closer, and then there he was, Petros, the vile little man who worked for the general. His eyes were dark, beady. His lips twisted.

"Don't look so scared, little one," he said in that heavily accented voice of his. "I'm not going to kill you."

She lifted her arms, pointed the gun at his heart. "Come one step closer, and I'll shoot."

He laughed. "All I want is what you gave Vellenti back at the house."

"I mean it, one step more and you're a dead man."

"One step more," he said, leering, "and you're mine." Then he lunged.

And Miranda fired.

But he slumped to the ground before she even squeezed the trigger.

A scream burned her throat, but no sound came forth. She stared blindly at the filthy man's unmoving body, then lifted her eyes to the man beyond. Lightning flashed in, stark, illuminating, garishly casting him in silhouette. Her heart beat crazily. She'd prayed for an angel, a miracle, but there was nothing holy or pious about the avenging commando standing alert and ready, savagery humming just beneath the surface, with hands that turned into lethal weapons even though his wrists were still cuffed together.

The man she'd deceived, just as he'd deceived her.

The man she'd left at the castle ruins, out cold.

The man who'd come after her anyway.

There was cold murder in his eyes, and her heart jammed into her throat. His clothes were plastered to his body. He stood so violently still he looked more stone than human.

But then he was moving, she was moving, and all doubts as to whether he was real or an apparition vanished. He was across the space separating them before she could blink, and then he was on the cold floor with her, taking her shoulders in his hands and practically dragging her into his lap like a rag doll. The second their bodies touched, something between a cry and a moan ripped from her throat. She wanted his arms around her. She *needed* his arms around her. His hands moving along her flesh. The heat of his body soaking into hers.

She needed…him.

No matter who he worked for.

She crushed him in her arms, held him to her, plastered her body against his as though she could fuse them into one. Even soaked to the bone, he was big and warm and clinging to him like that, sprawled in his lap like that, rocking, rocking, Miranda couldn't hold back the tears. Nor could she stop the violent shaking that ripped through her. Him.

She wasn't sure she could ever let go.

But he'd yet to put his arms around her.

"Jesus, God, Miranda," came his rough-hewn voice. "Are you all right? Did he hurt you?"

The question was coarse, pleading, the anguish in it damn near breaking her heart. She didn't want to move. She wanted to stay tucked against the heat and strength of his body forever.

But she also wanted to see his eyes, those mesmerizing chips of black ice. "No," she managed, pulling back slightly. No, she wasn't all right. No, Petros hadn't hurt her. No, she didn't want to let go. "No. He—" She glanced at the still unmoving man, saw a dark substance pooling out from under his head. "Is he de—" she started, but Sandro cut her off.

"Probably." His eyes met hers then, and the vile little man was forgotten. The old church was dark, but lightning flashed relentlessly, revealing the wet dark hair plastered to the sides of Sandro's face, the brutal scratches across his cheeks, the mud on his jaw.

The agony in his gaze.

She couldn't imagine what he'd gone through to reach her. The river had been deep and fast and cold. The woods dark and treacherous. But he'd come anyway.

I'm not going to let anything happen to you!

"You're real." She just barely managed to squeeze the words through the emotion knotting in her throat. "You came for me."

And then his eyes filled. Sweet God. His eyes actually filled. "You've got to get me out of these," he practically growled, lifting his wrists toward her.

She stared in horror at the cuffs she'd completely forgotten about, the streaks of blood littering his forearms. "Sandro—"

"...because if I don't get my arms around you in the next ten seconds, I won't be responsible for what happens."

She lost it then, what little control she'd scraped together. She had the key out of her pocket and was jabbing it against the little hole. She had to fight to steady her hands, but then the latch turned and the manacles fell open.

And then he had his arms around her. Not just his arms, either. He had his whole body around her, arms, legs, just holding her. Holding her.

And then they were both rocking.

"Why, Sandro?" she whispered, burying her face against the wet fabric of his T-shirt, warmed by the heat of his body. She could feel his heart beating. She could hear it. "Why?"

Why had he lied to her?

Why had he pledged allegiance to a criminal?

Why had he saved her from Petros?

Why couldn't she stop holding him? Wanting him.

He pulled back, cupped her face with his big battered hands. "I'm not the monster you think I am," he said, and the words sounded torn from him, torn from somewhere dark and hurting. "And I'm not going to let anyone hurt you ever again."

The tears overflowed then, hot, scalding. Affirming. Everything inside her felt raw, needy, stretched beyond the breaking point. She could barely even breathe, much less think coherently. But she didn't need to think, not when she felt. There was only one way to make the hurting stop. To make the pain and the doubt and the longing go away.

"Sandro," she whispered, sliding her hand through the damp strands of his hair and urging him down toward her.

He didn't need much urging.

Chapter 12

His mouth was on hers in a heartbeat, hot, rough, possessive. Glorious. He kissed her hard. He kissed her deep. He kissed her with the blind abandon of a man deprived of oxygen, greedily dragging in air.

She kissed him with the same urgency. She could feel his teeth against her lips, his whiskers scraping her jaw, but still she wanted more. She kept the one hand tangled in his damp hair, brought the other to his face. His hands were on her face, too, holding her while he drank of her. Took her. Claimed her mouth as intimately as she'd longed for him to claim her body. His mouth slanted restlessly, hungrily, as though something of monumental importance hung in the balance.

The need was relentless, driving, and she suddenly wanted more than just his mouth on hers, his hands on her face. She wanted him to touch her. Everywhere.

Primitive sounds tore from deep in his throat, empowering Miranda to grab one of his wrists and drag his hand away from her face, place it against her side. He groaned, sliding his hand to yank her shirt from her shorts. And then his hand was on her flesh, all hot and roughly possessive, sliding and stroking. Claiming.

She never wanted him to stop. Ever. She could no longer discern truth from lie, but she also realized she didn't care. Because in every corner of her heart, she finally accepted what instinct had been shouting all along. This man, this amazing, lost, ferocious poet of a commando, would not hurt her.

Touch her again, you son of a bitch, and you're a dead man.

A shiver ran through her at the memory, and Sandro gathered her closer. She wasn't sure it was possible to be any closer without slipping beneath his skin. She only knew that she wanted to hold this battered warrior close to her heart and never let go, no matter what lies he'd told. No matter who he worked for. No matter how loudly common sense screamed that she should run far and fast.

He tasted of strength and raw determination, a bone-deep ferocity that thrilled on a fundamental level. He tasted of sorrow and hope. He tasted of need and urgency. He tasted of everything she'd ever wanted but had never thought to find in the arms of a man who'd robbed her of fundamental liberties.

He tasted of freedom. Pure, raw, soul-shattering freedom.

There in his arms, body to body, seeking mouth to seeking mouth, hands groping desperately, she didn't let herself analyze why. She didn't let herself analyze, period. She simply kissed him with the same relentless hunger he kissed her. She let her mind shut down, her senses hum. She loved the feel of his mouth moving roughly against hers, his teeth against her lips, his tongue sliding with hers. She loved the feel of his whiskers scraping her jaw, his hands tangled deep in her hair.

She loved *him.*

It was as simple, as absurd, as impossible as that.

The realization should have stopped her cold. It didn't.

Nothing could, not even the fact she'd run from him. Because she hadn't, not really. She, champion of going with the flow and living life to the fullest, of tossing protocol to the wind and making her own decisions, her own judgments, had run from herself. From the fact that even during the darkest moments back in the bedroom of the safe house, when she'd bit and hit and shouted, all she'd really wanted was for him to crush her in his arms and hold her. Love her.

That's why she ran. And every step of the way, a fundamental piece of her had silently prayed he would come after her. Find her. Prevent her from escaping him.

Because she knew, *she knew*, the second she tasted so-called freedom, she would never see him again.

And that reality made her hurt in ways she'd never imagined possible. It was a ragged, tearing hurt, bone-deep, a chill that could permanently freeze everything inside her.

They had no future. They *could* have no future.

But Miranda had never constrained herself by logic, rules or plans. That was her sister's realm. Miranda was the dreamer.

And she knew no matter what else went down, when she dreamed from this day forward, she would dream of eyes like chips of midnight ice, a poet's mouth that kissed with soul-shattering intensity, a commando who carried an assault rifle in his briefcase and a carved statue of his childhood dog in his pocket.

She refused to think beyond that. She refused to think at all. She was safe. She knew that. Sandro had risked his life to save hers, not to reclaim a prize. She'd seen the violent, unchained emotion in his eyes. It had touched her, changed her.

For now, that was enough.

More than enough.

His hands were all over her, rough, but gentle at the same time. It was as though he was inventorying her body, cataloging the feel of her, making sure she was really safe and whole. And she knew that as long as she lived, she would never forget the sight of him standing in the abandoned old church, dripping wet, wrists cuffed in front of him, lightning illuminating the hard glitter in his eyes. The image was indelibly etched into her soul. Where she could keep it safe.

Just like he'd kept her safe.

She clung to him now, this man who had somehow swam a swollen river to find her, kissed him, loved him, knowing she'd never get close enough, not even if she crawled inside his skin.

Lightning brightened the church, thunder booming within seconds. Sandro pulled back abruptly, again took her face in his hands. His breathing was hard, labored, his mouth swollen, his eyes hot. "We've got to get out of here."

No. That's what she wanted to tell him. She wanted to stay, right there behind the old altar on the cold damp stone floor, sprawled between his legs. "I know," she whispered.

But he didn't move, just kept touching her, the longing and sorrow in her heart reflected in the steady burn of his gaze.

She tried to breathe, feared she might cry instead. "I'm sorry," she whispered. "I—"

"Shh." The moisture was back in his eyes, making the dark oddly bright. "I left you no choice."

"I...I didn't expect Petros to be waiting." *Didn't realize I loved you.*

Sandro let out a rough breath, frowned. "He probably put some kind of tracking device on the car," he said, and though he spoke gently, regret twisted through the words. "That's why we ditched it. I was going to get us new wheels in the morning." He paused, his jaw tightened. "I should have told you that."

She couldn't stand the self-recrimination in his voice. "It's not your fault. You're here now. We're together."

He squeezed his eyes shut, opened them a moment later. "I'm glad you didn't have to pull that trigger."

So was she. "I would have," she said. "I would have done anything to keep him from touching me." From touching what belonged to Sandro.

His hand was on her face again, gently stroking. "Killing another person is not a stain I want on your soul, *bella*. You deserve better than that."

There was a note in his voice she didn't understand, but that spoke to her anyway. Spoke to her deep. Her chest tightened. Emotion burned her throat. Slowly, she lifted a hand to his neck, skimmed a finger along the nasty, faded gash. "What of yours, Sandro?"

He glanced to the side of the altar, where Petros lay unmoving. "It's a little late to be worrying about my soul."

"You might as well ask me to stop breathing," she said through the hurt in her heart, determined not to let the tears break through. She tried to smile, knew she failed.

He stood abruptly, reached for her hand. "A man does what he has to do, *bella*. It's as simple as that."

She put her palm to his, rose to her feet. "So does a woman."

Even when doing so defied the very freedom she'd spent her entire life craving.

They drove south. They drove fast. They drove despite the driving rain and relentless lightning, the pounding thunder. They drove until sunrise chased the squalor away, the dark of the night giving way to an eerily beautiful storm-washed morning. The glare brightened the blue of the sky and the white of the clouds, the green of the grass, the red and orange and yellow flowers tumbling wildly alongside the narrow, single-lane road.

Sandro bit back a stream of virulent frustration. The vivid beauty contrasted sharply the dark, ugly edges inside him. The edges that continued to cut and slice even hours after he'd found Miranda crouched behind the altar in the old abandoned church. If he'd been just a few minutes later...

He tightened his hold on the wheel, his jaw. If his teeth weren't ground to bits by the time this was all said and done, it would be nothing short of a miracle.

Eyes burning, he glanced at Miranda, who lay sprawled across the front seat, sleeping. She rested her head in his lap, her hand curled around his knee. Her hair and clothes remained damp, despite the full blast of the heater.

His chest constricted painfully. Emotion stabbed his throat. She should have been out of the country by now. She should have been safe and warm and dry. She should be free. Instead she lay shivering in the front seat of a beat-up car, trying her damnedest to be brave, even though he'd seen the stark fear in her eyes.

It was that fear that had him taking matters into his own hands. He hoped to God and back Javier still lived, but could no longer be sure. Something inside him went cold at the thought, but he shoved the emotion aside, knowing it would only poison him now. He needed to stay sharp. He needed to stay focused. And his options were pitifully thin.

"My mobile phone," he'd said as soon as they'd retrieved his belongings from the castle. "I need my phone."

He'd seen the answer in Miranda's eyes before she spoke. "It's...gone."

They were so screwed. Something inside him had twisted, but he kept his expression blank, refusing to let her feel an ounce of remorse for tossing their only safe link to the agency, after discovering he'd removed the battery to prevent her from making a call that would place them in greater danger.

Now he had to rely on landlines, which meant he had to work through an elaborate network to keep calls from being traced. But he would do it. Because he had to.

For Miranda.

For the freedom she so desperately deserved.

He glanced in the rearview mirror, finding grim satisfaction in the deserted road behind him. No one followed him. Of that he was sure. Petros wouldn't be leaving the old church. When Miranda was safely out of the country, Sandro would call the authorities, make sure Petros was found and returned to his home country of Ravakia. He doubted anyone would truly mourn the man, but he hadn't lost his grip on humanity to the point where he wanted Petros to lie forgotten on the floor of the old church. True, a fundamental part of him had died that long ago, ominously beautiful morning in London, beneath a sky as starkly blue as the one above him now, but not the part that could let him take human life without feeling a shot of cold deep inside.

He just thanked God it was a feeling Miranda would never know.

"Sandro?"

He looked down at the sound of her sleep-roughened voice, found her gazing at him through those gypsy eyes of hers. They looked greener than usual, verdant, like the fields through which they drove. But red streaks marred the illusion. And the shadows beneath her lower lashes looked disgustingly close to bruises.

"Sleep well?" he asked as casually as he could.

She pushed up from his lap and ran her fingers through still-damp hair, glanced out the front window. "Where are we?"

"About a hundred miles away from where we were."

She wrinkled her brow. "Where are we going?"

Home. "Somewhere I can get you out of those wet clothes."

She blinked, her eyes going even darker. "I'd like that."

He wasn't sure how he stopped from groaning. His whole body tightened, painfully, forcing him to keep his hands clenched on the steering wheel and out of her hair, off her flesh.

"And into dry ones," he amended. "I can't have you catching pneumonia on me."

He would have sworn she frowned. She watched him for an excruciatingly long heartbeat, before a soft little smile curved her mouth and damn near cut his heart out. "I'm not afraid," she whispered. "Not anymore."

This time he couldn't bite back the hard sound that broke from his throat. "Maybe you should be."

Her eyes almost seemed to glow. "Maybe," she said, tucking herself up against him. "But that's never stopped me before."

No, it hadn't, a fact which left him alternatingly terrified and fascinated. She approached life with a gutsy joy he'd never before encountered. She was fire and life and deserved the freedom she treasured above all else.

The very freedom he'd walked away from five years before.

A smart man would leave it at that. A smart man would keep his hands on the wheel and his eyes on the road, his mind on the job. But Miranda was cold and wet and shivering, and no power on earth could have stopped him from draping his arm around her shoulders and drawing her close, holding her tight.

Under the circumstances, he figured, two out of three wasn't bad.

Twenty minutes later he hid the car in an old garage on the outskirts of a sleepy, white-washed village overlooking the Tagus river.

"We can shower up here," he said, as they exited an alley and faced what passed for a hotel in Coruche. "Change clothes, then hit the road again."

Miranda stopped walking, looked up to meet his gaze. "You're exhausted," she pointed out, skimming her fingertips along the increasingly dark stubble itching against his jaw. "When was the last time you slept?"

For some stupid reason, he felt his lips twitch. "If I

recall, you made sure I slept for a good couple of hours last night.''

He'd meant the words teasingly, but the shadow crossed her gaze so quickly, so violently, he would have given anything to grab the stupid comment back. "Miranda—"

"No," she said. "You're right."

"I left you no choice," he reminded. "You were doing exactly what I would have done in the same situation."

This time, the smiled quirked her lips. "What does that say about me?"

He didn't know how or why, didn't even know it was possible, but he laughed. "Good damn question." He refused to voice the answer that vaulted to his throat.

Kindred spirits.

They were about as kindred as shadows and sunshine.

Her eyes were sparkling now, but still heavy with a concern he didn't deserve. "You need sleep, Sandro. Maybe we should stay here longer."

"No." Because the word came out harsher than he intended, he softened it with a faint smile. "It's too risky, too public."

She held his gaze for a painfully long moment, searched deep, then sighed. "I trust you."

The words were soft, but they landed hard. It was what he'd wanted, what he'd maneuvered for these past several days. Her trust. But offered up like that, given so simply, twisted him up in ways he hadn't expected.

And couldn't afford to analyze.

"De hora?" the motel manager asked a few minutes later. An hour? She was a large woman, slightly graying, with a knowing smile that speared straight through him. Sandro found himself grateful Miranda didn't understand Portuguese.

"Seem," he told her. Yes. *"Tem quartos livres?"* Have you any vacancies?

Her gaze slipped to Miranda, who stood by Sandro's

side, silently holding his hand. She watched the two of them through wide, expectant eyes.

"Seem," the manager said at last. *"Tenho um quarto."*

"Fico com ele," he practically growled, reaching for the key she handed him. I'll take it. *"Obrigada,"* he said in thanks, then led Miranda down the hall. He'd made sure the motel rooms had two methods of access, just in case. If someone came through the window, he and Miranda could leave through the door.

That wasn't going to happen, though. They weren't going to be here long enough.

"Problems?" Miranda asked, hurrying to keep up with him.

He thought about lying, didn't see the point. "Senora Lopez doesn't believe we just want to shower."

They were at the door now, and as he slid the key into the lock, he felt Miranda's gaze on him, hot and insistent, offering promises he would never allow her to keep.

"Smart woman," she whispered.

He shoved open the door and strode into the small but clean room. Now was not the time for afternoon delight, no matter how tempting the bed looked. Now was the time to get her warm and dry, make a few phone calls, kick the final act into motion.

That was all.

The late-afternoon sun chased them south. Streaks of light slanted through the branches of gnarled olive trees, casting long shadows across the bumpy dirt road.

Sandro stared straight ahead, one hand curled around the bottom of the steering wheel, the other resting with deceptive casualness in his lap. At his feet sat the attaché case with his submachine gun tucked safely inside. Dark sunglasses concealed his eyes but not the scratches on his face, and while a Hawaiian shirt again stretched across his shoulders, this one brown with little tiki idols scattered about, the illusion of casualness that had come before with the brightly colored shirts didn't form.

He looked…tired. He'd only wanted to spend an hour at the hotel, but she'd taken a deliberately long shower, taken a deliberately long time getting dressed. To give him time to rest, she'd told herself. That was all. The fact she'd left the bathroom door unlocked hadn't meant anything. The fact she'd stood naked under the spray of lukewarm water, sudsing up her body while listening for Sandro, meant nothing.

Nor did the fact that while she'd left the door unlocked while she showered, he had not.

Of course, she'd had to cuff her ankle to the bottom of the bed before he would agree to leave her alone long enough for him to shower. She'd volunteered to go in the bathroom with him, sit on the commode while he stood behind the flimsy curtain.

He'd looked at her like she'd volunteered to shove splinters beneath his fingernails.

So she'd stood outside the door to the bathroom, knowing she couldn't shuffle too far from the bed. But that hadn't stopped her from putting her hand to the knob, and turning.

And finding that he'd locked her out.

A sane woman would be thankful. Because after her own shower, she'd stood in the foggy bathroom, listening to him speak on the phone. She hadn't understood the language, but the hushed tones were universal. So were the short, urgent bursts.

Their time together was drawing to an end. She knew that. But with every corner of her heart she also knew that whatever his allegiance to General Zhukov, he wouldn't hurt her.

There are many ways to hurt, bella. *Not all of them are physical.*

She knew that, too. She also knew in a few days their paths would part. They could have no future. She would return to life as she knew it, and he, this complicated, enigmatic man by her side, would return to his.

There could be no shared path for the daughter of an American ambassador and the right-hand man of an Eastern European militant responsible for the deaths of eight highly trained U.S. operatives.

But, God, how she wanted…

She bit back the thought, fought the emotion burning her throat, her eyes. She couldn't let herself think too far into the future. She had only the here and the now, and the precious few moments remaining.

"Where are we headed?" she asked for the third time.

He didn't look at her, didn't miss a beat. Just kept staring straight into the near-blinding sun. "Somewhere safe."

The vague answer frustrated her, but no longer surprised. They'd changed cars twice since leaving the hotel, making their trail almost impossible to follow. They'd been on a fairly major highway for a while, before taking a fork in the road and bumping down a gravel path through a dusty village that looked as worn down as she felt. Children had played soccer in a field, while a few thin dogs wandered alongside the road.

That was close to an hour ago. They'd been driving through a grove of twisted olive trees ever since. With the sun cutting through the branches and the horizon washed in the white of early twilight, they seemed to be driving into nowhere.

Until he rounded the corner.

And the standing stones came into view.

There were far too many to count, giant, misshapen monoliths towering toward the sky.

And they flat-out stole her breath.

"Oh, my God," she whispered as he stopped the car behind a rusty old trailer. "Where are we?"

Somewhere safe, she waited for him to answer. But he didn't.

"*Cromlech of Almendres,*" he answered, the words rolling off his tongue in the accent that still had the power to heat her blood.

"Like Stonehenge?" She'd planned to visit the massive site in England later in the summer.

Sandro took the key from the ignition and opened his door. "Maybe older."

She followed him into the cool breeze of early evening. The sun which had seemed so intrusive only minutes before now seemed softer, bathing the ancient site in an otherworldly combination of shadow and light.

Sandro moved to stand by one of the large monoliths, stepping easily into the puddle of darkness cast by the stone that looked far too similar to a tombstone.

"There's ninety-five of them," he said. "Supposedly they date back to the fourth or fifth millennia *B.C.* Probably a temple dedicated to a solar cult."

Miranda moved beside him, her photographer's eye roaming the megalithic structures. They ambled down the side of a slight hill, not in a circle like others she'd read about, but staggered, like a crowd gathered restlessly to hear a poet speak.

"How do you know all these places?" she asked, fascinated.

Sandro looked off toward the western horizon, lifting a hand to shield his eyes, even though he still wore the dark sunglasses. "I had a friend from Portugal. He brought me here many years ago."

The friend whose family had owned the villa she and Sandro had hidden in that first day. The friend who could only be summoned through a séance.

There really seemed to be nothing to say, so she didn't even try. Sometimes, silence said enough. Especially with a man like Sandro.

Instead, she reached for the camera she'd grabbed upon leaving the car and lifted it toward the grouping of monoliths. The early evening light was perfect, creating an apocalyptic feel to the stones modern man had yet to understand.

She was tempted to turn the lens toward Sandro, an equally confounding mystery, but knew he'd only turn away from her.

And that was something she didn't want.

Wandering away from him, she snapped a series of shots, going down on her knee to catch an angle looking skyward. The stones were weathered, all shades of gray. Patches of grass shot up between them, smaller rocks scattered about. A few of the monoliths boasted carvings, a series of primitive circles and lines in varying sizes.

"This isn't a field trip, Miranda."

She stilled, pushed to her feet, pivoted to find him standing mere inches away. She could literally feel the heat from his body, his breath. "I know that."

"Then what are you doing?"

"It's that old lemons-and-lemonade thing," she tried to explain. "Just because life threw a nasty curve ball doesn't mean I have to surrender. I came to Europe for a reason."

It was almost night now, but he'd yet to remove his sunglasses. "To take pictures?"

"To learn, and to record. There's a huge world outside the borders of the United States, a world many Americans never have the chance to experience. I thought…" She paused, frowned as she recalled her parent's horrified reaction to her plan.

"Thought what?"

"Thought I could share that world. Thought I could create a photo essay, maybe get it published." When he said nothing, she added, "I know, it's an absurd idea."

His jaw tightened. "Who told you it's absurd?"

Miranda looked away from him, toward the western horizon, where only red streaks of the sun remained.

"Who, Miranda? Who said it was absurd?"

She turned back toward him, lifted her chin, forced a smile. "My grandfather was a senator, Sandro, my father is an ambassador. My sister is a corporate attorney. My brother works for the Department of Justice. Carringtons don't put together coffee-table books for a living.''

He lifted a hand, and for a thrilling moment, she thought he meant to touch her. He did, but only long enough to ease a strand of brown hair from her face. ''That's exactly what a Carrington will do,'' he said very softly. ''Soon, you'll be home, safe and sound and ready to put together a photo essay that will knock the socks off your family.'' He paused, frowned. ''Until then, I'm taking no chances. We'll stay only where I'm sure no one will find us.''

He spoke with absolute certainty, but rather than warming her, assuring her, his words chilled. ''How will you know we're safe? How will you know for sure?''

He let out a rough breath. ''Because one, Petros isn't tracking us anymore. And two, I'll trust no one but myself.''

Not even her. He didn't say the words, didn't need to. She felt their sting clear down to her bones. ''Not even Javier?''

The stones cast longer shadows now, darker. ''Not even Javier.''

The pain in his voice was unmistakable. ''You think he betrayed you?''

He stiffened, much as he had when she'd pulled her knife on him. ''No,'' he bit out quickly. ''No. Just because the message directing us to the safe house came from his phone doesn't mean he sent it.''

Realization dawned swift and brutal. ''Oh, God, you think—''

''Don't say it, *bella*, okay?'' The command was rough, jagged. ''He's a good man, an even better friend.''

And every rigid line of Sandro's body screamed that he thought his partner was dead. ''But why would Petros—''

Sandro turned from her, lifted a hand to trace the circles etched in one of the stones. ''Petros used to be Viktor's go-to man, until he botched an important assignment. He resented that I'd been sent…for you. He thought if he could get you away from me, he could somehow regain Viktor's favor."

A wave of cold went through Miranda so sharp, so numbing, she braced a hand to one of the monoliths to keep from sinking to her knees. The slimy man had probably killed Sandro's partner as a way of finding Sandro, finding her. If Sandro hadn't found her— No. She broke off the thought violently, refusing to dwell in could-have-beens. "I'm glad you stopped him."

He turned back toward her, again brushed the hair from her face. "Lesser of two evils?"

She stepped closer. "You're not evil, Sandro."

"How can you say that?"

She hesitated only a moment before answering. "Take off your sunglasses."

"What?"

"Isn't that what you asked of me in Cascais?" she reminded. "To take off my sunglasses? Now I'm asking the same of you."

She couldn't see his eyes but knew that he looked at her, could feel the slow burn of his midnight eyes even through the dark lenses. Slowly, he slid his hand from her face to his, where he lowered the shades from his eyes.

And this time, Miranda felt the slow burn clear down to her soul. "Now give me your hand."

His gaze was hot, piercing, full of an uncertainty she'd rarely seen from him. But he did as she asked. Standing there beside the ancient standing stones, with night casting a blanket of darkness, he put his hand in hers, every movement, every breath, taking on exaggerated proportions. Seconds felt like forever.

"I know that here," she said softly, drawing his palm to her chest, where every beat of her heart hammered with near-painful precision. "You promised you wouldn't let anything happen to me, and I believe you."

He squeezed his eyes shut, opened them a moment later.

They were burning now, practically on fire. "God, you're amazing."

I'm in love, she correctly silently, holding back the words, keeping them close to her heart. More than anything, she longed to return to the magic of the wine cellar, but knew the innocence of before was gone. They had only the truth now, the impossible fact that even though he'd lied to her, she still wanted him.

"Don't prove me wrong, Sandro. That's all I ask."

His smile turned grim, but his hand remained against her heart. "Would you like the sun and the moon, as well?"

She didn't know why that question hurt. "Would you give them to me?"

"If I could," he answered quietly, then turned and walked away, vanishing within the cluster of standing stones.

"You need to get some sleep," she told him long hours later. He wouldn't stop pacing the perimeter of the site, just kept walking, walking, as though he didn't trust himself to stand still for longer than a second.

"There will be plenty of time for sleep later," he said as he passed her for what had to be the hundredth time.

She pushed to her feet and went to him, grabbed him by the arm, forcing him to stop or drag her along behind him. "Why later, Sandro? Why not now? You're exhausted."

The moon was full, casting enough light to show the answer register deep in his eyes, even though he said nothing.

He wouldn't sleep because of her. Because she'd run last night. Because he didn't trust her not to run again.

The realization pierced deep. She turned from him jerkily and hurried toward one of the larger stones, where he'd left the duffel bag containing their supplies. Moments later she caught up with him about twenty feet further along the perimeter and again took hold of his arm.

"Here," she said, lifting her free hand. "Use these."

He stared at her palm, where moonlight glinted off the cuffs. "What?"

She snapped one around her wrist. "You're exhausted. You need to sleep. And I'm not going anywhere." Before he could protest, she closed the other manacle around his wrist and tossed the key into a pile of rocks several feet away.

Chapter 13

"Miranda—"

"I know," she said, cutting him off and trying to inject a lightness into her voice she didn't come close to feeling. "I'm sure when you imagined spending the night with a woman and handcuffs, this isn't exactly what you had in mind, but—"

"Don't."

The warning glittered in his eyes, resonated in his hoarse voice. But she ignored both. "Don't what?" she asked, angling her chin. Prove to him she wouldn't run? Force him to sleep?

Love him.

"Don't pretend this is some big adventure," he bit out, then started to move away from her. His movements were rough, forcing her to stagger along behind him, bumping up against his side when he stopped abruptly. He looked at her for a long moment, his eyes darker than she'd ever seen them. Then he swore softly. "Christ, I'm sorry."

She tried to hide her surprise. "Sorry for what?"

He lifted a hand to her face, traced the line of her cheek. "That I've reduced you to this, to sleeping in a dirty field, handcuffed to a stranger."

Her throat tightened. "You're not a stranger, Sandro. And you haven't reduced me to anything." She went down to her knees, urging him beside her. "Now go to sleep."

It was one of those impossibly blue skies that if captured by a photographer, everyone would claim the picture was doctored. But it was real, and it was overhead, and against it, white clouds floated aimlessly. A warm breeze blew through the crowded city streets, the bustling café.

"Where to next, mate? Paris? Madrid?"

Sandro put down the small white cup and grinned at Gus. "What's with the mate crap? You suddenly think you're an Aussie?"

"He thinks he'll get more broads that way," Roger answered, surveying the surrounding tables. "There's a cute little redhead over there just begging to be approached."

"Begging for me," Sandro boasted, "not bonehead, here."

"That's Count Bonehead to you," Gus corrected. "You forget, I come from a long line of Portuguese royalty."

Roger coughed out a laugh. "Royal pains in the ass, that is."

Sandro picked up his cup again, finished the last of the now-cool coffee. Grinning, he glanced toward the redhead, ready to suggest she put them out of their collective misery and join them.

But her hair was no longer red.

It was…brown. And those round eyes of hers were exotic now, laughing, full of life. Almost like a gypsy.

He blinked, confused. His heart started to race. Panic speared deep. This was…wrong. She didn't belong here. Couldn't be here. In a heartbeat he was on his feet, throwing aside chairs to reach her before—

The bomb exploded.

"Miranda!" he shouted. "Sweet Jesus, no!" He was falling then, thrown to the concrete by the force of the blast. He fought against the debris, choked on the smoke. "Miran-da!"

"Sandro."

Her voice, so soft and sweet. So alive. He focused on it, thrashed against the tables and chairs pinning him down. "Hang on!"

"Sandro, I'm here! It's okay!"

He felt her then, somehow, soft hands running along his body, clearing away the rubble. She shouldn't have been strong enough to reach him, save him, but her arms were around him. He crushed her to him, held her tight, tangled his hands in her hair. "Sweet God, Miranda."

Her hands found his face, feathered along his cheekbone. "Open your eyes," she commanded softly. "*Please*. Open your eyes."

It took effort, but he would have given her the sun and the moon if she'd asked. His eyes burned, but he opened them, blinked several times before the world came into focus.

Darkness. That was his first thought. The blue sky was gone, replaced by a black as pure and impenetrable as death. The smoke, he thought, but then sucked in a breath and waited for the burn in his lungs, found only the sweet scent of grass. And Miranda.

"It was just a dream," she whispered. She was sprawled over him, her breathing as ragged as his own. "Just a dream."

"No," he ground out. "It was real. Gus and Roger were there, just like before."

More on top of him than not, she stilled. "Gus and Roger?"

He fought against the burning wreckage of the café, couldn't tear it away. "In London. After graduate school. We were just…playing. Killing time before real life started."

But it had ended instead, for Roger, and for Gus. And in many ways, for Sandro.

"What happened?" Miranda asked. "What happened?"

He blinked, but couldn't bring her into focus. "You were there…the bomb."

"What are you talking about?" she asked gently.

He was talking about General Viktor Zhukov, who'd decided to show the world he wouldn't go quietly into the night. Time to grab the spotlight. Time to demonstrate how far he would go, how many lives he was willing to take in the process.

"No," Sandro growled, pulling her down against him. His heart pounded hard and violent. Rage pummeled him like debris. *Not you, too, goddamn it. Not you, too.*

"Sandro—"

He didn't let her finish. He couldn't. He slid a hand to the back of her head and urged her down toward him, took her mouth with a desperation that ripped harder and deeper than the bomb that had killed his two best friends and prompted him to walk away from life as he knew it, to fight for a freedom and future he'd always taken for granted.

She didn't fight, didn't resist, just kissed him back with the same hunger, the same need. The same abandon. She lay sprawled between his legs, one hand holding the side of his face as though to prevent him from pulling away from her.

As if he could.

He'd tried. He'd tried so damn hard to do the right thing, to be noble, to keep his hands off her. To keep cold logic intact, to keep his heart from getting involved. But some needs ran deeper than honor, drove more relentlessly than integrity. Loving Miranda was a mistake. Wanting her was practically criminal.

But the thought of losing her shredded him to the bone.

Tearing his mouth from hers was impossible, not when she represented everything he'd ever wanted, but knew he could never have. Not after that sunny, bloody morning in

London. Not after he'd knelt before Gus's grave and promised to exact vengeance.

He would, too, if it was the last thing he did.

And if it was the last thing he did, he would go to his death with the sweet taste of Miranda on his lips.

His soul.

She tasted his need, felt a like need pour through her. He kissed her hard, he kissed her deep. He kissed her as if his very life depended on it.

She kissed him the same way.

Her right wrist remained cuffed to his left, the key hidden by darkness in the rocks somewhere beyond. She didn't care. She liked being bound to him, didn't ever want to let him go. With their free hands they explored each other's bodies restlessly, eagerly, fingers skimming flesh, grabbing at clothes.

No more denying. No more pretending. Miranda didn't come close to understanding how she could feel so strongly, want so deeply, a man who worked for a criminal, who'd kidnapped her for God's sake, but she knew feelings couldn't be analyzed. Nor could desire. It just…was.

Tomorrow offered no guarantees. She knew that. But she didn't care, didn't need guarantees. Only Sandro. Holding her. Kissing her. Driving inside of her, making her his. Tonight might be all they had, and more than anything, she wanted him to know that not everyone in his life was destined to forsake him.

She loved being sprawled on top of him. She loved being between his legs, feeling his body envelope hers. She loved the strength she felt in his thighs, in the bulge pressing into her stomach, the arm he used to hold her.

She loved the take-no-prisoners possession of his kiss.

Everywhere his hand skimmed, his fingertips teased, she burned. She wanted to touch him, too, to feel flesh not fabric. Fumbling with the buttons of his tiki shirt, she slid them free, until she could pull the cotton back and feel the heat of his skin. She shivered as she pressed her shaking palm to his stomach, slid up to his chest, tangled her fingers in the splattering of coarse hair there. With great effort she slid her mouth from his, cruised over the prickly whiskers on his jaw, down to the scar across his windpipe. There she kissed, and licked, and loved.

Something terrible had happened to Sandro. Something that shattered the boy with the dog and hardened him into the commando with the assault rifle. But that other part of him remained, buried below the surface. The part that made him swim a swollen river to prevent Petros from touching her. Hurting her. The part that enabled him to touch her with a mind-numbing combination of need and hunger and reverence.

The night was dark, but the full moon provided all the light she needed. She went down to his chest, opened her mouth over one flat, round nipple, and sucked gently.

A rough sound tore from his throat, sent everything inside her up in flames. Blindly, she reached for his jeans, worked at the fly.

"Whoa," he rasped, using their joined hands to pull her up from his waistband. "Slow down." His breathing was labored as his eyes met hers. They were unbearably hot. "I don't want you to do anything you'll regret."

She lifted a hand to his face, skimming his lower lip with her thumb, the whiskers on his jaw with her pinkie. "I'm not."

His eyes darkened, flickered. He clenched them shut, his body beneath hers going rigidly still. When he opened them a moment later, the struggle between desire and restraint remained.

"This isn't going to have a happy ending," he rasped in a voice more hoarse than usual. "You know that, don't you?"

Panic slashed in from somewhere unwanted. "I don't care about endings, Sandro. I care about now."

He let out a rough breath. "I don't want to hurt you."

"Then make love to me," she said, despite the tearing deep inside. She leaned down and pressed a searing kiss to his mouth. "The only way you'll hurt me is by pretending you don't want me as badly as I want you."

"Miranda—"

He was a man of iron will, but she was a woman of the same. In abducting her, he'd taken her body captive, but he'd freed her spirit. And her heart. No way would she let him take this fundamental freedom from her. No way would she let him save her from herself. She didn't want to abandon his mouth, but she did want him to see her eyes when she spoke. For him to see the truth and conviction burning in hers.

The irony was nearly unbearable, that this man who'd stolen her freedom had actually given her so much more. She didn't know why he'd turned down the path he had, but suspected his choice had something to do with the nightmare she'd awoken him from. The terrible dream that had brought those distorted, primitive sounds from his throat, made him thrash. The dream that had made him cry. The dream that had made him reach for her, hold her tight. And with absolute certainty she knew that beneath the bad-guy label, he possessed a heart and a soul purer, more loyal and dedicated than the majority of people commonly thought of as heroes.

What mattered lay inside. The man, not the label.

And it was that man she burned for, wanted with all her heart.

And her body.

"For the first time in my life," she told him, squeezing the words through the tightness in her throat, "I feel free. Free to be myself." She saw him wince, refused to let it deter her. "You make me feel alive," she went on, fighting the emotion twisting inside her, the tears gathering deep. "You make me feel special. Don't take that from me."

She waited for him to pull away, to push her from between his legs and put as much distance between them as he could. Instead, with their wrists cuffed together, he threaded his fingers through hers and squeezed. "You *are* special."

She could tell the admission cost him, which made the words all the more valuable. "Then give me now, Sandro. Give me now."

His lips quirked, but the motion looked more pained than pleasured. "I thought you weren't asking for the sun and the moon," he muttered.

She smiled, a curve of her lips that stemmed from deep inside. "I thought you said you'd give me them, if you could."

He swore softly. Again, she thought he meant to roll from beneath her, sit, turn his back to her. But he surprised her again, this time pulling himself up so they sat facing each other. She was still in his lap, though, her legs straddling his waist. And it was impossible not to feel the bulge that revealed he wanted her as badly as she wanted him.

"Tu hai le labbra le piu morbide del mondo," he said quietly, lifting a hand to her mouth. His fingers skimmed along her lips, parted them, slipped inside. *"Baciami."*

Her heart kicked, hard. Recognition flowed swift and deep. The memory from that first day, there in the alley, brought stinging moisture to her eyes. "Sweet nothings?" she asked, smiling, even though for some reason doing so cut viciously.

His eyes, those chips of midnight ice, took on a heated glow. "No."

"Then what?"

His gaze dipped to her mouth, where she continued to play with his finger. "You have the softest lips," he whispered. "Kiss me."

Surprise came first, followed by a rush of emotion so pure, so overwhelming, it jammed in her throat, making it hard to breathe. "Sandro—"

"Shh," he whispered, pulling his finger from her mouth and using it to press against her lips.

Her heart pounded mercilessly as he slid his hand from

her face and down her neck, down to the buttons of the yellow shirt with orange Bird of Paradise flowers he'd provided her in the hotel room. Boneless, barely able to move, breathe, she watched him slip the buttons free with surprising precision, one by one baring her chest. His fingers skimmed her flesh, flesh that had never really known the intimate touch of a man, turning her breathing choppy, her heartbeat irregular.

His own shirt hung open, the moonlight casting his chest in an erotic study of rigid planes, hard muscle and scarred flesh. The urge to touch every inch of him almost overwhelmed her. While he slid her shirt from her shoulders so that it dangled from their joined arms, she did the same with his.

Her body burned for him, screamed. She wanted him to touch her, everywhere. She wanted his hands on her, his mouth. She wanted to feel him push inside her, go deep.

Holding her gaze, he reached behind her and unfastened her bra, eased the plain white garment down her arms and freed her breasts. They pebbled in the cool night air, eager for his touch. First he skimmed his fingers around her nipples, applying barely any pressure at all. The touch made her tingle. The touch made her ache for so much more. Then he replaced his hand with his mouth, and the rush of sensation changed, deepened.

As he suckled, he eased her down to the blanket she'd spread out earlier in the evening. With the same finesse, he unfastened her white jeans and slid them down her legs. Instinctively, she reached for his, pulled the zipper and tugged them over his hips, laughing when he violently kicked them free of his long legs.

Somewhere in the distance, an animal howled.

They lay there more nude then not, surrounded by the ancient stones and the grove of gnarled olive trees. Sandro wore only a pair of tight jersey boxers now, she her panties, except for the shirts tangled around their bound arms. She cried out when his hand slipped between her legs and cupped

her, let out a jagged little cry when he slipped inside her
panties and eased a finger inside, discovering just how badly
she wanted him.

"Miranda—"

"Kiss me," she breathed. *Love me.*

He needed no more urging than that. His mouth took hers
again, while his fingers stoked her deep. She longed to feel
his other arm around her, hers around him, but cuffed together, they could only twine their fingers together and hold
on tight. She slid her free hand between their slick bodies,
found him hard and ready, curled her fingers around him.
The thrill was immediate, the promise intense.

Soon, he would be inside her.

They lay there intertwined in the darkness, sprawled on a
blanket in the shadow of the moon and monolithic stones
that predated time. And somehow, it seemed right.

She felt him against her thigh, hot, hard, heavy, and
shifted so that he was between her legs.

"Miranda," he gritted out, sounding like a man fighting
a weight that could easily crush him. "I don't have a con-
dom."

She laughed out loud. Otherwise, she might have cried.
"You don't need one," she said, wrapping her legs around
his. She loved how finely muscled they were, the feel of the
coarse dark hair scraping against her flesh. "I'm protected,"
she explained, acutely conscious of the heat of him.

A low sound ripped from him, and then he was pushing
inside her, stretching her, filling her. The pleasure ripped
through her in relentless waves, close to unbearable.

"You're so…tight," he rasped, pulling back to meet her
gaze. "You're not—"

"No." Not technically. A former boyfriend, a golden boy
handpicked by her mother, had known her body, but never
her heart. He'd not come close to making her feel like this,
on fire from the inside out, her heart and her soul stripped
bare. "No."

That was all it took. He was buried deep in a heartbeat.

She clutched him to her with her free hand, clenched her legs around his. Instinct had her lifting her hips, to which he pulled out slightly, only to push back in. Even more deeply. The tempo increased with every thrust, a rhythm at one with the crickets and cicadas in the woods beyond. The fingers of their joined hands twined together. And held. Tightly.

All that longing, all that emotion, the doubt and the uncertainty and the craving, melded into something more powerful than she'd ever imagined possible. Too powerful to be denied.

They came together on a rush of blinding sensation. There on the blanket beneath the midnight sky, he gave her far, far more than just the moment. Far, far more than the moon and the stars.

He gave her a gift she would never, never give back.

He gave her freedom.

In the fragile light of early dawn, Sandro found the keys, removed the cuffs. He wanted both his hands on her body. He wanted both hers on his. She smiled drowsily, pulled him down beside her, closed her arms around him. He loved the feel of her beneath him, all warm and soft and naked. Even more, he loved the way she kept her eyes open, watching him watch her.

During the night, they'd had only the hazy glow of the moon. Now, splashes of yellow and pink streaked up from the horizon, casting a soft glow to her skin, her eyes. He ran his hand along the smooth flesh of her stomach, up to the heaviness of her breast. There he cupped, his fingers teasing her puckered nipple.

A low mewl tore from her throat and damn near ripped him in two. There was a rawness inside him, a searing desperation that lingered long after he'd woken from the dream to find Miranda safe and sound. He should have found relief in that. He hadn't. Instead he'd violated a vow he'd made to himself, to make sure she came out of this ordeal unscathed.

She wouldn't. Not now.

She would hurt.

The only way you'll hurt me is by pretending you don't want me as badly as I want you.

The courageous words wound their way around his heart. The proverbial rock and a hard place took on a whole new meaning. He'd hurt her if he shut her out. He'd hurt her if he didn't.

He'd more than crossed the line. He'd shattered it. They could have no future. His life belonged to his fallen friends, to the vow he'd made to bring down the man who'd ended their lives. He couldn't turn his back on that. But nor could he let Miranda fall into enemy hands. The greatest gift he could give her was what she prized above all else.

Freedom.

Even if doing so meant she would hate him forever. Better she hate him, than live with dangling loose ends, always wondering, wondering…. Even more, better she hated him, than wind up in enemy hands.

"Now," she whispered, urging him between her legs. He kissed her deeply, his hand going down to find her slick and hot and ready for him. An honorable man would have found some way to resist. But no power on earth could have kept Sandro from slipping inside one more time, telling her goodbye the only way he could.

I'm Alessandro Vellenti, some place deep inside him burned to say. He refused to let it be his heart. *Heir to the Vellenti Vineyards. A man believed dead by the world. A man who thought he knew what it was to hurt, to sacrifice, until you came into my life. A man who would do anything to keep you safe.*

Anything.

"Sandro?" Miranda whispered, lifting a hand to cup his face. "What's wrong?"

Chapter 14

Only when Miranda spoke did Sandro realize he'd stopped kissing her, gone completely still. He was poised over her, his legs between hers, his arms holding him up. His *shaking* arms.

"I'm not inside you yet," he ground out, then rectified that and pushed deep. She accepted him readily, hungrily, as though her body already knew the size and feel of his. He loved the way she arched up into him, the way her gypsy eyes glazed over and her swollen mouth tumbled open.

"Better?" she asked with a husky smile.

She had no idea. "It's about to get even better," he promised, then returned his mouth to hers and carried her over the edge once again.

It was as close as he could come to the sun and the moon.

"Where do we go from here?" Miranda asked as she pulled on the ugly yellow shirt she'd worn the day before. Her whole body continued to tingle, burn. More than anything she wanted to lie down on the blanket with Sandro, to welcome him within her again, but she'd noticed the change in him within minutes of his last climax. He was pulling away from her, even before he pulled out.

"Evora," he said now. He had his tiki-idol shirt on again, though he'd only taken time to fasten the three lower buttons. She could see his chest, see the little marks she'd left throughout the night.

"Evo-what?" she asked.

He gathered up the thin blanket and shoved it into his duffel bag. "Evora. It's an old walled city about an hour from here. I have…contacts there. They can help."

Unease gathered, thickened. "Help what?"

"Help get you out of the country."

The words were curt and final and had Miranda taking a staggering step back. "To the general?"

Behind Sandro the sun flirted with a pale blue sky, but a large monolithic stone cast him in shadow. His jaw was set, his mouth hard. The whiskers which had scraped relentlessly over every inch of her body the night before looked thicker. Darker.

"No," he said. "To America."

Her mouth went dry. Numbly, she reached for one of the standing stones, braced herself. His words made no sense, but hope surged anyway. And a chill she didn't understand.

"To America?" she asked, working to keep her voice from shaking. "Are you going with me?" she asked, even though her heart already knew the answer.

"No."

He said it so simply, so…coldly. She wanted to run to him, hold him, never let him go. Instead she stood there by the huge stone and lifted her chin. "What will become of you?"

His gaze grew darker, but not dark enough to hide the secrets and the agony in those chips of midnight ice, the sure knowledge that he wasn't telling her everything. "*É hora para mim de morrer outra vez.*"

Fury flashed hot and bright. This time she did push away, marched right up to him and shoved her hands against his chest. "Don't do that to me, damn it!"

He didn't stumble back like she'd hoped, just took her shoulders in his hands. "Do what?"

She glared up at him, not giving a damn about the tears she knew sparked in her eyes. "Speak in a language you know I don't understand."

"Then maybe you understand this," he said roughly, and pulled her to him, kissed her hard, kissed her deep.

She understood, all right.

He kissed her goodbye.

In the shadow of an ancient aqueduct, a surprisingly intact, white-washed stucco wall embraced the centuries-old town of Evora. The city seemed squeezed inside, a veritable maze of white stucco buildings with red-tile roofs. The streets were cobblestone and narrow, most only wide enough to accommodate one car. In the center of the town sprawled a huge plaza, dotted by small round tables, tourists and pigeons.

Miranda and Sandro walked hand in hand, the shadows of twilight lending an element of anonymity. Here in such a public place, the glare of the sun had made Sandro uncomfortable. But now, now he'd agreed to show her a few of the sights before inevitability caught up with them.

Tomorrow they would part. Sandro had made the calls from a safe house, kicked his plan into motion. Two men would meet up with them in the morning, and in the privacy of the museum, the handoff would be made. She would be disguised once again, hustled out of the city, out of the country.

She would finally, at last, be free.

Her throat burned at the certainty of it all, but she bit back the tears, determined not to let Sandro see her cry. She knew he thought he was doing the right thing. They still had the long night ahead of them. There was still time to convince him to turn from this terrible course he seemed determined to follow.

"Here we are," he said as they rounded a corner. "The Temple of Diana."

Miranda fought a sudden chill and looked from Sandro to the plaza beyond, where an array of weathered Corinthian columns stretched toward the hazy twilight sky. She counted fourteen, determined from the size of a gap in the structure that four were missing. The columns stood on a crumbling stone base at least twice Sandro's height. And she easily judged him well over six feet. In the distance, the spired dome roof of a cathedral created a fascinating contrast between pagan and Christianity, early Roman and Gothic.

Instinctively, she lifted her camera and brought the structure into focus, snapped a few shots.

"Come on," she said, taking Sandro's hand and dragging him closer. Excitement bubbled inside her. "Right here," she directed, pausing a few feet from the base of the structure. "Just stand here for a minute and—"

"Miranda, don't."

The hard edge to his voice erased the moment of inspiration. She looked at him standing there in the shadow of the temple, saw that every line of his body had tensed. "Don't what?"

"You know I can't let you take my picture."

Wouldn't let her was more like it. Frustration battled with sorrow. The juxtapositions were back, the casual brown shirt with the tiki idols scattered about, the briefcase that turned into an assault weapon. The poet's mouth that could be so impossibly soft as it skimmed her body was now a hard line. And his eyes, those hypnotic midnight eyes, the ones that could reach clear down into her soul, were again concealed by rock-star sunglasses.

Even though the sun was just about gone.

Emotion scratched at her throat. He was pulling away from her, moment by moment, heartbeat by heartbeat.

"Tomorrow we say goodbye," she reminded. "What harm can there be in just one picture? What can it hurt?"

He didn't hesitate. Didn't pretend he misunderstood. "You. A picture can hurt you." Gently, he took the camera from her hands and slung the strap over his shoulder. "And no matter what anyone else thinks about me, hurting innocents isn't my style."

She lifted her chin, refused to surrender. "Take off your sunglasses."

"My sunglasses?"

"Your eyes," she clarified. "Let me see your eyes, then. It's the least you can give me after everything we've been through."

"*Bella*—" he said with a sigh, but then did as she asked.

And flat-out stole her breath.

It was all there, the emotion she'd seen the night before, the struggle she didn't understand, the bottomless sorrow that gave her the strength and courage to challenge an animal hell-bent on returning to his cave.

"Hurting innocents may not be your style," she said, refusing to let her voice crack on emotion. "But what about loving innocents?"

He winced, as though her question had been constructed of stones, not words. Then a sad smile twisted his lips. "Love doesn't have a role in this game."

Game. Inevitability pushed closer, wound deeper, but she refused to let the word hurt her, deter her. "For me it does."

"That's excitement," he corrected without skipping a beat. "Adventure." He paused, met her eyes with his. They were darker now, flatter. "Lust."

Something inside her broke. Restraint, dignity, she wasn't sure. She only knew the animal was loose, and she couldn't cage it in. Didn't want to.

"Don't," she said, stepping closer and angling her head toward his. She felt the fury sparking in her eyes, giving strength to her voice. "Don't you dare!"

"Don't what?" he asked mildly.

"Don't reduce this incredible thing between us to lust!" Don't insult what they'd shared. Don't pretend there wasn't something real and powerful and deep between them.

Don't make saying goodbye harder than it was already going to be.

His expression never cracked, became harder by the second. "Okay," he said without a shred of emotion. "No lust." Slowly, he lifted a hand to her face and smoothed a strand of flyaway brown hair behind her ear. "But no love, either."

All her life she'd struggled against being told what she should or shouldn't say, what to wear, where to go to school. How to think.

Whom to love.

She wasn't about to let Sandro join the parade of those who thought they could point her in a direction and wind her up like some inconsequential toy, set her down a course of action.

Life wasn't that cut-and-dried. Choices weren't that clear. And love...love wasn't that simple.

"You think it's that easy? You think you can just tell me what to do or not to do, and presto," she rolled on, snapping her fingers to emphasize her point, "that's the way it is? Just like magic? Just because you said so?"

"Miranda—"

"Don't!" she spat. "Don't look at me like that and don't you *dare* tell me not to love you. Because I do." She paused, searched his gaze. "I think you love me, too."

"A job, *bella.* I'm doing a job."

"Oh, that's right," she said acidly. "A job." The hurt was a jagged tearing pain now, a sharp inescapable force pushing her down a dangerous path. "I suppose midnight dancing in a wine cellar is part of your job description. And buying plumeria shampoo. *Shooting your own man.* That's right. Silly me. How could I have forgotten that's all part of Traitor Training 101?"

He took her arm, pulled her closer. "Don't you see, *bella?* That's just it! That's why this game *has* to end. Some paths can't be turned away from. Some choices really are etched in stone."

"You're wrong," she started, but stopped abruptly when an older man rounded the base of the temple. He wore a finely pressed white linen suit that practically glowed in the hazy light of the fading day, his long silver hair slicked back in a ponytail, emphasizing his high forehead and receding hairline. He walked slowly and deliberately, with purpose, carrying a single red rosebud in one hand, a pistol in his other.

"At last," the man she recognized from countless news reports said. "My pretty, pretty prize."

Miranda went absolutely, deathly still. Even her heart. She waited for Sandro to surge to life, to throw his body in front of hers like he had so many times before, to lift his briefcase and shower the man, the plaza, with bullets. To tell her to run.

He did none of that. He simply looked at General Viktor Zhukov. And smiled. "I always keep my promises."

Disbelief slammed in hard and fast, and for a cruel moment, the world, the temple, the man and the truth blurred into something dark and unrecognizable. She must have misunderstood. That was all. She must have misunderstood the looks, the words exchanged between the man she'd trusted her heart and her soul and her body to, and the desperate criminal who'd callously ordered the execution of entire villages in Ravakia, whose soldiers forced husbands to watch as their wives were raped then executed alongside their children.

Smiling faintly, Zhukov stepped closer and extended the rose in his right hand toward Miranda. "For you, my sweet. I've waited a long time to have you."

Horror crashed through Miranda with breathtaking swiftness. Stricken, stunned, appalled, she stared at the manicured nails of his fingers, realizing sickly that the stories she'd read were true. He'd cut off his pinkie to demonstrate to his men his disregard for pain.

"Worry not, my sweet," he murmured in that cruelly cultured voice of his, the one that belonged to a connoisseur of fine wine and art, not a man with eyes as lifeless and flat as the Dead Sea. Not a glimmer of emotion shone from their depths, not hatred nor anger, not anticipation, not victory. Nothing.

"I'll be very, very gentle with you," he promised with a slow, twisted smile.

She felt Sandro's hold on her wrist tighten, felt sickness back up in her throat.

"Once I'm done," he went on, "once I teach you how to beg, once my son is home, you'll never want another." He shifted his gaze to Sandro, but his eyes remained cold. "Not even your escort here." He laughed then. "I hope you enjoyed her while you could."

"What man wouldn't?" Sandro muttered.

Something deep inside Miranda shattered. Betrayal slashed hot and hard and deep, slicing clear down to the bone. On an animalistic cry, she wrenched away from Sandro and staggered back from him. She commanded herself to run, to fight, to get away from these men, this nightmare as fast as she could, but her legs were leaden. She could barely breathe, much less move. It was as though she'd been lifted from her body and could only watch the hideous scene unfold.

It was like stepping on a land mine.

"What's going on?" she demanded in a broken voice she barely recognized as her own. There had to be some mistake, she kept telling herself. Sandro would not turn her over to this man.

Standing there in the shadows of the ancient temple, with a kooky Hawaiian shirt on his back and his lethal briefcase in his hand, Sandro looked at her with absolutely no emotion in his eyes.

"Some paths," he said again, slower this time, softer,

his voice more accented, more vacant than she'd ever heard it, "cannot be turned from." He started to say something else, but a hard sound broke from his throat as his eyes flared wide. His body went horribly rigid for a punishing heartbeat, then just as quickly, he collapsed at her feet.

Gunfire, she realized in a stunned rush. From behind him.

"Sandro!" She dropped to her knees and lunged for him, horrified by the puddle of red seeping against cool stone. "No!" she cried. "Please, God, no!" Around her, chaos exploded much like that day on the promenade in Cascais. There was shouting and running, more gunfire.

"Come," Zhukov barked, curling his hand around her upper arm and dragging her along the cobblestone. "Now."

Jagged edges ripped into her skin, but she fought him, not caring about the pain. Desperately she grabbed for Sandro's briefcase and pointed the weapon at Zhukov, her fingers shaking as she fumbled with the trigger disguised by the handle.

Zhukov laughed. "Do not fight me," he warned, his voice no longer mild and cultured, but hard and authoritative. "I do not have to be so gentle."

She tried again and again, but nothing happened. Zhukov kicked the briefcase from her hand and dug his fingers more deeply into her flesh. She struggled against his surprisingly powerful hold, the rocks tearing into her skin.

"No," she said again and again, trying to break Zhukov's grip and reach a hideously still Sandro.

"Someone help us!" she pleaded, finally inching close enough to press two fingers to the base of Sandro's throat. His skin was hot and damp, but her hands shook so badly she couldn't tell if she felt a flutter of a pulse or her own hideous fear. "Please!"

Zhukov smashed the muzzle of his gun to the side of her face. "You leave here with me," he growled in a low menacing voice, "or you do not leave here alive."

Fear sliced cruelly, the inevitability of a death she hadn't expected for a long, long time, but Miranda wasn't about to go anywhere with the man who'd made it clear what he had in store for her. She'd die before she let that man touch her.

"Go ahead and shoot me," she challenged, twisting against his grip with a superhuman strength born of love and determination, through midnight dances and making love in the shadow of standing stones. She glared at him, for the first time noticing several men positioned around the temple, all in black, all carrying submachine guns. The general's men, there to see his will be done.

A child for a child.

"What happens to your prize if I'm dead?" she challenged. Sirens wailed and droned in the distance, and from the maze of narrow streets she heard shouting. Running. If she could hang on for only a few more minutes, help would arrive. "How will my death help get your son back?"

Abruptly, the pressure of the gun against her temple eased. Relief bubbled hot and fast, but as she glanced behind her, she realized her mistake. Zhukov wouldn't kill her, but he would kill Sandro.

"Now," he said firmly, pointing the barrel at Sandro's chest. "Or he dies."

Miranda went hideously still. Her heart hammered so hard it hurt, making breathing almost impossible, but with punishing clarity she knew Zhukov meant what he said. If she didn't go with him, he'd execute Sandro in cold blood, just like he'd done hundreds of others.

If she went with him, he'd put his hands all over her. And worse.

She realized it then. She had only one choice, one chance. A chance Sandro had returned to her just that morning.

"Miranda!"

More gunshots then, closer, louder.

Zhukov's eyes finally came to life, going wild. He signaled to his men and swore viciously, then curled his finger around the trigger of his gun.

Miranda acted without thinking. She grabbed the knife from the holster around her ankle and lunged for Zhukov, plunging the sharp blade deep into his thigh. He howled in pain and lost his balance, but the gun fired anyway, shards of cobblestone spraying mere inches from Sandro's head.

"No, Miranda, no!"

Everything happened so fast then, Miranda didn't have a chance to scream. Three of Zhukov's men lunged forward, but a rapid spray of gunfire sent two to the ground and one running for cover.

"You stupid bitch!" Zhukov roared, pivoting toward Miranda. "Now you pay."

She scrambled back from him, knowing she would never escape the gun pointed at her head.

The sound of gunfire deafened her. She rolled from the gun's trajectory, waiting to feel the white-hot sear of pain, the burn of a bullet ripping through flesh and shattering bone.

But didn't.

Gasping for breath, she shoved the hair from her face and looked up to see one of Zhukov's henchmen dragging him backwards, firing his gun to prevent anyone from stopping them.

Relief pushed hard and fast. Dragging air into her lungs, Miranda crawled back to Sandro. "Help us," she cried into the now ominously silent plaza. "Please!"

Footsteps then, loud and hard and closing in on her. Then arms, closing around her waist and dragging her away toward one of the narrow streets.

"No!" she shouted, thrashing wildly against Zhukov's henchman. Dear sweet God, she couldn't let it end like this. "Let go of me!"

"Don't fight me," barked a boldly familiar voice that sent her head spinning. The man broke into a run, in one smooth move swooping her from her feet as he sprinted toward the far wall of the city.

Reality cut Miranda to the quick. "We have to go back," she shouted, fighting desperately, kicking, hitting. "We can't leave him there like that!" Hurt. Bleeding.

Dying.

Like they'd left the man who'd gone down that day in Cascais, the man who now ran with her through the streets of Evora.

"The hell we can't!" Hawk Monroe growled. "If he's still alive, Zhukov's men will be all over him. No way was that bastard here alone."

"But—"

"Quit fighting me, Miranda! He's probably dead anyway."

No. "No!" Her heart slammed painfully against her ribs. She could barely breathe. "Hawk, please—" She saw it then, the huge black beast of a helicopter waiting just beyond the city wall. Its blades whirred horrifically, promising escape. "No!"

Breathing hard, Hawk ran through an opening in the stone and practically lunged into the open side of the chopper.

In the same heartbeat, they were off the ground, climbing into the hazy twilight sky.

Away from Sandro.

"No!" Miranda screamed, her vocabulary reduced to that one word. The chopper steadily gained altitude, leaving Evora, and Sandro, far behind. She could see the ancient columns jutting up against the crimson-streaked sky, people scurrying around like ants. "We have to go back!"

"Miranda," came a deep booming voice.

Startled, she blinked through her tears, turned, saw her father open his arms wide. "Dad…"

"You're safe now, sweetheart," he said, enveloping his youngest daughter in his arms. He pulled her to his chest, held her against his heart. "You're free."

Chapter 15

Terrorist Blast Kills Eight

The horrifying headline glared at her from her unyielding computer screen.

The accompanying picture chilled.

Miranda's throat burned with an emotion she didn't want to feel. Her heart bled. After her rescue, she'd searched for information about a man left bleeding on the cold streets of Evora. At night, she'd lain awake in the once-comfortable bed of her Richmond, Virginia apartment. There, she'd relived every moment they'd spent together. Every touch. Every lie. She'd braced herself. And she'd prayed.

But nothing prepared her for the truth she found on the third day.

Sandro, the man who'd taken her captive but promised her freedom, who'd strolled straight out of her fantasies but shattered her dreams, was dead.

Killed five years before.

Blinking against dry eyes, Miranda stared at the results

of her Internet search, as she had so many times over the past two weeks. For the first few days everything inside her had felt raw and shredded, but now, now, there was only numbness. She was free, her father had told her. Free.

She didn't feel free.

Sitting cross-legged on the overstuffed sofa she'd once loved, with her notebook computer in her lap and a glass of untouched iced tea to her side, with the sun shining brightly from a shockingly blue sky and a robin singing for all the world to hear, she might as well have been locked in the dingy room hidden in the abandoned villa.

A lie, she told herself. It had all been a lie. In the end, Sandro had merely told her what she wanted to hear as a ploy to gain her cooperation. Had it not been for her father and Hawk, she'd be in the general's hands now.

The evidence was irrefutable. She'd been there herself. She'd heard the exchange, seen the glimmer in Sandro's eyes.

But Sandro was dead, killed five years before.

That was the real lie.

Discovering his true identity had been easy enough. She doubted he even realized how many clues he'd given her. Bombings always made the news. All she'd had to do was go to her favorite search engine and type in London Bombs. A horrifying number of matches had greeted her, but she'd plowed through them, determined.

And found it.

Five years ago, a car bomb had exploded outside a London café, killing eight, including three American tourists. The names Sandro had mentioned—Roger and Gus—had glared at her from the computer screen. And his own. Sandro. Alessandro Vellenti. Heir to the renowned Vellenti Vineyards in California's Napa Valley.

There'd been a picture.

And the picture had been of Sandro.

Younger, happier, those midnight eyes not so haunted. Smiling. Laughing.

A man the world believed dead.

But Miranda knew that wasn't true.

She'd tried to contact his parents, but they were out of the country and the receptionist at the vineyards sadly said master Sandro had gone to Europe five years before but never came home.

She looked at the Web site again, at the picture of a younger Sandro, his hair longer, mussed. His mouth not so hard. He looked…innocent. Far more innocent than a mere five years should tarnish. And this time when she blinked, tears escaped.

She knew it was him. Despite what everyone said, she knew the man who'd been killed in a hideous act of cowardly terrorism five years before was the same man who'd danced with her in a musty wine cellar. The man who'd killed for her.

The man who'd lain broken and bleeding in the shadow of an ancient temple, while Hawk had raced her to safety.

To freedom.

Away from Sandro.

É hora para mim de morrer outra vez.

She knew what the words he'd muttered that misty morning by the standing stones meant now. She'd had them interpreted within minutes of touching down at a military base in Germany.

It's time for me to die again.

The reality chilled her. He'd planned to die that day in Evora. That was hardly the mark of a ruthless criminal. A man as vile as Sandro pretended to be would do whatever it took to protect himself, all else be damned.

But Sandro had taken her to Evora, despite the foreknowledge that he might not walk out alive.

Had he been successful, she wondered with a sharp stab to her heart? Had he died alone there that day, abandoned on the cold cobblestone sidewalk? The question tortured her, shadowing her by day, slicing through her dreams when she sought sleep.

She would know if he'd died, she told herself. She would *feel* it.

But didn't.

You're free, her father had told her. But she wasn't. Didn't know how she could be free when memories flanked her more tightly than her father's security personnel. She'd tried every avenue imaginable to discover the fate of the man left shot and bleeding at the base of those crumbling old columns, but could find nothing.

It was as though he'd never even existed.

Or rather…died five years before.

Not for the first time she wished for her camera, the film inside, but the sleek little 35mm had not made it out with her.

But something had, something more tangible and precious than any picture in the world.

Swallowing against an uncomfortably tight throat, Miranda leaned toward her coffee table and picked up the object she'd found stuffed in her purse several days after her return. *Virgil.* The carved statue of Sandro's boyhood dog felt smooth and sure in her hand, and it promised her that, despite all the evidence to the contrary, Sandro was not the criminal he pretended to be.

She was still holding Virgil when a loud knock echoed through her quiet apartment. Startled, she blinked, then stood and hurried to the door. The rapid-firing of her heart was ridiculous. The rush of adrenaline misplaced. She knew that, but could not stop the physical reactions.

"Mir," her sister said as soon as she opened the door. "Are you okay?"

Miranda smiled tightly. "I'm fine." Elizabeth looked gorgeous, as always, her long sable hair twisted off her face to highlight killer cheekbones and flashing green eyes. She was dressed to the nines, wearing a chic little black dress that hugged all the right places. "I'm flattered, E, but you didn't need to get dressed up just to come see me."

She expected her sister to smile or laugh, not to frown. "Oh, Mir, you've forgotten, haven't you?"

"Forgotten what?"

"The party."

"Party?"

"You know, the party Mom and Dad are throwing to celebrate your safe return?"

She remembered then, didn't know how she'd forgotten. "Oh."

Her sister pushed inside and closed the door, pulled her into a hug. "It's him, isn't it? You're thinking about the man who kidnapped you."

"He didn't kidnap me," Miranda immediately protested, but the claim sounded weak even to her own ears. Of course he had. "He saved my life."

Elizabeth pulled back and gently wiped the tears from beneath her sister's eyes. "Time heals all wounds, sweetie. You'll see."

"Does it?" Miranda instinctively challenged, and knew she'd hit pay dirt when she saw her oh-so-poised sister wince. Elizabeth hadn't healed yet, despite what she wanted the world to think. Her sister hadn't forgotten. Miranda herself had heard Elizabeth cry out Hawk's name in her sleep, seen the tears.

Miranda doubted she'd ever forget the shock, the profound relief of discovering he'd not been killed that day in Cascais. He'd been shot in the shoulder, a bullet that went clean through. And when he fell, he'd hit his head on the concrete and blacked out.

"Are you really over Hawk?" she now challenged.

"Don't be ridiculous," Elizabeth said in that smooth, cultured voice of hers, the one that announced a subject was closed and she wasn't about to reopen it. "How many times do I have to tell you that man was my bodyguard, nothing more?"

Until the lie caught up with her. But Miranda let the subject drop. Now wasn't the time.

"Come on," her sister was saying, tugging her toward the bedroom. "Let's get you dressed and out of here before Father sends a search party."

"...the Pentagon is confirming that General Viktor Zhukov was killed overnight after an exchange of gunfire with elite U.S. Special Forces involved in a covert operation...."

Five weeks after the nightmare in Evora, Miranda sat upright in bed and cranked up the volume on the morning news program. Adrenaline shot through her, clearing the cobwebs of sleep and making her heart pound so hard it hurt.

"...an ongoing mission to apprehend the man responsible for war crimes and the deaths of eight undercover operatives..." the anchor was saying. But Miranda barely heard.

General Viktor Zhukov was dead.

Killed by Special Forces.

A covert operation.

Ongoing mission.

Blindly, she reached for Virgil sitting on the chest by her bed and clutched the carved dog to her heart. Because she knew. In that moment she knew, deep, deep in her heart, she finally, at last, had her answer.

Sandro may have lied about his identity, but that lie had concealed a dangerous truth. He hadn't planned to turn her over to Zhukov, but he had been straddling a thin dark line. And he had planned to die that day, if that's what had been necessary to give her the one thing she'd claimed to want above all else.

Freedom.

The tears started then, hot, salty, wrenching. Her throat tightened. She couldn't believe how naive she'd been. How foolish. All her life she'd dreamed of being free, of living her life outside the fishbowl of the Carrington prestige, but now she knew true freedom had nothing to do with the body, but everything to do with the spirit. And the heart.

Loving Sandro, losing him, had taught her that.

Miranda shoved back the thick ivory comforter and scrambled out of bed.

She knew what she had to do.

He didn't want to be found. That much was clear. His family refused to back off the claim that Allesandro Vellenti died one sunny morning five years before. The Department of Defense refused to acknowledge that he worked deep undercover for the U.S. government, that he'd been part of a covert operation to bring down General Viktor Zhukov.

For once in her life, Miranda had been grateful for her family's political clout, certain it could break through the web of lies and intrigue. But not even her father could find the truth.

As far as the world was concerned, Alessandro Vellenti was dead. Which only meant one thing.

He was a man of the shadows. He couldn't allow sunshine into his world.

"Your father will have my hide for helping you do this."

Walking down a narrow street in Cascais, Portugal, Miranda waved off Hawk Monroe's concern. "Let me handle my father."

The familiar sights and sounds and scents greeted her, the local vendors with their wares proudly displayed in stall after stall, two men having an animated conversation in bursts of Portuguese, the smell of French fries from an American hamburger joint. It was all so achingly, painfully familiar.

Past the perfume shop and around the corner, the Atlantic ocean glimmered in the early afternoon sun, the fleet of rainbow-colored fishing boats bobbing in the harbor, just like before. The fountain still sprayed upward. Pigeons still hobbled around the cobblestone piazza.

Lovers strolled hand in hand.

Everything was the same as that morning six weeks before, when her life had changed so irrevocably. Everything was *exactly* the same. Except her. She wasn't the same. Would never be again. Still, she could almost hear the gunfire, see the blood.

"Are you okay being here?" she asked Hawk.

He didn't break stride, just kept walking toward the ocean. As usual he wore aviator sunglasses, but Miranda knew he scanned the busy open-air market with that unerring intensity she'd once found so offensive. Now, the semiautomatic tucked into his shoulder holster brought her comfort.

"I'm not a flashback kind of guy," he answered in clipped tones, "if that's what you're asking. Lightning never strikes twice."

She didn't know whether to hope he was right or pray he was wrong.

He stopped then, turned to face her. She couldn't see his eyes, but she would have sworn his expression gentled. "You're looking for him, aren't you? You're looking for Sandro."

It was the concern that got her, maybe even a trace of sympathy. The question was far more brotherly than that of the bodyguard she'd clashed with not that long ago. Before her ordeal with Sandro, she'd thought Hawk evil incarnate. He'd hurt Elizabeth. He'd made her cry.

Nothing seemed quite so black-and-white anymore.

"No, I just...needed to come back." To retrace their footsteps, visit the places she'd been with Sandro.

To say goodbye.

Now, at last, she understood why Elizabeth had been so lost after Hawk left. She looked at him standing there against the vivid blue sky, all tall and rough around the edges, dark blond hair queued behind his neck, looking more like a Viking than a former Army Ranger. Normally she didn't find blond men attractive, but there was an energy to Hawk Monroe, a wildness. A presence. It was as though a fire burned deep inside him, smoldering from his eyes, his very flesh. She almost thought that if she touched him, he would sear her fingertips.

Just like he'd seared her sister's heart.

"Did you see her?" she blurted out.

He was looking toward a vendor hawking seashell wind chimes, which tinkled in the breeze. "Did I see who?"

"Elizabeth," Miranda clarified. "Did you see Elizabeth?"

Hawk went very still, his voice very hard. "No."

Once, Miranda would have let it go at that. Once, she would have celebrated. Until Sandro, she'd never understood what had drawn Elizabeth to bold, blunt, brutal Hawk Monroe, never understood why her sister gave the time of day to a man who rattled her by merely walking into a room. Now, though, now that she knew what it was like to be carried away by emotion, by desire, she understood a little more.

"Will you when we get back?" she asked.

"No."

"Do you want to?"

Hawk's jaw tightened. "No."

"But—"

"Don't, Miranda, okay? Don't look for something that's not there." He hesitated, staring down at her through those damnable mirrored sunglasses. "Your sister would rather walk barefoot over hot coals than see me again. She made that abundantly clear when she had me thrown out of her engagement party to Nicholas like I was some no-good piece of trash."

Miranda just stared. Right there, in one hot angry breath, Hawk Monroe had spoken more to her than he ever had. And no matter what he said with words, she knew he lied. The hard line of his mouth and rigid stance of his body made that abundantly clear.

"She's not with Nicholas anymore," Miranda said softly.

Hawk looked off toward the ocean. "It wouldn't matter if she was."

"She's not the ice princess you think she is," Miranda pushed on. "She's never been the same since you left." Her sister would kill her for interfering like this, but Miranda couldn't let that stop her. There'd been enough suffering already. "Maybe the two of you should talk."

Hawk whipped back toward her. "And maybe you should just leave it alone," he said angrily. "Your sister and I have never talked, Miranda. We only f—" He bit back the words with near-violent force. "Fought. We only fought." The muscle in the hollow of his jaw jumped furiously. "Now come on. I don't like you standing in the open like this."

"I thought you said lightning never strikes twice," she reminded.

He didn't answer, just cut her a look that warned he'd said all he had to say.

And Miranda let it drop. She recognized a dead end when she saw one. For now.

They wandered over to the boardwalk, where she curled her hands around the railing and gazed out over the ocean. The salty breeze was cool, just like before, carrying with it the scent of fish and dreams.

"Here."

She turned to see Hawk with his arm extended toward her, a camera in his hand. *Her* camera.

Her heart pitched, hard. She took the 35mm and checked the little window, saw that film remained inside, tangible proof those dangerous days with Sandro really happened.

"Where did you get this?" she asked, surprised by how breathless her voice sounded.

Hawk shrugged. "It showed up a few days ago…must have gotten left behind in Evora."

Miranda lifted the camera, looked through the lens, saw memories. There was Sandro standing in this very spot. Sandro carving a block of wood in the musty old wine cellar. Sandro eating mint-chip ice cream at the basilica in Fatima. Sandro making love to her beneath a mammoth standing stone.

Sandro lying still as death at the base of the temple in Evora.

Moisture stung her eyes, forcing her to blink rapidly, but the tears spilled over anyway. She turned toward the ocean, not wanting Hawk to realize she was crying. She didn't want his comfort. She didn't want his advice. She didn't want to hear him talk about lightning never striking twice.

Because, dear God, she needed to believe it could.

The sky was obscenely blue with no clouds in sight, weathered old fishing boats bobbing on the water in the cooling breeze. Like that day that now seemed more dream than memory, they were practically begging to be photographed.

"No, no, no. That's not right at all."

The voice was low, drugging, almost made her drop the camera. It was the voice of memory, the voice of countless nights alone in her bed, dreaming. Instinctively she closed her eyes, wanting to hold the moment as long as possible. *This* was why she'd insisted on coming to Portugal. Not closure, but to prove to herself that what she'd felt those magical days had been as real and powerful as she remembered.

"Aren't you even going to turn around?"

Miranda went very still, all but her heart. It kicked, hard. Her chest tightened painfully. Her throat constricted. Imagination had always been her friend, bright, vivid, full of promise, but now it turned enemy.

Swallowing against the emotion lodged in her throat, she kept the camera to her face and slowly turned toward the voice that made her heart strum low and deep and hard.

Only a few minutes before, when Hawk had given her the camera, she'd looked through the lens and seen memories.

But in her memories, Sandro had never stood on crutches.

She blinked, but the image didn't go away. He stood much closer than American manners dictated, tall, dark, battered, the weight of the world in his midnight eyes. Dark whiskers covered his jaw. On the left side of his face, there was a scar that hadn't been there before.

The sight almost sent her to her knees.

"The picture you were about to take," he said in that low, hoarse voice of his. The one that warned of violence and danger. "It's all wrong."

Shakily, she reached behind her to clasp the railing. Her heart was pounding so hard its echo roared through her, blurring her vision and making her dizzy.

"Wrong?" She wasn't sure how she managed the word, where it came from. "How so?"

"Because you're not in it."

The breath stalled in her throat. Her chest hurt. Not because of the painfully familiar words, but because of the way he looked at her, like she was the coveted trophy at the end of a long, hard-fought battle. Only once before had she seen a gaze so full of secrets and promises, eyes that dark, like chips of midnight ice.

Wake up, the survivor in her commanded. This man wasn't what he seemed. He wasn't real. He was only another dream.

Slowly, with great effort and dread, she lowered the camera from her eyes, certain that without the aid of the lens, Sandro would vanish. Because he wasn't just standing there in broad daylight, reenacting their first conversation. He couldn't be.

But dear God, he was.

"I see myself in the mirror every morning," she mused, memory supplying the words. "I hardly need a picture of myself."

His voice dropped an octave. "But I did," he said. "I needed to see you standing here like this, with the sun in your hair and a smile on your face, to remind me why I was such a goddamn fool.''

All those walls she'd tacked up deep inside, the hard, impregnable barriers to the hurt and the pain, came tumbling down.

"Bella," he whispered. "Did I say something wrong?''

She couldn't take it anymore, couldn't play a game when her whole world had just shifted.

"Sandro…'' She had to touch him, just touch him, put her hands on his body, feel the warmth of his skin. Assure herself he was real. And alive. *Here.* He'd visited her so many times in her dreams, dissolving into shadows the second she lifted a hand.

"You're here,'' she murmured thickly. "You're alive. You came back.''

He shifted on his crutches. "I never left you, *bella.* I was always here,'' he said, lifting a hand to put his palm against her chest. "And you were always here,'' he said, drawing her hand to the wrinkled cotton of his black shirt.

Miranda wasn't sure how she stayed standing. "Your leg—''

"Nothing that won't heal,'' he said matter-of-factly. "A small price for making sure Zhukov never hurts another.''

Beneath her palm his heart beat strong and true. She could feel the warmth of his body seeping into hers. More than anything she wanted to eliminate the scant distance between them, put her arms around him, feel his arms around her.

But first she needed to understand.

"You lied to me,'' she whispered. "You let me believe you were a criminal.''

He winced. "I did what I had to do to make sure you got out alive. That's all I cared about.''

"You tried to make me hate you.''

Those midnight eyes went even darker. "I loved you,'' he said, his voice pitched low. Very slowly, he slid his hand from her chest to her neck, up farther to cradle her face. "I love you more than I knew possible."

Something deep inside her went hot and liquid. "Sandro—"

"I tried to forget you," he went on, "but it would have been easier to quit breathing."

Now he looked at her standing there, with the ocean glimmering behind her and the sun shining on her and had to remind himself to do just that. Breathe. He'd thought he could walk away from her. He'd thought he could turn her over to Hawk and her father and go on with his life. He'd thought he could walk away from her like he'd walked away from his life five years before.

He'd never imagined how wrong a man could be.

After finding and rescuing a badly beaten Javier from Petros's men, the two had completed their plan to bring down the general. Everything should have been over then, but thoughts of Miranda had refused to diminish. If anything, they'd grown stronger. Still, he tried to stay away, tried to pretend their lives hadn't touched for a few brief days, changing everything. But couldn't.

Through Hawk, with whom Sandro had orchestrated the exchange that ensured her safety and protected Sandro's cover, he learned of her safe return to the States. Hawk had also told him of her endless string of questions, her tireless efforts to find him. And finally he could stay away no longer, not when he knew that in setting her free he'd subjected both of them to a hellish prison neither expected.

Loving Miranda didn't mean betraying his friends or his quest for justice. The two were not mutually exclusive. He owed it to the memory of his fallen friends to live his life to the fullest. Anything less was granting Zhukov and his men a victory they didn't deserve.

Sandro stepped closer, lowered his face toward hers. "Some paths," he murmured, "...they cannot be turned away from. Some choices really are etched in stone."

''I love you,'' she whispered as their mouths came together.

He slid his free arm around her shoulders and kissed her slow, deep, savoring the feel of her, the taste of coffee and desire and hope.

He'd been wrong that day in Evora. It wasn't time for him to die again.

It was time for him to live.

* * * * *

And look for Elizabeth Carrington's
story later this year when
author Jenna Mills pens another heart-pounding
tale of adventure and romance!
Don't miss it!

If you enjoyed what you just read,
then we've got an offer you can't resist!

Take 2 bestselling love stories FREE!

Plus get a FREE surprise gift!

COMING NEXT MONTH